If
I Ruled
the
World

ALSO BY JOY

Dollar Bill

If
I Ruled
the
World

JOY

St. Martin's Griffin
New York

www.stmartins.com

ISBN 0-312-32879-6
EAN 978-0312-32879-5

P1

This book is dedicated to my
damn self!

I put more into this novel than any other work that
I've ever written.
It was absolutely draining at times.
I became the character of Harlem. I fought this
character's battles.
I cried for this character. I hated for this character.
I triumphed with this character.
I sacrificed so much to write this particular novel.
I hope it makes a difference in just one other person's life.
It made a difference in mine.

Acknowledgments

For Martina, and all the others out there struggling in their youth, in their adulthood, and in life, period.
Keep ya head up,
He has a plan for you.

I promise.

If
I Ruled
the
World

Prologue

I'm a fine ass young black female and I have everything I need. Having everything I want is a bonus, an extra perk in this venture called life. I have a three bedroom house, an automobile that's in mint condition, a little extra spending cash, nice jewelry that includes a Movado watch and a five-carat tennis bracelet, a jazzy wardrobe with a few name brand clothes thrown in the mix, and just all around nice shit.

Hell, I should have it going on. I do own my own business, a music/bookstore. And before you get it twisted, no, some drug slinging nigga didn't front me the money for it, or, should I say, invest in it. It's all me.

It's a nice little café type hookup over on East Main Street in Columbus, Ohio. It's a pretty decent size. In addition to the book and music shelves, it's big enough for a latte bar with five tables that seat four each. My partner, Morgan, who helps me run the shop, smokes a joint every morning before coming into work, so she always has the munchies. Needless to say, we sell sugar sweets, and snacks and shit too. Her favorite munchies are the chocolates we stock from a local company called Chocolates and Stilettos. I don't think one box has ever made it to a customer because Morgan inhales them all.

Everything I sell is legit. Muthafuckas be trying to come up in my store to sell me bootleg shit to flip. Fuck that. If the artist don't get a cut, then I don't fuck with it. I know what it's like for someone to take food from my mouth and I can't see myself turning around doing it to someone else who done put in work in the game. That's how a lot of these businesses keep their doors open, by pushing bootleg CDs, DVDs, and, believe it or not, books. The game is dirty. Even though I don't participate in that type of thievery, my business profits are just fine. It helps that my location is in between all the major hair salons and barbershops in the city. Because I sell snacks and whatnot, the chicks and dudes come in all day long for change and shit. I make them make a purchase before I give them change though. In addition to the basic bag of chips, soda, or coffee that they purchase to break their large bills, they end up buying something to read or listen to, so you can best believe that I makes my money.

Now, what can I say about myself? I'm your average inner-city princess who made an early come up in life. I'm twenty-six years old and I've got things that fifty-year-old women have yet to obtain. But I know, I know, there are plenty of women my age who have what I got and then some. So what makes me so special you're probably thinking? The thing is, I ain't never had to give up no pussy to get what I got!

People look at me and see my light skin, long hair, thick waist, and gray eyes and automatically think that I'm a stuck-up gold digging yellow girl. As a matter of fact, I think I've been called that once or twice. For some strange reason, others have this automatic perception that I think my shit don't stank and that I'm better than everybody else is, especially black chicks. If I speak to sistahs walking by, because of the delayed reaction of their being in shock that I even spoke, I'm long on my way before I'm able to hear their faint replies. Bitches always end up hating me. They stay mad at me 'cause they can't be me. I ain't never did nothing to nobody, nobody who didn't deserve it anyway. So how I've managed to attract so many haters is beyond me. It's cool though. I still handle mine, take care of business every day and count money all night. On those nights I can't get to sleep, fuck sheep. I count dollars.

"Harlem," Morgan, who is not only my partner but my best friend, always says to me, "you gon' die with a wad of cash in your hand."

Some people want to die in their sleep. Some people want to die fucking. Me, Harlem Lee Jones, I want to die rich, or, like that rap superstar 50 Cent says, die tryin'.

Today, while I was out browsing at some of the shops in the Short North area, I paid a psychic for a five-dollar reading. She told me that I was going to live to be eighty-nine years old. I'm only twenty-six now so I suppose I should be ecstatic. But no, not me. My comment to her prediction was: *What the fuck am I supposed to do for the next sixty-three years?*

1. The Suga Shop

"If he takes me to the suga shop, kisses gonna buy me ice cream," Morgan sang as she sat on her couch polishing her toes. She was singing along with the CD of the female singing group, Vanity 6. Morgan is obsessed with that old ass chick group that were crooning in camisoles and garter belts when we were still playing hopscotch in our elementary school yard. Ever since she saw them on VH1's *Where Are They Now* segment four years ago, she hasn't gotten them out of her head. She went out and bought their album, as well as Vanity's solo album, and even went through that lacy garment stage for a minute. I finally had to tell her that it was the fingerless lace gloves or me. I refused to walk through the mall with her broke down Cyndi Lauper looking ass wearing those damn gloves. She grew out of dressing like them, but she's still head over heels in love with their bubblegum songs.

I personally hated the hell out of that group back in the day. They were so damn sexy and beautiful that they made even Tamara McNair, the most beautiful girl in middle school, look like Aunt

Esther from *Sanford and Son*. Dealing with feeling inferior to girl groups and magazine models as a youth ain't no joke. I pity the youth who have the Halle Berrys, Beyonces, and Tyra Bankses to contend with.

Morgan ain't no hater, though. She sees things for what they are and judges solely on that. As a matter of fact, she's attracted to beauty, beautiful things. She's more interested in learning how to achieve and maintain the beauty rather than be jealous of it. I'm just the opposite, but I mostly don't voice my opinion. On top of that, I'm a grudgeable bitch. If someone does me wrong, I'll never forget it, nor will I forgive. Don't get me wrong. I love everything and everyone in the beginning. But once I'm crossed, that's it. When I cut a muthafucker off, you best believe they cut the fuck off for life. I sever their hand so they can't reach me.

With Morgan and I having totally different attitudes and outlooks on life, how she and I ever remained best friends for so many years is beyond me. Not only that, but I'm from a home that started off sweet, but then ended up bitter. Morgan is from a home that started off sweet and is still sweet.

Her parents got married when they were twenty-one. They had her two years after they both graduated from law school. By then they had started their own corporate law firm, Travese & Kleiningham. Morgan's mother used her maiden name, Travese, and her father used their family name, Kleiningham.

Morgan was born into money. She never wanted for a thing. She went to private school all of her life and even had a nanny. Go figure, a black girl with a nanny.

Money was never on Morgan's mind. Her parents provided her with everything a child could want. She got all the new toys a day before they hit the shelves. She knew how to spell the names of clothing designers before she could spell her own name. She took gymnastics and ballet classes like every little girl dreams of doing.

She had carnival carousels at her backyard birthday parties. At sixteen her parents bought her a convertible car. And with all that being handed to her on a silver platter, she still managed to stay grounded. Nothing went to her head and she took nothing for granted.

As soon as she turned eighteen her parents told her that she had to get a job for her own spending money. They wanted to start teaching her about being independent. After all, they were paying the rent and utilities for her apartment off campus. Morgan earning a full academic scholarship at Ohio State University had made them proud and had saved them thousands of dollars that they had planned to spend on her higher education. So they had no problem paying her living expenses while she attended college.

To appease her parents, Morgan took a less than part-time job selling magazine subscriptions door-to-door. It was something sweet, simple, and that didn't entail much work. It didn't pay much either. So, 'spite her parents attempt to teach her to have some independence, she still relied on them for the majority of her spending money.

Morgan earned a bachelor's degree in business administration and I don't even have a high school diploma. We are from two completely different walks of life, but we have one struggle in common: being young black females. No matter what side of the track you came up on, having black skin is always a challenge. Fortunately for Morgan, though, she had two parents who loved one another, and who loved her dearly, to support her.

To this day Morgan's parents are still happily married. Their relationship is what gives Morgan confidence that there is a good man out there waiting for her, to spend the rest of her life with. But until she runs into him, like any other good girl, she doesn't mind entertaining herself with as many bad boys as she can sink her claws into.

Morgan does truly adore her parents' relationship. That has a lot to do with her being the outgoing vibrant woman that she is today. Not to take anything away from the single parents putting it down, but growing up in a loving two-parent home is priceless. I wish people would realize that before they went fucking just anybody.

I wish they would take a deep look into the person they are about to give their bodies to and ask themselves, is that the person they would want to be the parent of their child? There is always that possibility when having sex. Especially when doing it raw. But all in all, it doesn't matter how differently Morgan and I came up, she is definitely my ace boon coon. She helps me run my business, and in return I help her run game. If it weren't for me, the poor girl would get run over by every thug who winked at her. She's so gullible that it's sickening. I told her that not every man out there is like her father. So it was my duty as her friend to let her know how to work a nigga rather than be worked by one.

Morgan is as smart as a whip when it comes to book and business smarts, but as far as the streets are concerned, she's still working on her GED (Ghetto Education Degree).

It was actually solely Morgan's business idea to add coffee and candy sweets into the mix of things at the bookstore. I plan on adding a couple of computers next year. My five-year-plan is to start a chain across the United States, kind of like The Shrine of the Black Madonna bookstores, only better. When I do start up my chain I'm going to sell Jackie Collins and John Grisham, too. Right now I only supply African American books, but I got the idea to add Caucasian authors one day while I was in Philly. I had gone into this bookstore called Ligorious Bookstore. Although most of their titles were African American books, they had a Caucasian section. For the first time, I had gone to a bookstore in a mall where my section of books was not the minority. White readers were going to walk into that store and finally know what African American readers feel like when they walk into a bookstore in the mall and have to seek out the one row of books dedicated to their culture.

I've only been running the bookstore for two years and already I'm sick to death of Uncle Sam. How does he expect a sistah to keep her bank account thick with his ass pinching on it? Who made up taxes anyway? I got to pay to be free. What kind of shit is that?

"You wanna go to Second Wind with me?" Morgan asked, removing a piece of candy from the hot pink Chocolates and Stilettos box. "I'm meeting DC and his boys up there. Rashad is going to be there."

"You know I don't go to no clubs," I said to Morgan, flicking the channels with her remote. "And if you're trying to use Rashad to convince me, try again. He's a loser."

I held up the L with my index finger and thumb and Morgan laughed. I continued trying to find something to watch. I swear I had clicked through two hundred channels. Morgan had some Direct Television Satellite cable that provided her with a zillion stations. Who could memorize all of those stations? Trying to find the channel you were looking for was hell.

"You are just too picky when it comes to men," Morgan stated, biting down on the piece of white chocolate. "Rashad was a good catch and you blew it. He had a good job, nice whip, and no kids."

"Sure, he worked for the post office. Yes, he drove a BMW, and no he didn't have any kids. But what he did have was a broke ass, bumming ass family. Next time, before I decide to start diggin' a guy, remind me to do a background check on his family. That fool might as well have had kids because he was always shelling out money to his peoples. I think he paid his mama's car note more than he paid his own. His brothers and sisters were always crying broke, and with him being the oldest, he felt that it was his duty to take care of them. Fuck that! They weren't the ones fucking him, cooking for him, and washing his nasty drawers. I couldn't get nothing for him giving everything to them."

"But, girl, that was his family," Morgan said in Rashad's defense. "Don't you want a man who treats his mama and his family good?"

"Not if it means he ain't got shit left in his pockets to treat me with," I replied. "I mean damn, you know me, Morgan. I don't ask for much. I enjoy being able to do for myself more than anything. But when I do need a brotha to come through for me and he can't, then, Houston, we have a problem."

"We'll that's you, and if you just keep doing you, then it's always just gonna be you."

"And I'm cool with that. I don't mind my own company. As a matter of fact, you can leave," I said jokingly.

"Forget you," Morgan said, snapping her neck and twisting up her lips. "And besides, you're at my house. You leave."

Morgan winked at me and popped another chocolate in her mouth. She closed her eyes and allowed it to melt and slide down her throat. This girl could do a commercial for Chocolates and Stilettos.

"I do need to get going, though," I said, standing up to stretch.

"Girl, you know I was just playing."

"No, really, I need to get up out of here. Tomorrow is Saturday and you know the store is going to be off the hook. I'm going to go home and listen to some R. Kelly and veg out."

"You still listen to that fool?" Morgan asked.

"Yeah, why wouldn't I?"

"After all that drama and talk about him having sex with fourteen-year-olds and shit," Morgan said, turning her nose up.

"Look, that man don't owe me shit but good music," I said. "What he does in his spare time is between him and his God. I don't even worry enough about my own ass getting into heaven. I don't have the time to worry about whether R. Kelly is getting let into the gates too. But anyway, I do have to worry about you. Now don't get too crunked tonight at the club. You bringin' your ass into work in the morning, hangover or not."

"Yes, boss," Morgan said, saluting me. "I'll see you in the morning at eight-fifteen sharp."

"Eight o'clock damn it," I said, giving her the evil eye.

"Same difference." Morgan winked, her hazel eyes sparkling.

Morgan knew she was gorgeous, a chocolate delight. With the complexion of Naomi Campbell and the body of Tisha Campbell in her earlier days on the *Martin Lawrence* show, she was the perfect catch. Not to mention the girl had the brain of a genius and she loved to read. She read to me like I was her child. Every book she had read, I had listened to her read out loud. Actually, that's what we had just finished doing before she started polishing her toes, and I started trying to find something to watch on television.

She had just finished reading *Twilight Moods* by Jossel Flowers Green. It was a book of erotic stories. No wonder she was fixin' to race off and hook up with DC. Those stories had both of our clits throbbing. Hell, if I got down like that, I could have even fucked Morgan after reading those tart tales.

Speaking of which, even chicks were attracted to Morgan. There was just something about her that was so adorable and crazy sexy cool. But at the same time, she put out this free ride vibe, so instead of guys wanting to make her their partner for life and do things for her, they just wanted her as their partner for right now so that she could do shit for them. And that right there was the attitude I was trying to teach her not to project.

She was just too damn nice. Nice is good, but sometimes it gets you nowhere. A bitch gotta put her foot down and squash everything up underneath it sometimes. I was a firm believer of that, right along with the belief that a person should work hard and take everything that comes their way and give nothing.

After a couple of hours lying in my bed sighing with boredom, I decided to get up, shower, and throw on some going out gear. I had already listened to *Twelve Play* and *TP2.Com*. After putting in the Jay-Z and R. Kelly *Fiesta* remix, I was amped. Morgan would be all too surprised when I showed up at Second Wind.

I hadn't been there since it was called The Classic, so I had no idea how to dress for the scene. I'm very conservative, so I threw on some heather gray slacks from Lerner New York and a white ribbed sweater shirt. I decided to play my sling-back signature Ralph Lauren shoes, and the matching handbag was so necessary. I pulled my hair back in a long ponytail and curled the ends under. It looked like a perfectly groomed horse's tail. I put on a little Mary Kay foundation and some light makeup. I decided to play my diamond studs. They made me look more ladylike. After a few squirts of Fendi cologne, I was ready for the world.

Although summer had pretty much wound down, I still didn't need an evening jacket to tolerate the night breeze. There was no breeze. It was a stiff dry night caught in between summer and fall. As I started up my black four-speed Mustang, I indulged in its purr. I closed my eyes and gave a shout out to myself, not God, for making it possible for me to own my dream car. I had traded in the pink Cadillac that I had inherited from my grandmother for it. Well, I hadn't actually traded it in. While I was on the car lot test-driving Mustangs, some woman, who happened to be a Mary Kay cosmetics consultant, inquired about the pink Cadillac that was sitting on the lot. She offered to give me five thousand dollars more than what the dealership was willing to give me on a trade-in for it. In addition, she threw in some Mary Kay freebies. Needless to say, I took her up on her offer.

After giving my shout out, I opened my eyes only to be greeted by a full moon. I should have known right then and there that this was going to be one crazy ass night.

I could hear the words to Tupac's "All Eyes on Me" as I approached Second Wind. A more perfect song couldn't have been playing because that's exactly how I felt. There were about twenty people in line. The parking lot wasn't even full so I knew the club owners were perpetrating. They wanted passersby to think that the spot was jumping and required a wait. Ain't no club in Columbus worth a wait in line and that's exactly why you'll only catch me doing the club scene every blue moon.

"Miss Lady," a dude sportin' a cream linen hookup said to me.

"I know you ain't going to the back of the line. Bring your fine ass up here with me."

"Oh, I'm good," I said, winking at him. I thought the lil' wink would let him know that I wasn't trying to act stuck-up, I just didn't want to be bothered with his ass hanging on me all night. I guess his boys laughing at my turning down his offer pumped him up. He was angry with them, but he lashed out at me with the normal, "Fuck you then, bitch."

I stopped in my tracks because I was going to clown on this fool, but I didn't know if I could get to the gun that was in my glove box soon enough if this fool really decided to get stupid. I kept the gun at the store, but then at night I took it back home. I was good for accidentally leaving it in my glove box. So instead of tripping on the dude, I threw him a slight snicker, brushed my shoulder off, then proceeded to the back of the line. While waiting in line I scanned the parking lot for Morgan's gold Toyota Camry. I spotted it in a matter of seconds. My girl was in the club. I was looking good, and as long as no more niggas got out of line with me, it was going to be a good night. But that would have been too much like right.

I stood in line for about twenty minutes before I finally got admitted in. There wasn't a cover charge so that was a good thing. I let security hit up my purse with a flashlight and I was good to go. As soon as I walked in I spotted Morgan in the back by the window where food could be ordered. She was sitting at a table with DC, three of his boys, and some other chick that looked like she was on the hoe stroll.

Morgan spotted me and her eyes lit up. She was looking absolutely adorable in her Donna Karan white bandeau top with matching slacks. Her white strappy stilettos were killin' the outfit. She had the full Naomi Campbell look going on with her long straight hair, bangs and all. Her hazel eyes looked like cat eyes. She was crucial up in that bitch.

I could see all the fellas eyeballing her when she got up to meet me halfway to her table. Most people thought that just because she was dark skinned that her hair was weave and she wore contacts. They were color struck prejudgmental assholes if you asked me. Some people would even have the audacity to ask her if her shit was fake. It takes a lot of balls to ask a woman if her hair or eyes are fake. That's some ghetto stupid ass shit right there.

"You came," Morgan said, hugging me and kissing me on the cheek. DC must have been filling her up with the sloe gin fizzes because she was buzzing like a bee. She was staggering and shit. She might as well have had a free pussy sign taped to her that night.

"Yeah, I decided to grace Columbus with my presence tonight," I said.

"Come on over to where we're sitting," Morgan said, leading me by the hand.

She was in her touchy-feely mood so I knew she was good and full. Whenever she got drunk, she hung all over me, hugging me and kissing on me and shit. Some people even thought we were on the down low *girlfriend* girlfriends.

"Look who's here," Morgan said to DC, throwing her arm around my neck. "My girl came out to kick it with us tonight."

DC gave me the what up nod. He really didn't like me and I really didn't give a fuck. We just stayed cordial because we had a common denominator in our lives, Morgan. DC owned an urban-clothing store, plus he played the role of promoter and brought R&B groups to town on occasion. He considered himself to be the man. He had done well for himself. I had to give him credit. He was straight legit. I mean, yeah, at first he hustled to come up with the funds to set his business off, but once the legitimate money started rolling in, he gave up the dope game all together. He even pulled a few of his homies out with him. At least he says he ain't in the game anymore.

But he was known for his Ike Turner mentality. He thought women were put on this earth for three things: to look pretty, to suck his dick, and to look pretty while sucking his dick. I had warned Morgan over and over about what the word on the street was about him, but she sounded like an old eighties song talking about she didn't care what he did to them (other girls) as long as he would just be good to her. A woman is going to do what she want to do. Sometimes they have to learn the hard way. But why did it have to be tonight?

"What you drinking, Harlem?" DC asked in his hard Suge Knight demeanor.

"Long Island," I said with a cordial smile.

DC nodded for one of his boys to go order my drink.

"You don't see nobody else," I heard a voice from the end of the table ask. "You don't see me down here, Ms. Harlem?"

"Oh, hi," I said when I saw Rashad chillin' with a cigar hanging out of his mouth. That's all he was getting was a hi out of me. He was the clingy type. He would sit up under me all night and then think that he was going home with me. He got me once before and I'll be damned if I was going to let him get me again.

Out of all of DC's boys, I was most attracted to Rashad. At first, we would just always speak to one another in a flirtatious manner. Then he took me out a few times. I would sometimes go to his house and cook for him and even do his laundry. We were just really good friends. Of course we were attracted to one another, but we had never done the do . . . had sex. It wasn't until one night, after drinking and playing cards at Morgan's, that I ended up in Morgan's guestroom with him. His foreplay was on point, but when he pulled out his uncircumcised dick I thought I was going to throw up.

It wouldn't have been so bad if I had just let him fuck me and not seen what the dick looked like, but I was giving him a little foreplay and worked my way down to his dick. I pulled it out and started rubbing on it. I wasn't going to suck it or anything, because I don't do that. I was just going to tease it a little. But when I held it in my hand, it just felt saggy. And to top it all off, it had the nerve to have this weird odor. I had to pretend that I had drank too much and had to go throw up to get out of that predicament. Any mother who doesn't get their son circumcised at birth should be stoned. Do it for your son. Do it for the women who he will choose to fuck.

When I only said hi to Rashad, he could tell I was being short with him, so he just left it alone. Pretty soon DC's boy came back with my Long Island. But while waiting, I had to watch Morgan dance and grind up against DC while he ignored her to stare at every other chick walking by.

It was pissing me off, but I let it go. Morgan couldn't stay blinded forever.

"Thank you," I said when the guy sat my drink down. "Thank you DC."

"No problem," he said, looking into my eyes. "A friend of Morgan's is a friend of mine."

I smiled. Maybe I shouldn't have, because he read more into my smile than it really was. I could just feel his eyes burning a hole through me. I was like, *damn, do this nigga want his drink back or what?*

"Come on, baby, let's go dance," Morgan said to DC, kissing on him.

"You know I don't dance," he said, sipping on his Hennessy straight. "I only fuck."

Morgan laughed, but I thought it was disgusting and downright degrading.

"And that you do well," Morgan said to DC's comment.

I turned my head to see what was going on in the front of the club. As I turned back around to sip on my drink I felt a hand on my knee. I looked at the guy sitting to my right, and both his hands were on the table. I looked at the guy sitting on my left, and both his hands were around his drink. I looked across at DC and he winked. I think he was giving me what he thought was a sexy smile, but to me, there ain't nothing sexy about a mouth full of gold teeth.

"Get your hand off of my muthafuckin' knee," I said loud enough for everyone at the table, including Morgan, to hear. I was staring dead at him so that everyone knew exactly who my words were geared to.

"Oh, my fault," he said, swigging down his Henney like it wasn't nothing but a thang.

"Yeah, your fault all right," I said, rolling my eyes.

"Bitch, I said my fault," DC replied, twisting up his mug.

"Come on now," Morgan said, rubbing on DC's shoulder. "You don't have to call my girl out of her name."

"Fuck him, Morgan. Let's go," I said, standing.

Morgan hesitated. I could tell she didn't want to leave.

"You trying to stay up in here with him?" I questioned her.

Morgan hurried over to my side in an attempt to hush me. She put her arm around my neck, hugging me, and began whispering in my ear.

"That's right," I heard DC say. "Go on over there to your little girlfriend. I bet she knows what your pussy taste like better than me. Do she know you keep that muthafucka faded?"

"Morgan, I swear to God. Let's go," I said between gritted teeth.

"Come on, Harlem. He's just had too much to drink. He didn't mean any harm," Morgan pleaded.

"Why are you sticking up for that asshole? What has he ever done for you?" I asked Morgan.

"Look, Harlem, you know how much I like DC," Morgan said sadly, putting her head down. But I wasn't even feeling sorry for her. "Why are you doing this?"

"Come on, Morgan. Open your eyes."

"He's not like the others. He does nice little things for me. Remember just last week he got my hair done for me."

"And he just ought to have," I said. "You had just gotten it done the day you sweat it out fucking him all night. He should have gotten it done. You told me yourself that you didn't even get to cum. You wasted a perfect hairdo for a little dick man. Where's your come up?"

"Oooh, sometimes I hate you," Morgan said sharply. Once she realized the words that had slipped from between her lips, I could see guilt taking over.

"You can hate me now," I said, shrugging my shoulders. "But go tell that nigga *asta la vista*."

Morgan twisted her lips up and rolled her eyes as if to let me know that she wasn't going nowhere. She walked back over to DC and said, "Baby, just apologize to my girl for calling her a bitch. I want us all to stay and just get along."

"What?" DC said in disbelief that Morgan had the audacity to ask him to apologize to a female. "You gon' be the next bitch if you don't put your girl in check," DC said to Morgan. "You need to let her know that I'm that nigga."

"Oh, baby," Morgan said while laughing and kissing on DC's neck. "Just say you're sorry."

DC mugged Morgan dead in her face. She landed right on her inebriated ass. It was instinct, but I picked up my Long Island and threw it at him. I threw the whole fucking glass at him, but it missed, crashing against the wall. Security made it over there just in time. DC was about to come around the table and demolish my little ass, but I had no fear in my heart.

One of DC's boys helped Morgan up off the floor. She was dusting herself off. Then, unbelievably, she walked back over to DC and asked him if he was okay, if any of the glass I had thrown at him had cut him.

I snatched her drunk ass up by the arm and dragged her right out of that club. I couldn't wait to get her ass outside and let her have a piece of my mind. The minute we got out of the door, I let her have it.

"Don't you ever put a man before me!" I screamed. The folks in the line waiting to get into the club all stopped their chitchatting to see what was going down.

"I wasn't putting him before you. You my girl," Morgan whined.

"As many times as you've pissed me off and I've wanted to knock your ass down, I ain't never put my hands on you. If you think for one minute that I was about to stand there and let some grimy ass nigga do it, then you got me twisted. Fuck that, Morgan."

I was pissed. I wanted to cry. But tears don't fall from eyes. I don't have time to sit around and cry. I'm all cried out thanks to my earlier years. I'm all about action now.

"I was just tipsy and these shoes," Morgan said in DC's defense. "I lost my balance."

"No, bitch, you done lost your mind," I said angrily.

Morgan just stood there looking down. I gripped her chin and pulled her face up to me.

"Has DC ever put his hands on you before?" I asked. Morgan wouldn't respond. I took that as a yes, so I took my shoes off and headed back into the club.

"Harlem!" Morgan screamed after me. "Harlem!"

But I was halfway back to that son of a bitch's table by the time she caught up with me. He was already kissing on some other chick by the time I got back there. I was so glad Morgan had followed me back in there to witness it, too.

When he saw me coming he just sat there with his "I'm that nigga" smile on his face. He didn't know what hit him when the heel of my shoe whacked him across the forehead. I stunned his ass. I got in about four good blows before his boys got me off of him. Security quickly got me away from them.

"That's enough of you, lil' mama," the security guard said. "You got to go and make sure you don't ever come back."

Morgan was standing a couple feet from DC. I gave her the "are you coming with me" look. She stood frozen, then she hawked up a nice wad of spit that landed smack on DC's nose, then she followed right behind me.

DC stood there heated. What he would have done to us if security hadn't intervened is something I never want to find out.

The patrons who had seen me clock on DC thought that I was

just some angry broad clownin' on my man because he was up in the club with another bitch, but that wasn't the case. A woman needed to fight his punk ass to let him know that he wasn't going to beat on all of us. I couldn't save all the other dumb women that were sure to cross his path. But I saved one that night, my friend.

Morgan had drank way too much to drive her own car, so I walked her staggering ass to my car and laid her across the back seat where she went to sleep. When we got to my house I helped her walk to my upstairs guestroom. My house is a split-level, three bedrooms, but I turned one of the two upstairs bedrooms into an office/library.

After taking off Morgan's shoes I tucked her in. I wasn't even halfway out of the door when she started gagging. I raced over to her and helped her out of bed. We got to the bathroom just in time. I lifted the toilet seat and let her rip. I held her hair out of the way while she puked her guts out.

I got her a cold rag, made her swig a couple capfuls of mouthwash, and escorted her back to bed. I tucked her in once again and turned off the light on my way out.

"Harlem," I heard Morgan faintly call. "Thank you."

I smiled and walked away. Morgan didn't need to thank me. It was my duty as her friend to have her back no matter what. She was like a sister to me. And as long as I can remember it's always been just her and me. I've never been one to run with a pack, crew, or so-called clique. My mentality is way too dominant for that. I'm the leader and the follower, so besides Morgan, my only other posse members include me, myself, and I.

About five years ago, though, Morgan and I used to roll with this one broad named Yvette, but she tried to cross me so I had to fire her. With Morgan and I being like sisters, and with blood being thicker than water, Morgan fired her, too. There wasn't no love lost with Yvette. I had always considered her more so Morgan's friend and my associate. I never hung out with her outside of anything we all three did together. She wasn't someone I would even just call up to holler at on the phone. I mean we were cool, but only because of Morgan.

Morgan had met Yvette through some dude she was fucking. Yvette was one of his boy's girlfriends. After several double dates, Morgan and Yvette started hanging out. At first it made me sick, them two running around calling themselves those fools' wifey. If they only knew how stupid they looked. And perhaps there was a part of me that was jealous that Morgan was spending more time with Yvette than with me. But even aside from all of that, I hated Yvette just because she was a self-serving opportunist. She was always on the grind trying to see what she could get out of life for free, scamming and hustling and shit. And I don't have a problem with the dirt she did to other people, but when she tried to cross me, it was war.

That bitch tried to see me in jail. What had happened was that the three of us had taken a road trip to Canada in a rental car that Yvette got in her name. Well, on our way back home we were in a car accident. Some guy changing lanes didn't look and rammed right into the side of us. I was asleep in the back seat, leaning against the door when he hit us. My head jerked and rammed back into the door. I was pretty dazed. My jaw locked up and everything.

Yvette was driving and Morgan was in the front passenger seat.

They didn't get hurt at all. I had to make an emergency visit to my dentist and get some minor surgery. I ended up having to file a claim with the guy's insurance company to cover my medical bills.

Yvette was under the impression that her insurance company was going to have to get involved. She claimed that her policy didn't cover rentals, that her premium would go up, and all other kinds of dumb shit that she could think up. So one day she had the nerve to call me up and ask me to drop the claim. I told her cool, just as long as she paid for my medical bills. That bitch had the nerve to say, "Well, I don't think you're really hurt anyway."

I wanted to jump through the phone and bust her in her muthafuckin' jaw. I wanted that hoe's jaw to lock. Instead, I replied with a fuck you and hung up. We eventually spoke again because Morgan kept trying to play peacemaker and eventually got us back in the same room again. We still weren't as close as we had been before, and that wasn't even close. Two months hadn't gone by when the claim adjuster who was handling my claim called me to go over the final settlement offer. In the beginning, the claim adjuster kept trying to downplay my claim like it wasn't worth nothing and I couldn't figure out why. Finally, the adjuster told me that Yvette had called her and told her that I was filing a false claim with the insurance company and she wasn't going to be a part of it. Yvette said she felt that it was her duty to inform the company and that they should take any measures they needed to take for my fraudulent act.

Did that bitch know that I could have gone to jail for her trying to plant a bug like that in their ear, let alone a bug that was an outright lie? I mean, I had to wear a brace in my mouth that cost me eight hundred dollars out of pocket. I had needles stuck in my jaw and all kind of other crazy shit. For that bitch to say that I was faking, it hurt. I was so pissed that it physically hurt. But I didn't get mad. I got even.

The claim adjuster told me that Yvette's statements were not going to affect the claim because medical records and X rays showed that I did, in fact, obtain the injuries that were stated in my claim. We settled for a nice lump of change, but that still didn't take away from the hate that I was feeling towards Yvette.

As much as Yvette hustled and ran schemes, even if I had been faking my injuries, she was the last shiesty bitch to be turning a muthafucker in. She had rigged pay stubs and tax returns to get a house. She even had Morgan's dumb ass pretend to work at Chase Manhattan Bank, in the human resources department, to help get her a car. She had given the dealership Morgan's cell phone number. I told Morgan not to get involved, but when Ricart Ford called to verify Yvette's employment, Morgan was right there on the other end of the phone feeding them lies. It worked out just fine for a while.

The scheme enabled Yvette to get the car off of the lot, but when the bank that had approved her car loan contacted Chase directly, the shit hit the fan. The bank was told that Yvette didn't work there and never had. Everything ended up being traced back to Morgan's cell phone. The bank threatened to prosecute her for fraud right along with Yvette. Yvette managed to worm her way out of it by paying off the balance of the car, which she had planned on doing anyway, eventually. She had just wanted to establish some type of line of credit for herself so that she could start running bigger and better scams. Plus she said that she didn't want to just walk onto the car lot and buy an Acura with cash money. I don't know why not. She had already made the dumb mistake of putting thirty thousand dollars down on her house. Eventually Uncle Sam wanted to know exactly where that large lump sum of money had come from.

Supposedly, Yvette had this brother who lived out of town that was sending her money that couldn't be accounted for. To Morgan and I that only meant that it was drug money. But with all the men that came in and out of her life and her pussy, Morgan and I thought that it was possible that she was straight up hoeing. We thought that Yvette just didn't want to tell us so she made up this phantom brother, of whom we never saw one time while we were rolling with her.

So with all the dirt Yvette had done, I couldn't believe she tried to cross me with the insurance company. So of course I had to cross her right back. I hated to do it, but when you're back is up against the wall and someone is firing at you, you have no choice but to fire back.

I ended up placing a call to the IRS and that bitch's shit was on the curb in a matter of weeks. Only scraps were left to put on the curb. Anything of value was seized based on the suspicion of illegal activity. Uncle Sam put her shit in his warehouse until she could come up with proof of income. Even then they threatened that she might face tax-evasion charges. Her shit was a mess.

I don't know if she knows that I was the one who put the call in or not, but I'm sure I was the first person to come across her mind. But that's the kind of person I am. You cross me and I cross you. And that's all I have to say about that.

The next morning Morgan sobered up, but she had the hangover of a lifetime. Mostly everything that had happened the night before was a blur to her, but she knew that we had gotten into some shit with DC.

We got up and chatted about the situation over some toast and ginger ale, which my mom used to call sick pop when I was little. After that, I drove Morgan back to the Second Wind parking lot so that we could pick up her car.

When we pulled up, her car was the only one in the lot and the fucker was sitting on bricks.

"Oh, my God," Morgan said, putting her hand over her mouth. "That son of a bitch," she said, jumping out of the car. Her car wasn't literally sitting on bricks, but the tires were slashed, busted, and flat.

"Looks like somebody borrowed Michael Meyers's knife for this job," I said as I observed the deep wounds in the tires. I looked up and tears were running down Morgan's face.

"I know DC did this shit," she said crying. "How could he do this?"

This wasn't the time for an I told you so, but I sure did want to say it. When Morgan met him I expressed to her that he was a wolf in sheep's clothing. Yeah he dressed nice and smelled good, plus had a little change in his pocket. But he seemed like the type that would do some ole grimy shit to get back at somebody.

I don't know why he slashed Morgan's tires. I was the one who clocked him. But I guess spit in the mug hurts worse than any shoe upside the head. I'm sure that if it was my car that had been left there overnight, I would be the one on my way to Goodyear tires.

Morgan called Triple A and they towed her car to Goodyear tires. I followed behind, but not before we filed a police report. We knew there wasn't shit that they could do at this point because we didn't see who actually did it, but at least it was documented.

Once we got to Goodyear, Morgan had all four tires replaced. I paid half. I felt half responsible. But neither of us really minded replacing the tires because it was material. We both knew that DC was capable of far more than that, so we let it slide. We knew that was his way of sending a message to us. One way of sending us a message, anyway.

For a couple of weeks after the incident, DC did some old bitch shit, calling Morgan's cell phone to harass her. He told her that four flat tires wasn't shit to repair compared to the damage he planned on doing. Morgan eventually got her cell phone number changed and never heard much more from DC again. But he was one of them grimy, snakelike fuckers. He liked to make his enemy think that he'd forgotten all about them, but then out of nowhere, he'd strike. So I told Morgan that for a while she would have to sleep with one eye open. Me, I'd sleep with both mine open.

2. I Want Candy

It would be wrong of me to lead you on to believe that Morgan is the only one who could ever get caught up with the wrong type of man. I never knew just how easy it was to feel so right about Mr. Wrong.

I'm not some young, impressionable chick, but believe it or not, a sistah like myself can get caught up in the game too . . . the game of love. What makes the game even harder to play is when there are one too many players involved and no rules to follow.

My preference would be to tell you how this game called love ends before I tell you how it begins. But I guess we all have to go through the particulars and pleasantries.

I've never believed in any of that love conquers all shit. Hell, I never even believed in love. I suppose deep down inside, everybody feels as though they have a soulmate somewhere out there in the world. You know that one, that person who was put on earth to catch your drift.

I suppose it wouldn't be storytelling etiquette if I didn't walk barefoot over the hot coals just for you and put all of my business on Front Street. So fuck it! What have I got to lose?

Mmm. He's like candy to me. From the moment him and his boy walked into my store he was the sweetest thing I had ever known. His eyes told the greatest story ever told.

I'll never forget the day. As Morgan and I are standing behind the counter going over the inventory log, two guys walk into the store. One was wearing a red Nike Just Do It shirt and the other was wearing a thin Sean John short-sleeve sweater. They were both sportin' jeans.

"Hello," the one in the red shirt said, eyes wide as if trying to determine which one of us, Morgan or myself, he was going to spit game to.

"What's up fellas?" I replied, as the other one moseyed off to browse the store.

"So, love, what do they call you?" the guy in the red shirt asked me. He had some sexiness about him. He wasn't extremely cute in the face, but he looked good. He had these slanted dark-brown eyes with lashes that I would have killed for. His thick dark eyebrows complemented his eyes. I could tell that he found his way to the gym a few times because he had the body of boxer. But even with that being said, I wasn't feeling him.

"Harlem," I replied in a hard tone, like I was D'ing up to a prison inmate or something.

"Harlem, huh?" he snickered.

"What's so funny?" I snapped.

"Oh nothing. I was just thinking to myself. You see, my name is

York and now I got a lady friend here named Harlem. Ironic isn't it?" He said, winking at me. "Harlem-York. Harlem, New York. You get it?" He laughed.

I think he cracked himself up more than he did Morgan and me as we stood there watching him. I could see right then and there that he was going to be one of those cats that thought he was a pretty boy and could suck his own dick. I must admit. He was a little fine. He was a chocolate creamy brotha. He was about the complexion of a buckeye. He had a nice little mustache growing in. I could tell he had good hair because of the smooth baby hair that edged his zigzag braids.

"So what's your friend's name?" Morgan asked him, biting her bottom lip in delicacy. She had fuck me for free written all over her face. Had I taught this hoe nothing? I nudged her. She immediately took the hint and straightened up, wiping the drool from her bottom lip.

"Oh, him," York said. "That's my boy, Jay. Yo, Jazzy. Come here, man."

"Mmm, Jazzy," Morgan said under her breath. "I like that nickname."

Jazzy looked up from the book he was flipping through. His eyes immediately focused in on me. He smiled at me. I put my head down in embarrassment. He noticed me noticing him and that shit caught me off guard. I had never bowed my head down to no man. I guess there's a first time for everything.

He put the book back on the shelf and headed our way, lightweight giving me the eye the entire time he strolled. I promise the shit was in slow motion. I noticed everything about him from his well-groomed high fade haircut to his manila envelope skin tone to his embellishing left dimple. That's right. He only had one dimple. I found that to be unique. I was finding everything about this Jazzy unique. He was the first yellow brotha to ever turn my head. Call it a prejudice if you want to, but I always had a color preference for any man that I even thought about giving the time of day to. I enjoyed me the company of a chocolate brotha. But for Jazzy, oh a sistah was more than willing to make an exception.

"So Jazzy, where are you from?" Morgan said, licking her lips, calling dibs on him immediately. "By the way, I'm Morgan."

Morgan put her hand out to shake Jazzy's. He put his hand out and grabbed hers then placed it to his mouth. As he planted a juicy slurp of a kiss on her hand, which left a hint of his saliva, he was looking dead into *my* eyes. I envisioned him doing what he had just done to Morgan's hand to my pussy. I wouldn't mind him branding my pussy with his lips. I'd wear that badge proudly fo sho.

"I'm from around the way," Jazzy said in this mellow ass, down south voice. "But how did you know I wasn't from here?"

"Oh, I would have definitely remembered seeing you before," Morgan said, batting her big hazel eyes with a huge smile on her face. Morgan, who had two dimples, was all teeth. Her medium brown skin was glowing and the nipples on those big ass titties of hers were pointing straight at Jazzy. His eyes were staring right back at them, too. But that could have been because Morgan was a towering five feet ten inches to his five feet eight inches.

"Funny you ain't never seen me and I see you all the time," Jazzy said to Morgan, but once again looking at me.

"You gon' introduce yourself?" Jazzy said to me.

I took a deep breath before replying. "Harlem. And I've never seen neither one of you before," I said as if I could care less about ever seeing them again. I was playing.

"Well, we be around," York replied.

"Hey, I'm looking for this book called *No Strings Attached* by Nancey Flowers. Do y'all have that?"

"No," I replied at the very same time Morgan was replying "Yes."

Morgan and I both gave each other an evil look.

"I think Culture Plus or A&B once sent us that book with our order that just came in," Morgan said, giving me this bug-eyed look. "I'll check in the back storage room. Come on, Jay. You can come with me."

"Not unless you call me Jazzy," he said with a smile.

"Okay," Morgan said, blushing. "You can come with me, Jazzy."

As Morgan led Jazzy back to the storage room she turned at me and smiled. That bitch knew damn well we had sold out of that title. It was one we couldn't keep on the shelves. She was probably taking him back there to suck his dick. Now here I was standing in the store with boo-boo the fool.

"How come I've never seen you with no dude before?" York said as he grabbed a red blow pop from the candy rack, opened it up, and popped it in his mouth. He had a tongue like a serpent as he intentionally showed me that he definitely had skills with it by moving it about the blow pop like a snake. He wanted me to feel like he had me on a stick going to work on licking all over me like a lollipop. "I only see you with ole girl. You ain't into chicks are you?"

"Nigga, you don't know me like that to be coming at me like that," I said, snapping my neck and making my lips crooked.

"Now I understand why you ain't never seen me seeing you before," York said, shaking his head.

"And why is that?" I asked.

"Because your head is stuck too far up your ass to notice anything. I'm surprised you even know when it's daylight."

"See, there you go again. You talkin' shit and you don't know nothing about me," I replied, dippin' and dabbin' with hand motions.

"Then let me get to know you," York said, flipping the script, turning into this smooth ass character right before my eyes.

I leaned in closer to York over the counter. I pushed my sex kitten button and decided to play with him a little.

"And just what is it about me that you want to get to know?" I said almost in a whisper. "Is it what's in between my ears or what's in between my thighs?"

York licked his lips then smiled. "A brotha ain't even gonna lie. I wanna get to know both heads. But first let's start with your mind. What was the last book you read?"

"Your Blues Ain't Like Mine," I said.

"Who's your favorite music artist?"

"Phyllis Hymen," I replied.

"Enough about that head. What's your favorite position that turns on that other head, doggy style?"

We both cracked a smile.

"What? I got you to smile. I must be doing something right," York said, proud of himself.

A few minutes passed before Jazzy and Morgan came out of the storage room.

"You ready, York?" Jazzy asked as he came from the back with Morgan with two books in his hand.

And on top of being a smooth, sexy muthafucker, he also reads. My panties were getting wet.

"Yeah, man," York said to Jazzy, but his eyes were saying no to me. He could stand there all day long hollering at me if he could. But he never got the opportunity. York had made his move on me and Morgan had made her move on him. "Did they have the book you were looking for?"

"Nah, but I'm gonna cop one of Triple Crown's new shits, this novel *Dollar Bill* and this other book I had been looking for, *Rich Dad, Poor Dad*. And let me get some Mary Janes. Nigga got a sweet tooth now," Jazzy said, throwing the books on the counter while pulling out a huge wad of cash.

I could smell the sticky icky reeking from him. Once Morgan made her way back behind the counter I could smell it on her too. I looked up at her and she tried to hide her glossy red eyes. Them fools was back there sparkin' the izm and didn't even offer a puff. How rude!

Jazzy proceeded to scoop up a couple dollars worth of Mary Jane caramel chews while I rang up the books.

"This is one of our best sellers," I said to Jazzy, holding up *Dollar Bill*.

"Oh yeah," he replied, nodding his head.

"It sure is," Morgan said. "These ghetto books are damn near what keeps our lights on."

"Have you read it yet?" Jazzy asked me, trying to figure out my taste in literature.

"It was good, but you know I'll take that old school Donald Goines shit over any of this new jack shit," I said in a thuggish tone.

"Oh, so you one of them gangsta bitches," Jazzy laughed. "No offense. I meant that in the Tupac or Ja Rule sense."

"None taken," I said, bagging up his stuff. "That will be thirty-three dollars and three cents."

Jazzy peeled off a one hundred dollar bill and handed it to me.

"Do you have anything smaller?" I asked.

This sexy look came across Jazzy's face. His eyes traveled down to his privates and replied, "Naw. Nothing smaller."

Just then York's cell phone rang. He looked at the number then walked over to the door to answer it. The caller ID must have read baby's mama.

"If this book ain't no good I'm bringing it back and I'll expect a full refund," York said, directing his comment to me.

"Triple Crown don't drop nothing but hot titles," Morgan interrupted, drawing the attention back to herself. "So you definitely won't be returning that."

"All right then. Good day, ladies."

Jazzy picked up his bag from off the counter and walked over to the door. By this time, York was in a heated conversation with whomever had just called his phone. It was obvious that he wanted to holler at me some more, but there was no getting off of that phone call. So instead he gave me a nod and a wink, then he and Jazzy were out the door.

"Damn! Damn! Damn! Those were some fine ass menses," Morgan said with excitement. "I know dude asked for your number didn't he?"

"No, he didn't," I said as I pulled the inventory log back out.

"Then you got his number didn't you?" Morgan said anxiously.

"Nope," I replied as if I didn't have a care in the world.

"You've got to be shittin' me," Morgan said almost angry. "For once I don't push up on a brotha and ask for his contact info because

I think you're out here handling things on your end. Now you're telling me that we don't even have a way to get into contact with them?"

"Don't worry. He'll be back," I said, scanning down the log, but not reading a thing.

"You seem pretty confident about that," Morgan said. "What makes you so sure of yourself?"

I held up the $66.97 and said, "Because he forgot his change."

Ever since York and Jazzy left the store, Morgan's pussy gets wet every time a customer comes through the door, hoping that it's them. One would have thought that the five minutes she spent in the back room with Jazzy had been a lifetime.

When they were back there getting their smoke on she told me that she found out Jazzy owned a few car washes in town and that York ran one of them. I didn't run the streets, but I knew enough about those car washes to know that several of them were fronts. A car went in dirty and came out even dirtier.

A lot of hustlers used businesses like car washes, beauty shops, and carry-outs for drug money fronts. They had to prove to Uncle Sam that they were making money somewhere. They usually gave the businesses to their girlfriends, who were happy to run things and make a name for themselves in the community as a big baller's wifey. I didn't stereotype Jazzy and York by assuming they sold drugs. I didn't want to prejudge the brothas. I got my own business and it's straight legit. I thought that perhaps they were on the same type of level. But after Morgan told me exactly which car washes they manned, I did start to have my suspicions. They were each located in some pretty drug infested areas and I had heard a thing or two about a couple of the spots.

I wasn't all gung ho on seeing them again as much as Morgan was, but a little part of me wouldn't have minded. They seemed cool. But on the same token, I was straight that we hadn't hooked up with them if it turned out that they were a couple of street pharmacists. Yeah, I would be straight on them fo sho.

My shit is too tight to be getting mixed up with the wrong people. That's where some young women like me make their mistake. They get caught up. Well I owed it to myself to make sure that neither Morgan nor myself got caught up in any bullshit. But it's amazing that no matter how fast you run from it, bullshit can still manage to catch up with you.

3. Who's That Lady?

It was 9:00 A.M. Saturday morning and I was ready for the over-whelming store traffic that the beauty salons and barbershops would generate for my store. Morgan's ass hadn't made it in yet and she knew damn well that Saturday was the busiest day of the week for the store. She was always late. On a Tuesday, Wednesday or some-thing like that, I didn't mind, but not on no fuckin' Saturday. If she wasn't my girl, tight like glue, she would had long been repri-manded for her constant tardiness.

I got nervous when I heard the bell on the door ring, which meant that customers were about to start pouring in. I knew it wasn't Morgan because she used the back entrance with her key no matter what because that's where she parked her car. When I looked up and saw who the customer was my nervousness turned to complete disgust.

It was dirty crackhead Reese. She came into the Suga Shop at least twice a month, sometimes three, begging me for money or snacks. I even caught that bitch trying to boost some books and

CDs out of here one time. I told her not to ever come into my place of business again for as long as she lived, but evidently that didn't stop her. There she was, smiling at me like I was her best friend in the whole wide world.

"Harlem, Harlem, Harlem," Reese said as if she was singing a song. "Baby girl, Harlem. What's happening?"

"Ain't nothing happening in here, Reese, and ain't nothing for free so don't come up in here asking for shit," I said firmly. "So before you take any more steps up in here, show me the money."

"Why you so goddamn mean?" Reese asked, as if her feelings were hurt. "Why do you have to talk to me like that, Harlem?"

"Sometimes a bitch gotta be mean to get her point across. Otherwise people will try to step all over me. People like you. And speaking of steppin', why don't you get to steppin' right up on out of here?"

Reese sighed. "Look, I didn't come in here to fight with you."

"Then what do you want? And if I'm so goddamn mean, why do you keep coming back?"

"Look," Reese said, getting to the point. "Do-Rag who lives over there on Kelton owes me twenty dollars. I was wondering if I could hold twenty dollars from you until I catch up with him. Do-Rag is always good for what he owes. It's just hard catching up with him is all. But once I catch up with him, I'll pay you back with the twenty dollars he gives me."

I couldn't help but start to ask myself, what is it with crackheads and always trying to borrow twenty dollars? I bet if a crackhead found a bag full of one hundred dollar bills and there was one twenty dollar bill in the bag, their ass would take the twenty and leave the rest.

"I don't have no money to just be givin' you. Even if I did, why would I give it to you? I have to take care of my damn self. I'm tired of you coming in here like I owe you something. I owe you shit! Now get the fuck out of here!" I shouted to the nappy-head dopefiend. "I told you to stop coming around here begging. I mean it this time, Reese. Don't make me have to get a restraining order on you."

"It's cool," Reese said sadly. "I'm sorry. I'm sorry, baby girl. I truly am. I just thought. Never mind what I thought. Never mind."

Reese exited the store and I saw her stagger across the street, damn near getting taken out by a Honda.

I hated to see her coming towards my store. I hated how she came into my store like she was welcomed. I hated how she ignored my words over and over again and kept coming into my store begging all of the damn time. I hated how she would sometimes stand out in front of my store and beg for change from my customers, sometimes scaring them away. I hated her nappy dirty hair that looked like it hadn't been washed in ages. I hated the black blemishes that were scattered about her face. I hated the stale pissy smell that rose from those stupid denim overalls she always wore. I hated her. But what I hated most was that she was the woman who had given birth to me twenty-six years ago. I hated that she was my mother.

"You okay, Harlem?" Morgan asked, putting her hand on my shoulder. She had entered the store through the back storage room. When she saw that I was talking with Reese, she didn't interrupt.

"Yeah," I said, shrugging her hand off of me. "You're late."

"I know you hate to see your mother like that. I know how hard you try to forget about everything she put you through. But look at you, girl. You're okay. There's no need to be so angry and bitter anymore. Life's too short, babe."

I looked at Morgan without comment. She had such sincerity in her words, like it hurt her to see me hurting. I think seeing her hurt was more painful than my own hurt. I quickly brushed pass Morgan. I had to run to the back and go to bathroom. I had to catch my breath.

I went into the bathroom and closed the door behind me. I went over to the sink and looked at myself in the mirror. I had Reese's eyes. I had her fuckin' eyes. I wanted to claw them out of my sockets. I wanted no part of her.

I could feel my eyes beginning to water. I turned on the cold water and splashed my face, ruining my lightly applied makeup. But I had to freeze those tears up. And just in case one got away I didn't want to see it. I didn't want to be able to determine if it was water droplets or a tear running down my face. No way was I going to shed a tear. I had shed enough growing up.

At first when I was coming up things weren't so bad. Actually, they weren't bad at all. My early childhood years were wonderful. Reese and my father, Ray Jones, was the most envied couple in the family. Out of all of my cousins, I was the only one whose parents were married, or even together for that matter. My other cousins were always so jealous of that. I guess that's why I never really got close to any of them. All the while I'm thinking that they liked me, they simply wanted to be me.

I'll never forget my cousin Amerie. She was deemed the cutest of all of the cousins. All of my aunts loved to show her off. They would take her places that they didn't take the rest of us. They would buy her things that they didn't buy the rest of us. But I was cool with that. Reese and Ray gave me all the love and material things I needed to make me happy, so in my opinion, I still had more than Amerie would ever have. She knew it too and she hated it.

She used to love to come and spend the night with me. I was only seven and an only child at the time, so I looked forward to her company even though she was a mean, spoiled little girl. The neighborhood boys that I normally climbed trees with could have cared less about me and a dumb old tree when Amerie was around. All they cared about was feeling on her bootie.

I must admit, she was a cute little project chick. One would have never known that she was project breed. That's one thing I can say about Aunt Mary, Amerie's mother. She made sure that all of the ten boyfriends she had not only kept her laced, but bought her daughter just as many nice things. So Amerie stayed in frilly little dresses with matching purses, patent leather shoes, and white lace bobby socks. Her hair was always pressed, curled and shiny from this grease called Liv that her mother did her hair with. Her mother even allowed her to carry lip gloss in her purse, which Amerie constantly applied.

Amerie kind of reminded me of the youngest daughter on *The Fresh Prince of Bel-Air,* Ashley. She always wore two long curled ponytails with ribbons and fluffy bangs. She would have been a nice catch growing up if she just hadn't been so devious.

One time when she was over spending the night she and I stayed up until two in the morning playing with my extensive collection of Barbie dolls. I was a diehard Barbie fan. Back then, there weren't as many Black Barbies and Black Barbie paraphernalia as there is today, so most of my Barbies were white. I even had a Barbie coat with a picture of a white Barbie on it.

My favorite Barbie accessory was my Barbie dream house. It was pink with white window shutters and it even had a working elevator. Amerie and I played for hours with the Barbie Corvette and the Barbie Winnebago. But for some reason it seemed like every time Amerie left after sleeping over, some of my Barbie merchandise would disappear. I never used to say a word. I didn't want to cause any trouble and make Amerie not want to come over and play with me again. I guess my keeping quiet made Amerie feel as though it was okay to keep stealing from me or that I was afraid of her. So around me, she felt like the baddest bitch.

Well on this particular night that we were up until two in the morning, I had to excuse myself to go to the bathroom. Halfway down the hallway I forgot that I didn't have my house slippers on. Reese drilled it into me that a lady had to keep her feet in the best condition and that walking barefoot wasn't the way to do so. Well, when I went back into the bedroom to retrieve my pink Barbie slippers, my sudden return caught Amerie off guard. There she was, stuffing my Skipper doll, Barbie's little sister, into her overnight bag. I couldn't believe it. I didn't say anything. I just stood there looking at her and she was looking right back at me.

"I'm just going to borrow it for a spell," she said, smiling a fake smile as she zipped my Skipper doll into her bag.

That's when I knew that the longer I went without saying anything to her, the more she would take. I just wanted to be nice to her. I loved my cousin. But she was a prime example of how people can mistake kindness for weakness so it was time to shut that little bitch down.

I put on my slippers and went on to the bathroom as planned. I came back, kicked my slippers off beside me and sat back down to play with Amerie.

The bottom of my Barbie dream house had two drawers that I used for storage. I kept Barbie clothes and whatnot in there.

"Amerie, will you get me the red Barbie dress with the black fur on it from the drawer?" I asked her nicely, pointing.

"Sure," she said, bopping her head so that her ponytails bounced.

I picked up one of my slippers and just as soon as Amerie stuck her hand in the drawer to grab the Barbie dress I slammed the drawer back close, right with her hand in it. When she opened her mouth to yell my slipper fit perfectly.

"That's what happens to the hands of people who steal," I whispered in Amerie's ear. "I'm tired so I'm getting ready to go to bed and when I wake up in the morning I want to see my Skipper doll, along with anything else of mine you have in your bag, back where it belongs."

I released her hand out of the drawer and removed my slipper from her mouth. She sat there crying damn near the entire night while I slept with a smile on my face.

Okay, now who's the baddest bitch, I said to myself.

That was the first time in my life I had ever stood up for myself, but it wouldn't be the last.

Needless to say, Amerie stopped coming to my house for sleep-overs. Reese asked if the two of us were mad at one another and I denied it. I think a year later I confessed to Reese what had happened. I wasn't sure how'd she react because Reese had always been a pushover herself. She always felt that God would punish people with evil ways, that it wasn't up to mankind. Well, God was taking too damn long if you asked me. I would have been down to one Barbie by the time he handled Amerie's ass.

But Reese didn't get angry with me. As a matter of fact, she felt bad that I had to keep dealing with Amerie stealing from me for as long as I did. I remember her kissing me on the forehead and telling me that I could always tell her anything no matter what. That there would never be secrets between the two of us. I loved Reese so much then. Man, I loved her.

She was the nicest and the most beautiful mother in the world. And her smile, it was show stopping. I was young, but I knew what love felt like because of her. I knew I loved my mother and that she loved me. Reese had the kind of love that I could wrap myself up in twenty-four hours a day and keep warm with.

No one could have convinced me that any of that would have ever changed. I would have killed for her then. But it would be a few years later when I would want to kill her.

4. The Reason Why

I looked up and through the store window I saw Reese leaning into the window of a tan 1987 Cadillac. She had her hand on her hip and was smiling a big white smile like she was the finest broad out there turning tricks. She always did have a beautiful smile. She might be a crackhead, but she still took care of her teeth.

It wasn't long before she negotiated the transaction and hopped into the car and rode away with the male driver. Nine times out of ten she was going to screw him for a hit or some cash. If it was for a hit, he was probably only going to be able to tap that ass from the back. A trick only got to lay on top and fuck if he was paying cash money, fifty dollars at least. I had heard her negotiate enough transactions in my time to know how she did business. I would have never believed if someone told me the things that a person would do for a crack rock if I hadn't seen it firsthand myself.

Let me take y'all back for a minute and explain why I feel the way I do about Reese. Why I talk to and about her the way I do. Why there is so much hate in my heart for this woman. I know it's hard for anyone to truly ever comprehend how a child can feel so much hatred toward its mother. It's not every day you hear a girl lashing out so badly about the person who gave birth to her. But I believe that I have just cause. Maybe if you walked in my shoes a mile or two, you'd know exactly where I'm coming from. So feel this.

You see, I lost everything because of Reese's love for that damn drug. She's the reason why I lost weight and fit perfectly into this five feet six inches medium frame I own today. I had always been a chubby kid all the way up until my fourth grade year of school. That's when Reese discovered crack. That's when the money she used to spend on groceries started getting spent on her newfound habit. That's when my luxury of being able to indulge in snacks such as Little Debbie oatmeal pies and Mike Sells potato chips ended.

If you knew Reese way back in the day, her pre-crack days, you would have never thought in a million years that she would have turned out to be a drug abuser. I mean, Reese had always gotten her smoke on, but it was just weed. Hell, even I toke every now and then myself. I remember how she used to save up her doobies, break them open and reroll them into whole joints. She even taught me how to clean the seeds out of the bags of weed she bought. I used to take an album cover and a pack of tops, empty the bag of weed onto the album, and let the seeds roll down as I titled it. I used the pack of tops to keep the weed in place. Reese used to pay me fifty cents for that gig. I got an extra quarter if I was sure to get every last seed out. I got an extra dime off the top if the bag of weed was homegrown, because those were certain to have a ton of seeds in them, not to mention give the smoker a headache.

One day Reese's weed smokin' buddy, Sharmane, talked Reese

into smoking a primo, a joint laced with cocaine. For all the years Reese had known Sharmane, she hadn't done anything more than smoke weed either. But she had taken up with a new boyfriend, a small-time pusher, and he hipped her to primos. She liked the extra feel-good kick it provided. But Sharmane didn't want to feel good all by her lonesome, so as a favor to Reese, she hipped her to primos as well.

Reese enjoyed the extra kick just as much as Sharmane did. Eventually, Sharmane convinced her that it was an even better feeling straight up the nose. So Reese started doing lines. She'd keep the coke folded up in dollar bills until it was time to blow. Then she'd roll the dollar bill up as tight as a virgin's pussy and snort up the coke.

With a pusher for a boyfriend, Sharmane stayed up on the game. She couldn't wait to school Reese on the ultimate high, cooking and mixing the coke. Soon, doing crack became mind over matter for Reese. She became dependent on the type of feel-good smoking crack provided. Reese forgot all about how good her life was without the drug. She forgot about how good she felt without it. Eventually she forgot about me. Who knew that some white powder would have that much fuckin' power to just take over someone's life? It took over Reese's.

Reese was the reason why I never finished school. I was too busy baby-sitting my little brother to go to school. How I did it, I have no idea. I was a baby my damn self. I was only eleven when she gave birth to him.

Reese wouldn't come home in time in the mornings for me to go to school and I couldn't leave my baby brother there alone. Daddy worked twelve-hour shifts, from twelve midnight to twelve the next afternoon. Those became my mother's going-out hours. No sooner than my dad left the house on his way to work, was Reese out the door to hit the streets.

His friends used to try to tell him how she was out running the streets and fuckin' for that crack, but he never believed them. I don't know if he didn't believe them or if he didn't want to believe them. Besides, they were the same men she was fucking and sucking in order to get money for crack. They weren't telling my daddy that though.

Reese was my daddy's queen. She could do no wrong in his eyes and he loved her strong. He provided her with everything she needed and then some. He made sure that she never had to work a day she was with him. Reese threw it all away though. Crack is the muthafucka. It's a mind drug. It makes a person think in their head that they need it. The body doesn't crave it like it does heroin. The mind craves it. Crack makes a person believe that it is the only good thing in their life. The only thing they need to feel good. I guess it told Reese that me and daddy wasn't good no more.

My daddy was good though. He was the best thing that ever happened to Reese. Reese and my daddy started dating in ninth grade. She was the pretty light-skin cheerleader and he was the handsome football jock.

My daddy was a hardworking man. He was too busy keeping a roof over our head to pay much attention to street gossip. If only he had listened to the warnings. If only he had seen what wasn't there. For example, he used to be greeted with a big lunch every time he came home from work. Pretty soon he was scraping together a bologna sandwich. If ever he did try to question Reese about where the money he was giving her for groceries was going, she would turn on the charm and make up some lame excuse.

I used to get nice, cute little outfits and shoes on the regular. When my daddy didn't see that I was getting those things anymore he should have known something was wrong. All of a sudden a pair of shoes had to last me until my toes damn near busted out of them. Even then, Daddy was the one who would take me to get a new pair.

Reese had my daddy in the palm of her hands. She's the reason why I don't have a daddy anymore. He's dead and she killed him. No, she wasn't the actual one who shanked him, cutting his jugular until he bled to death. But if it had not been for her, he would have never been in the position to lose his life.

My father was murdered in prison after serving only six months of a ten year sentence. He was in jail for the death of my baby brother, only he wasn't the one who killed him.

I'll never forget the day I came home from school to find cops and detectives in our yard. An ambulance was parked in front of our house. We lived in a yellow duplex on 26th and Cleveland Avenue. By today's standards, we would be considered poor. But I never felt poor coming up.

Crime-scene tape was streamed across the yard. It was even blocking the entrance to our door. Cops were maneuvering over and under it to go in and out of our house. As I walked up the sidewalk, still a couple duplexes from my own, I saw two EMTs carrying out a body on a stretcher. I could tell that it was a little body. A body that belonged to a ten-month old. A body that belonged to my little brother.

I tried to pick up my pace so that I could catch up to them and ask them what the hell was going on. Where in the hell were they taking my baby brother? But I couldn't. I was cold and stiff. I got right up to the ambulance when the men closed the back door, leaving my brother back there all alone. They each climbed into the front of the vehicle and pulled away.

As I watched them drive off I knew my baby brother was dead. If he was alive, one of them would have been back there trying to make sure that he was doing okay, that he wasn't scared. But instead, they left him back there, alone.

As the ambulance drove off I could now see the police car that was parked on the opposite side of the street that it had been blocking. In the back seat of the squad car was my father. Tears were running down his face. I could tell that his hands were handcuffed behind his back. Reese was nowhere in sight.

When my eyes finally met with my father's, he smiled at me. I thought I was smiling back at him, but I don't think I was. I didn't want to smile. I wanted answers. I took a step towards my father. I needed to talk to him. I was scared.

Before I could take another step the squad car began to pull off.

"No!" I tried to scream. "Where are you taking my daddy?"

My eyes said it, but my voice box wouldn't let go of the words. I watched the police take my daddy away.

I needed to find Reese. Where was Reese? Where was my mother?

I was so afraid. Finally an officer approached me.

"Do you live here, little girl?" he said. "Are you the daughter, Harlem?"

I nodded yes and said, "Where's my mommy?"

The officer never answered me. He just took me by the hand and led me over to a female officer.

"Will you keep an eye on her?" he asked the female officer. "She's the little girl who lives here. Put her in the back of your car or something until we can locate the mother."

"Yes, sir," she replied, following his orders.

She walked me to her car and put me in the back seat.

"You're not in any trouble," she said to me. "Everything is going to be okay. We're just going to keep you with us until we can locate your mommy."

She closed the door once I got situated in the back of the cop car. Her telling me that I wasn't in any trouble didn't make me feel any better. Nothing feels like it's going to be okay when you're sitting in the back of a police car.

I stared out the window for what seemed like forever, praying that Reese would just hurry up and come home so that I could be with her. I, just like my baby brother and just like my daddy, was in the back of a vehicle alone.

I had dozed off to sleep when the police car door opened. Standing there was Reese. Tears were flowing down her face like a stream, but she still managed to smile at me. Her beautiful and comforting smile let me know that everything was going to be okay. Yep, now I knew that everything was going to be okay.

Reese scooped me up from the back of that car and held me in her arms for what felt like forever and a day. I didn't want her to let me go, ever.

Eventually I would learn that my brother had been left in the bathtub unattended where he drowned. I was absolutely devastated. I felt like my baby brother was more like my own child. I had spent more time with him than Reese had.

Reese had done a good job at managing to keep the entire details surrounding my baby brother's death from me, but later I would find out that my father confessed to leaving my baby brother in the tub for only a minute. He was charged with neglect, child endangerment, and manslaughter. He pled guilty and was sentenced to ten to twenty-five years. He would have been eligible for parole, though, in only five years.

I understood a little about death and my baby brother being in heaven, but whenever I asked Reese where my daddy was she would tell me that he was away in the service, that he decided to join the army. I guess she never planned on taking me to see my daddy.

It wasn't until the day of my father's funeral that I found out what had really happened. After the funeral everyone came to our house bearing food, flowers, and cards with money in them that Reese would later smoke up. I went upstairs to use the bathroom and through my mother's cracked bedroom door I heard the truth.

She was sitting there talking to my aunt Mary, who was comforting her. I couldn't believe what my mother was telling her. Come to find out that it was my mother who had left my little brother unattended. My father hadn't even made it home from work yet by the time he was dead. When my father got home he found Reese in the bed shaking from complete shock. He thought someone had harmed her. After questioning her about what was wrong with her and getting nowhere, he finally asked her where the baby was, if he was sleeping or something.

He went to check the baby's crib and he saw nothing but an empty crib. He went back into the room and started asking Reese over and over again where the baby was. Still she wouldn't answer. She just sat on the bed shaking, biting her nails and staring at the closet.

An eerie feeling came over my father.

"Is he in there, Reese?" my father said shaking her. "Is the baby in the closet?"

When she wouldn't answer my father walked slowly over to the closet and opened the door. He didn't see anything out of the

ordinary. He sighed a sigh of relief. But as he turned to close the
closet door he noticed water dripping down from the top shelf of
the closet. That's where he found my baby brother wrapped in a
towel, dead.

Reese had started bathing him when a knock at the door tore her
away from the task. After seeing who was at the door and answering it, she meant to go right back and get the baby, but it was Sharmane, her geeker buddy. Seeing Sharmane at her door with pipe in
hand, Reese's mind was set on nothing but getting high. While she
and Sharmane were downstairs on the living room couch sucking
up poison through a glass stick, my brother was in the upstairs
bathtub gasping for one last breath.

Sharmane had come and gone before my mother remembered
what she had been doing before Sharmane knocked. She prayed all
the way up the steps that her baby boy was okay. She listened for a
splash, something, anything. She heard nothing. But what she saw
was her baby floating in the tub.

She grabbed a towel and pulled him out of the water and placed
him in it. He was blue. Instead of even attempting CPR or calling
911 she pronounced him dead. She panicked. She was already trippin' off of the drug so she decided to hide my baby brother and
hoped that no one would miss him. First she hid him under the
bed. She knew Daddy kept his work shoes under the bed and
might see him if he kneeled down to get a pair so she moved him
over to the closet.

My father came home about a half hour after Reese had hidden
my baby brother. When he finally got her to tell him the details of
everything that had happened, he knew his queen was going to jail
for sure. There was no way her act could even be considered as an
accidental death.

I remember hearing my mother say, "Ray said that people would expect for a father to do something that stupid so they wouldn't be as hard on him as they would be on me. But a mother is expected to know better than to leave her child in a tub of water. Ray insisted on taking the blame."

I was only twelve, but I knew the repercussion of what I had just heard. I had lost a brother and a father because of Reese. That's the reason why I hate my mother with every being of my soul. I never told Reese that I had heard her speak the truth. Back then she was all the family I had and I was all the family she had. I didn't want her to think that I looked at her any different than before. Besides, I heard her telling Aunt Mary everything that had happened had been life altering, that she was a new woman now.

I hated the fact that I had lost a brother and a father, but perhaps that's what needed to happen in order for me to get my mother back. So I would continue to love her and cherish her, and hopefully she would do the same for me, her now only child.

But to make matters worse, Reese let the man take me away. About two weeks after my daddy's funeral Reese went on a crack binge. Franklin County Children's Service had already had their eye on our family since the death of my baby brother. Her going off on a drug-crazed binge was all the excuse they needed to snatch me up. A neighbor had reported me having been all alone for days. To make it worse, there wasn't any food in the house and the electricity had been turned off. I tried so hard to cover for Reese. I tried to keep going to school, but I was only twelve and there was no one there to make me, so finally I just stopped going, missing four days in a row. This raised an eyebrow with my school.

I didn't go outside and play or run the streets, but when there was absolutely no more food in the house and my stomach cramped with hunger pains, I had to go next door and ask Miss Laura for some food.

Miss Laura fed me well, but while I was getting my eat on in the kitchen, she was in the living room calling Franklin County Children's Services. They came by and scooped me up before I could even wash down the meal with a glass of milk.

I was sitting at the kitchen table when there was a knock on Miss Laura's door. I was hoping that maybe it was Reese coming to get me. I had left her a note saying where I was just in case she came home while I was gone. But when I turned to look it was some white lady in a suit and a police officer. Miss Laura pointed me out and they came over to the table where I was sitting. The white lady sat down and the officer remained standing.

"Hi, Harlem," the woman said in a soft, caring tone. "My name is Hillary."

"Hi," I said shyly. All of a sudden I felt like my twelve-year-old body was being run by a six-year-old mind.

"Miss Laura here tells me that you stopped by for dinner."

"Umm hmm," I said softly.

"Where's your mom, Harlem?"

"Home asleep," I lied, not wanting to get Reese in any trouble.

"How long has she been there asleep?" the woman asked.

"I don't know," I said, looking down, not wanting to make eye contact. I never did know how to lie right.

"You know what, Harlem? I don't think your mom is at home."

I stayed silent.

"Am I right?" the woman asked, placing her hand softly on mine.

"Umm hmm," I said with a nod.

"Well, Harlem, I know you're pretty grown up, but you're still not grown up enough to be left alone for a long time. So I'm going to take you with me until your mom comes home. Will you come with me, Harlem?"

The woman seemed so kind and sincere. She talked to me as if she was really concerned about my feelings. Like Reese used to talk to me. So I trusted her.

"Will you take me back home when she gets back?" I asked.

"Of course," the woman said. So I agreed to go with her.

It would be weeks before I ever saw Reese again. Needless to say I spent my thirteenth birthday in a foster home, with a white family at that. It was the pits. I mean the family was cool and all, but they were white. I was black. We couldn't relate, therefore I spent most of the time in my room so that I wouldn't have to try to have a conversation with them.

There were three other foster children in the home as well. A little Asian girl and two white boys. What I do remember about the foster family is that they were very hard with the boys. I remember one of the little boys always used to leave the toilet seat up after taking a piss. If the foster mother caught the seat up she would call him into the bathroom and scold him. But instead of making him put the toilet seat down she would do it for him, after making him grip the rim of the toilet bowl with his hands. Then as hard as she could she would slam the toilet seat down on his hands. He would scream bloody murder. At the time I didn't see it as that bad of a punishment. Hell, I used pretty much the same technique to get Amerie to stop stealing my Barbie stuff.

One day the white foster mother picked me up from my predominantly black school and that was the beginning of hateful torment from the other kids at school. Those black kids teased me so bad about having a white mother that it was ridiculous. They made me start to hate my foster family even though they were kind to me. I started turning out so bad in school and in the home that they sent me away. To this day I wish I could apologize to them. I shouldn't have let those stupid kids at school take me out of character.

All the while, while I was at that foster home, Reese had been trying to get me back through the courts. They made her go to rehab and everything until she could prove fit to take care of me. Eventually I was returned to her. I was so happy the day they released me to her.

I couldn't wait to get home to my old room and play with my old friends. Before going home Reese took me to McDonalds and bought me a Big Mac Combo. It felt like fine dining. I loved her and had missed her so much. Over lunch she promised things would be different and that she wouldn't ever let anyone take me away from her again.

We had to catch the bus home because Reese didn't have a vehicle. The longer we rode the bus the further out of the nicer part of town into the hood we drove. We got off the bus in front of an apartment complex called Greenbriar. It looked like the projects I had only seen on television, like some *Good Times* Cabrini Green shit.

"I know this isn't where you're used to living," Reese said. "But this is all I can afford right now. With your father gone, I had to get on welfare. But they're going to help me find a nice job here soon and we're going to move back to our old neighborhood."

Reese smiled at me with that sincere genuine smile I had always trusted. I nodded okay and she led me into our two bedroom roach infested cracker box.

It wasn't even a good two months before Reese was back to running the streets. She'd leave at the wee hours in the morning and not come back home until the next day. I didn't mind as much when she ran the streets, but what I did mind was when she decided to bring the streets into our house.

I'll never forget walking into the house after school one day. When I opened the front door Reese and some Chinese man were butt ass naked in the living room. The man had Reese bent over the couch fucking her from behind, while Reese was sucking on a pipe.

I couldn't believe my eyes. I had never seen two people have sex before. Not on television, the movies, or anything. And my initial thought was that sex was something that was very painful because whenever Reese was sucking on her pipe she was screaming bloody murder. The louder she screamed, the faster the Chinese man would hump her.

When Reese finally turned around and saw me standing there, she didn't even look embarrassed. It was as if she felt the scene was normal. She didn't even stop having sex with him. She just let him keep humping on her while she continued sucking on the pipe and moaning and groaning. I just stood there and watched in shock before finally running into my bedroom and closing the door behind me.

When I turned around, once again I was aghast. Right there on my bed was some stringy hair white girl. She was facing me. She looked like a skeleton. I swear I could count her ribs she was so skinny. Lying underneath her was some huge, fat black guy and she was just humping him away. He was moaning and groaning calling her all sorts of white bitches and she didn't seem to mind.

The fat man's stomach was so big that she had to lift it out of the way to get to his penis. Instead of sucking on a pipe while she handled her business on top of the big fat man, she was sucking another black guy's penis. He had her by the hair and was forcing himself down her throat.

My presence didn't seem to bother them one bit. As a matter of fact, I remember the guy who was getting his dick sucked saying to me, "Come on over here, princess. We got something for you, too."

He winked and started laughing.

I immediately ran back out of my room and into the bathroom. I closed the door behind me, locked it, and hopped into the bathtub. I pulled the shower curtain closed and sat in the tub all night until I heard them all leave. And that's what I did every time Reese decided to bring the streets home. Sometimes she would even have my pillow and blanket in the tub waiting for me.

It was four months before I found myself alone in the house for days at a time and hungry. This time I called the muthafuckin' police on Reese my damn self. One officer showed up to answer my call and it was just so happen that Reese had finally decided to return home only five minutes before the officer had arrived. On top of that, she showed up with a bag of mediocre groceries.

"Honey, I know Mommy has been gone a couple of days but I had to get some groceries," Reese said as she took the groceries into the kitchen. This was the first time I had ever seen her look so bad. I mean, before, I could see her starting to deteriorate, but now her appearance was just full-blown sickening.

Her long beautiful hair was capped up and matted as if she had sweat it out. My guess was that she did sweat it out, on her back.

She had on the same clothes that she had worn out of the house three days ago, minus the socks. I'd bet the farm that she still had on the same nasty drawers too. There was this hideous herpes cold sore on her mouth that looked painful and her skin was starting to get bumpy. Looking at her broke my heart.

No sooner than she had started whipping up some ninety-nine cent bologna sandwiches there was a knock on the door. I knew it was the police. And looking at Reese, I didn't care if she had come home with a pack of bologna, cheese, and a loaf of bread, she had abandoned me for the second time. I knew there would be a third, a fourth and a fifth. I had to save myself this time or else no one else would. There was no Miss Laura at Greenbriar.

"Yes, may I help you?" Reese said, answering the door for the police officer. She was all smiles. The rest of her might have looked tore up from the floor up, but her teeth were still beautiful and white.

"Good evening, ma'am," the officer said, tilting his hat. "I got a call about a neglected child."

"I don't know what you're talking about," Reese said with a chuckle. "There's no one here except for me and my thirteen-year-old daughter. And as you can see, she's not neglected. She's clean. She's healthy and look, she's eating."

Reese held up the sandwich like it was a steak dinner. She was proud of the little spread she was able to provide.

"I called you," I said, finding the courage to speak up. "My mother left me again. I didn't have any food until just now. She's on crack and I need you to help her. Please help her."

"Harlem," my mother said, putting her arms around me. "I know you're angry at me, but that's no reason to call the police on me."

Reese turned her attention back to the officer who was starting to buy her act.

"You see, officer, my daughter here was misbehaving in school and I put her on punishment, forbidding her to leave the house. She's just rebelling."

The officer looked at me with a frown. "Well, everything looks to be fine," the officer said.

"And everything is fine," Reese said.

"Young lady," the officer said to me. "There are real matters out here that need the attention of the police. You can't use us just because you're mad at your mother. I'm going to let it slide this time, but I suggest you never pull a stunt like this again."

I couldn't believe this officer and how quick he was to believe Reese. He didn't even take me into another room and question me like I had seen it done on television.

"I'm sorry about this, ma'am," the officer said to Reese. "You might want to gain a little bit more control over your daughter."

"No problem, officer," Reese said as she began to close the door. "You have a good night."

"No!" I screamed as I pushed Reese out of the way to keep her from closing the door. "Wait!"

I followed the officer down the stairs as he headed for his squad car.

"Please don't leave me here," I begged him. "My mother needs help. She's only going to leave me again. She uses crack and sometimes while she's out on a binge, she doesn't come home for days. When she is here, sometimes she brings in men and they do things, right there with me in the house."

The officer kept walking and trying to ignore me. I think a part of him knew that I was telling the truth, that's why he wanted to hurry up and get the hell out of there before his conscience could become involved.

"Please, just listen to me," I said, grabbing the officer's arm.

"My mother hasn't been home in three days. I was there alone. I haven't even been to school in three days. Call them and find out. I'm too scared to walk out here in the morning dark alone and wait on my school bus so I don't even go."

"Your mother is home now," the officer said in a matter of fact tone. "I know a bologna sandwich isn't a gourmet meal, but it's food. There are some kids who don't even get that."

"Just come back into the house and look," I pleaded with him. "The refrigerator and the cabinets are bare. After that bologna is gone, I don't know when the next time we eat will be."

I'll never forget that officer's face. I'll never forget him trying to hold back his tears as he looked into my teary eyes. As big and strong as he was he couldn't hold back that tiny weak little tear that formed in his left eye. I pitied him just as much as he pitied me. Soon enough I hated him. My tear dissolved before it could even make its way out of my eye.

The officer patted me on the shoulder and said that everything was going to be okay. He got into his car and drove away. Why? How could he? He was abandoning me. He saw where I lived. He knew deep down that I wasn't lying about Reese and my home situation. Maybe he was a new cop and didn't know what to do or where to take me. Hell, he should have taken me home with him if he had to. He could have saved me from the humiliation of becoming a ward of the court, belonging to nobody. But instead, he left me there to have to face Reese.

That night Reese no longer believed in her saying that God takes care of people who commit evil acts. She saw my calling the police on her as an evil act of betrayal towards her. She beat me so badly that a neighbor called the police from all of the ruckus and my screaming.

Reese had never laid a hand on me in all my years. She had never had a reason to discipline me. I was an obedient child. Who knew she had one hell of an uppercut?

She busted my lip and pulled out patches of my hair. My ribs were cracked and black and blue bruises covered my body. This time, when the police were called, a couple of different police officers showed up. They took one good look at me, and with no questions asked, they took me away. They took Reese to jail.

That would be the last time I would ever live with Reese.

5. Over the River and Through the Woods

While Reese went to jail, I went to another foster home, and at first, I didn't mind one bit. Miss Myla, my foster mother, was as nice as nice could be, and not just when the social workers came around for home visits. She was nice all of the time.

She took great care of me from the moment I stepped into her house. She had clothes, books, and board games already waiting for me on my bed. And Lord knows that woman could cook. I didn't miss a meal and neither did Penny, her biological daughter.

Miss Myla treated Penny and me one in the same, like we were blood sisters. Miss Myla did our homework with us, read books to us, and was still old fashioned in the sense that she felt the need to tuck us into bed every night.

Penny and I shared a bedroom and every night Miss Myla made sure we were nice and comfortable before lights out. We even said a prayer together every night. Penny always asked God to keep the boogieman away and I always thanked God for Miss Myla and Penny. I wished that I could have lived the life a child deserved

with Reese, but since I couldn't, I was glad God had put me in
Miss Myla's way.

One night, after Miss Myla turned out the lights and left Penny
and I to sleep tight, Penny asked me, "How come you never pray
that God keeps the boogieman away?"

I was going on fourteen so I had long gotten over the boogieman. But Penny was two years younger than I was, so I suppose
that was normal.

"There's no such thing as the boogieman," I responded.

"Yes there is," Penny insisted as if next she was going to try to
convince me that there was a such thing as Santa Claus, too.
"Pretty soon you'll be praying that God keeps him away because
he's going to come for you, too."

Penny's words were chilling because of the sincerity she had behind them. Hell, she had me checking under the bed and in closets
for a couple of days. But I wasn't about to let her scare me with her
wild imagination.

By just looking at Penny, one would never know that she was the
eleven-year-old and I was the thirteen-year-old. She was well de-
veloped for her age. Her boobs were twice the size of mine and she
had even gotten her period. I was as flat chested as a board and
didn't even know what menstrual cramps were.

I liked Penny very much. She wasn't funny acting like the kids
at the last foster home I was in. She shared all of her things, including her clothes, which she had a nice collection of. The only
time Penny didn't talk much was when Wilber, her mother's
boyfriend, was around.

I could see how he could possibly intimidate a small child. He
was a very large man, standing about six feet six inches tall and he

was pretty much overweight. My guess was that he was about three hundred pounds.

Penny never said two words around Wilber. And because she was so fun and outgoing any other time, I found it strange that she would clam up around Wilber. So one night after Miss Myla saw us to bed I decided to ask her why.

"Penny, don't you like Mr. Wilber?" I inquired.

"He's okay," she said in an insincere tone.

"How come you never talk around him or anything?"

Penny didn't answer me. She laid in her bed quiet for a moment then she sat up.

"If I tell you something, do you promise not to tell anyone?" Penny asked me in a whisper. "People will think I'm crazy and I might get taken away from my mother like you did yours."

"Sure," I whispered, ears open.

"Well, you know how every night I pray that God keeps the boogieman away?"

"Yes," I said, feeling that chill again.

"Well, Mr. Wilber is the boogieman."

Penny laid back down and put the cover over her head and went to sleep. I could see her little body trembling through the covers. I was scared to death. Before having that conversation with Penny, I had slept sound, like a baby. Now I couldn't sleep a wink. I always kept one eye open on the door, watching for the boogieman.

Then it happened. The boogieman finally came to pay me a visit. I had been tossing and turning all night trying to stay awake like I had been for the past two weeks. The sandman got the best of me and I caught myself dozing off. When I looked up out of my sleep I saw his silhouette standing in the doorway, fixin' to enter the bedroom. I immediately sat up in the bed. He raised his hand to his mouth and whispered, "Shhh."

I looked over at Penny and she had her covers over her head pretending to be sleep. I knew she wasn't really sleep because she was breathing too heavily, and I saw her little body trembling the same as it had trembled the night she first told me about the boogieman.

As the boogieman's huge silhouette towered over me I didn't know what to do. I was only thirteen years old. I had never been taught about good touches and bad touches. But when that fat bastard put his hand on my warm ripe pussy and started rubbing himself and moaning, I knew that wasn't good.

The next thing I knew he was attempting to climb on me.

"Let me make you feel good," he whispered in a soft friendly tone, still fondling his penis. "This is going to feel real good to you."

I did what my instincts told me to do and that was to scream. I screamed so loud that my own ears were ringing. Could you believe that Penny still didn't budge? I guess she didn't want to jump in and help me because she didn't want to turn any of the boogieman's attention to her pussy. She was out of sight and out of mind as far as she was concerned.

"No! Help!" I screamed while I began to kick at him.

Before I knew it, Miss Myla was in the doorway turning on the light switch.

"Baby, what's wrong?" she said in her genuine sincere tone.

By now, Wilber was standing between Penny's and my bed.

I jumped up out of bed, still screaming.

"Oh, baby," Miss Myla said. "Were you having a nightmare?"

Miss Myla opened her arms for me to come to her so that she could comfort me, but instead, I ran past her, knocking her out of the way.

Miss Myla always made us take our shoes off at the front door so the pair of loafers I had worn to school that day was sitting right at the door. I put them on, unlocked the door, and ran out, not even closing it behind me.

I didn't run far because I had no idea where to go and it was pitch black outside. I was scared to death. I ended up running behind the house into the alley and hiding in some bushes. The house was still in clear view from where I was hiding. I figured I could wait there until morning and then, when everyone left, I could get in some how and get some of my clothing and things.

The sleep shirt I was wearing could double for a cotton dress, but I still needed my things so I cropped down in the bushes and waited patiently, keeping my eye on the moon hoping it would be replaced by the morning sun soon.

An hour hadn't even passed when I saw red and blue lights flickering. I knew those lights were a prelude to the police. Soon I saw two police cars pull up to the house.

"The boogieman is going to get it now," I said out loud.

At first I had the right mind to run up to the police and tell them all about the boogieman and what he tried to do to me and what he had been doing to Penny. But then I thought about that time I told them about Reese and they left me with her anyway. I didn't want to play the odds so I kept still.

Miss Myla and them were probably in the house trying to put some type of blame on me for the entire situation. Any moment now the police would be out here looking for me and make me go back in that house to live. So knowing that the police would be searching for me shortly, I got from behind the bushes and ran.

I didn't know what to do or where I was going, but I ran. I was young and didn't know much, but what I did know was that I wasn't about to be forced to live in that house and let that fat fucker rip up my little thirteen-year-old pussy.

I probably ran a mile before finding what I thought was another safe haven. It was in a lot behind a building that had huge containers lined up. They were like garbage containers only they weren't. They were containers for people to donate items to, such as clothes, and there were a couple that took aluminum cans and paid out money.

Behind the containers was a wire fence fully contaminated with weeds so no one could see through the fence. That's where I hid my body, in between the fence and one of the containers. It was still dark so I knew no one would spot me. I tried to keep my eyes open because I was too afraid to close them, but eventually they managed to shut and I was able to get in a few z's.

Eventually I was awakened by the sound of aluminum cans clanking together. Slowly, I peeked my head to see what was going on. I could see the legs of a person that looked like a male. They were feeding cans to the container I was lodging behind.

He would set them on the ground, stomp them, and then place them in the opening on the container.

Afraid to death that he might see me, I kept still, damn near not even breathing. Every time he stomped a can, my heart jumped.

Right when the man got down to the last can he went to stomp it and it rolled back to where I was. I closed my eyes as I heard the man's footsteps coming closer and closer to me.

I could hear him pick up the can and then there was silence. I opened my eyes and there he was, standing there looking dead at me. I closed my eyes again, hoping that this time when I opened them, he would be gone.

"Little girl, are you okay?" he asked with concern.

I opened my eyes and peeking behind the container I was stationed behind was a middle-aged white man. He had on some jeans, a plaid shirt, and an apron. He looked to be friendly, but had a terribly concerned look on his face at the same time.

"My goodness, child," he said, wiping his hand across his forehead. "I thought you were dead at first. You should feel how fast my heart is beating."

I just stared at him, saying nothing.

"Are you okay? Do you need to go to the hospital?"

I didn't say a word.

"Are you hungry?" he asked. He saw that he wasn't going to get two words out of me so he sighed. "I'll tell you what. You see that sandwich stand right over there?" He pointed to what was a white small-sized trailer. It had a sign posted on it advertising his business.

"Well, I own that and if you're hungry, then you can follow me over there and I'll put something in that belly of yours."

The sandwich man smiled then walked away.

"But I don't have any money," I stood up and called to him.

He paused then turned to me and said, "It's free!" Then he continued walking until he disappeared into the trailer.

I was a little hungry and I didn't have a dime to my name. I figured that if I was going to take the sandwich man up on his offer, then I better hurry up and do it before he changed his mind. Eventually I walked over the to trailer and went to the window where orders were taken. I couldn't see the man. I looked down and saw where there was a little bell with a handwritten sign on it. I hit the bell and the cling summonsed the man to the window.

"I was wondering how long it would take for you to make it over here." He smiled. "Don't be afraid. Come on in through the door over there on the side. I'll whip you up something nice."

I walked over to the door he had instructed me to and he was waiting there to let me inside the trailer. I entered slowly and skeptical as I peeped the place out.

The front of the trailer was solely for business purposes. It had a nice little kitchen with a flat grill, microwave, and a little refrigerator he kept the sodas in.

The back was nothing but a bed. There was a table slash ironing board that pulled out from the wall. And in between the so-called bedroom from the kitchen area was a small bathroom with only a sink and a toilet.

I sat on the bed while the sandwich man made me up some bacon, eggs with cheese on buttered toasted white bread. It was delicious and it was free.

Reese had once told me that nothing in life was free. Well at the time, as I devoured that free meal, I thought that she couldn't have been more wrong.

The sandwich man waited on customers while I gobbled down the breakfast sandwich he had prepared for me. Right after I had taken the last bite he came back and joined me by sitting on the other end of the bed from where I was sitting.

"Do you want to talk about why a little girl like you was sleeping behind an aluminum-can recycling bin?" he asked as he handed me a cold can of Orange Crush.

I shook my head no.

"So where are you headed?" he asked.

I shrugged my shoulders.

"You got any money?" he asked.

I shook my head no.

"Then you ain't going far that's for sure," he said with a chuckle. He began to stare at me and I started becoming a little uncomfortable with his piercing gaze.

"I'll tell you what," he said, digging down into his pockets. He pulled out a wad of cash. "I'll give you some money. Would you like that?"

I spoke this time. "Yes," I said.

"Will twenty dollars be enough?" he asked.

"Sure," I said. To a thirteen-year-old, twenty dollars was a whole lot of money.

"Okay, then it's yours, but first you have to do something for me," he said, smiling a wicked smile.

"What?" I asked with a worried look on my face.

"Oh, don't worry, it's nothing like that. I don't want to do it with you or anything. I just want you to touch it a few times. That's all. And then maybe put your mouth on it. I promise it won't hurt you. I'm not going to do anything that might hurt you that you don't want to do."

The sandwich man seemed pretty convincing at the time. I mean, it's not like he wanted to do to me what the boogieman wanted to do. He wasn't standing there wagging his penis in my face or anything like that. I'm sure it wouldn't hurt me any just to touch it or put my mouth on it. And he was right. I wasn't going to get far without any money. So after carefully considering his offer I decided to take him up on it.

"Okay," I said nervously.

He looked like a kid on Christmas when I agreed to his proposal. He couldn't stand up fast enough and whip his peter out.

"Now just touch it real soft. Real soft like this," he said as he began to demonstrate by gripping it in his hand and rubbing it up and down.

It looked scary. It was a soft pink color and pointed out, looking straight at me. He moved in closer to me.

"See, did you see how easy that was?" he asked me. "Now you do it."

I put my index finger on it and stroked it. Then I put my hand around it and repeated that act he had just done.

"Squeeze it harder," he moaned. "That's it, just a little tighter."

I tightened up my grip.

"Now yank it," he said. "Come on, yank at it. It won't hurt me, I swear."

I began yanking at it. It was kind of fun. It was like a piece of elastic. And the more I yanked at it, the more noises he made.

"Now just lick it," he said, as he started to pump himself in sync with how I was yanking him. "Go on, girl. Just pretend it's a lollipop and lick on it. You do want that twenty dollars don't you?"

He held up the wad of money that he still had in his hand. He was using it to remind me of why I was doing what I was doing in the first place. Kind of like how a dog's master does when he's trying to teach him tricks. This was a trick all right.

I took a deep breath, and just when I was about to put my mouth on sandwich man's peter, the service bell dinged. A customer was ringing the bell for service.

The sudden noise startled me. I jumped.

"Forget about them," he said, holding his peter in his hand, tugging it towards me for me to continue.

"No, they might see," I said with a timid look on my face. He could tell that no way was I going to proceed with someone standing out there.

"Damn it, okay then," he said with a grunt. He sat the money he had been holding in his hand down on the table/ironing board. He then proceeded tucking away his little wrinkled up peter. The service bell rang again.

"All right. All right. I'm coming," he said. He headed up toward the front then he stopped, turned to me and said, "Don't move. I'll be right back."

As he went to wait on the customer I looked up and my eyes locked on the wad of money he had laid down. I wanted to just take it and run, but I was scared. What if he caught me? He might call the police on me and I'd have to go to jail. Or he might try to kill me.

I had to think quickly. I knew he would finish up with the customer soon so that he could come back for me to suck him. Maybe it wouldn't be so bad to just suck his peter for twenty dollars. I'm sure girls did it all of the time, and for free on top of that. I wondered what it tasted like. I was hoping that it didn't taste yucky or anything like that. Maybe I could get him to put ketchup on it or something so that it wouldn't seem so bad. But something told me, and I felt in my gut, that for now it would be me rubbing on and sucking on his peter, but sooner or later, he'd want from me what the boogieman wanted.

After the sandwich man finished up with the customer, he put a sign in the window, pulled down the blind, and headed back to the bed of the trailer. Once he got back there he noticed that the side door was swinging open. I was gone and so was his wad of money.

Once again I was alone on the streets, only this time I had money. I didn't know how far it was going to take me, but it had to take me far enough.

I remembered a hole in the wall motel about two miles from where I was. You could rent rooms by the hour. I didn't know whether they would give someone my age a room or not, but it was worth a try because I had no other options but back to Miss Myla's and that was definitely out of the question. Maybe I could pay a grown-up to get the room for me like I saw kids paying grown-ups to buy them beer.

The only other option I could have even considered was to try to find Reese, if she wasn't still in jail, and at the rate she was probably going, she would more than likely willingly hand me over to the boogieman for a crack rock. So I decided to try my luck with the motel. But first I had to stop at the store and get a few items to hold me over just in case I did get the room.

On my way to the motel I stopped in a little convenience store to get a few snacks, a toothbrush, toothpaste, and a comb. My total came to $22.57. When I went to pay the clerk I pulled out the wad of cash I had stolen from sandwich man. The clerk gave me a curious look. I could tell that she wondered where a thirteen-year-old girl had gotten all that loot.

I peeled off a twenty and a five and told her to keep the change. I was good to go. Now it was time for me to see if I could get one of those rooms at the motel. I hadn't gotten out of the store parking lot when a guy came up behind me and tapped me on the shoulder. I turned around to see what he wanted.

"Excuse me, sistah, but do you have change for a twenty?" he asked.

"I think so," I said, setting down my bags. "Let me check."

I pulled out my wad of cash and before I could even check to see if I had change, the man grabbed the entire wad of money from my hand and ran off.

"No!" I screamed in an attempt to chase after him. "Come back here. That's my money, thief!"

I yelled and screamed hoping that someone would join in on helping me to chase that fool down. No one did.

I chased him a couple of blocks until he was out of sight. It was evident that I wasn't going to catch up with him. He had gotten away with my money and there was nothing I could do about it.

Once I got older I would understand that what had just happened to me was called karma, only I was paying for the sins of this lifetime, which was stealing the sandwich man's money.

I headed back to the store to get my bags that I had sat down before I went in pursuit after the thief. As I cleared the corner and walked back to the lot, there were three or four boys raiding my bags.

"Hey, that's my stuff," I shouted as I sped up my pace.

They looked at me and started running.

"Sucka," they shouted back at me as they ran off with my things laughing.

I stood there and I wanted to cry. But I remembered my father telling me one time after I had fallen off of my bike and scraped my elbow that crying wasn't going to get me nowhere. So instead of crying, I moved on without a clue as to what my next step would be.

For a while I walked the streets, then I came to a public library. There I could go in and relax for a few hours. I could use the bathroom, drink from the water fountain, and hide in the back corner of the library and sleep. I think I looked at the pictures of every magazine in that library before an announcement came over the intercom that they would be closing in five minutes.

I knew what that meant. It was back to streets for Harlem. I went to the bathroom one last time, got a sip of water and headed out the library door. I was actually the last one to leave. The security guard locked the door behind me.

Night had fallen so quickly. It was pitch black again and I was scared. I walked through a neighborhood that had fairly nice houses. Each of them had a garage and either a swing set or a basketball court. I noticed that one of the houses had left their garage door open. It was dark and the night air was getting the best of my skinny little legs, so I figured it was the perfect opportunity to snatch up a spot to lay my head for the night.

My stomach was grumbling. That breakfast sandwich had long worn off and my snacks were history. I figured the best thing to do would be to go to sleep, that way I wouldn't be awake to entertain hunger.

I went inside the garage. There was a white Chevy pickup parked inside of it. In front of the pickup were stacks of trash bags. They were filled with clothing and linen. I made a pallet with some of the bags and used the others to cover up as much as my body as possible, then I fell off to sleep. Although I was sleeping on trash bags on a cold, hard ass cement ground, it was the first night in weeks I was able to sleep comfortable and without fear of the boogieman.

The next morning I was awakened by a police officer. Apparently the homeowner spotted me when their headlights hit me as they were backing out of the garage. One of the trash bags had fallen over during my sleep, exposing my leg. I never even felt it fall. I was sleeping like a baby.

The homeowner called the police and reported a young girl in their garage. Miss Myla had placed a report for her runaway foster child, so immediately they put two and two together and assumed that it was me. After giving them my name, I was, once again, marched back into the county's custody, waiting to be shipped off to yet another foster home.

Never before had I feared being placed in foster care, but now that I knew there were chances that I would have to fight to protect myself, I would have rather been given back to Reese to starve to death and get beat.

When the social worker informed me that she had been able to place me with another foster family I begged and pleaded with her not to send me to any more foster homes. I wanted Reese. I wanted my mother. She had birthed me. If anyone was going to hurt me in this world, I at least wanted it to be the person who grew me in her womb. But the social worker wouldn't listen. She had seen hundreds of other kids throw the exact same tantrum that I was throwing. She was immune to it so my desperate actions didn't affect her decision to send me to another foster home one way or the other.

On the day I was to be sent to my new foster family I was sick to my stomach. I was literally throwing up. I didn't know what kind of hell I had in store for me there and the fear of the unknown was getting the best of me.

I remember when the social worker came to pick me up her having this huge grin on her face. I saw her coming for me and I wanted to run, only there was no place to run to.

"Well, hello, Little Miss Harlem," she said as if the world was treating her far better than it had been treating me. "I've got a surprise for you."

I could tell she wanted me to ask what the surprise was, but instead I just sat there.

"You're still going away today, Harlem," she said, still in a cheerful voice. "But there's been a change of plans. You're going away, but not to the foster family that was originally set to take you. Guess what, Harlem? We found your grandmother, Mrs. Jones."

She put her hand on my shoulder and smiled. "Honey, get your things. You're going to live with your grandmother."

I had never even met this grandmother I was going to live with. I had seen her once, at my father's funeral. Supposedly she was my paternal grandmother, Ray's mother. For some reason or another she had never accepted Reese's pregnancy with me and her marriage to her son. But she was willing to take me in all the same.

When the social worker pulled up to my grandmother's house I felt like Alice in Wonderland. The house was a huge pink house trimmed in white. It had white shutters and a white picket fence. There was a swing on the porch that had little white pillows on it with pink flowers. There were beautiful flowers planted in the yard and butterfly windmills. And that chime, that beautiful angel chime that greeted every guest with a warm tune orchestrated by the wind. Sometimes, just the memory alone of the sound of those chimes still wakes me up out of my sleep.

I felt like I was dreaming, like I was getting to live in a real live Barbie house. This was the house that all little kids like me coming up dreamt about.

Maybe God didn't hate me, I thought to myself as I got out of the car. Up until that point in my life, I thought that God saw me as evil. After all, Reese said he always took care of evil people. I assumed that meant that he would do something bad to them. Well, with all of the bad stuff that was happening to me, I thought for sure it was God's way of punishing me. But looking at this big beautiful home and the fact that my grandmother was taking me in and I wasn't going to some scary foster home, I had to reconsider.

Maybe it was the devil that didn't like me and now God was finally saving me.

The day I arrived at my grandmother's, conversation was at a minimum.

"Child, your room is upstairs to the right," Grandmother said in a stern but at the same time loving tone. "Once you go right, keep straight back down the hall."

I nodded okay, then headed up the steps.

"I hope you like pink," Grandmother said to me as I climbed the steps. "Most girls do. I got you a pink bedspread and curtain and things. Hurry up and unpack, although it doesn't look like you have much. Looks like we're going to have to go shopping."

I looked down at my one suitcase and continued on up the stairs.

"Dinner's on the table, so look around, but don't be long."

That was pretty much all that was said that day. She wasn't mean or anything, just short with her words. After all, she didn't know me and I didn't know her. She had gotten a call out of the blue being informed that her granddaughter was part of the system and that if no kinfolk wanted me, I would remain in the system until I was eighteen. By now I was fourteen and I guess my grandmother figured that she would only have to deal with me four years herself so she agreed to take me in.

She didn't waste any time getting me into school, but by then I was so far behind that not even the special classes did me any good. Those lazy teachers didn't give a fuck though. They felt it was easier to shift me on to the next grade and teacher, rather than to invest the that little extra attention I needed that just might have made a difference in my educational skills.

The next thing grandmother made sure of was that she got me plenty of nice little dresses for church. The dresses reminded me of the ones Amerie used to wear. I hated them. To this day I hate wearing dresses. I'll play a skirt, a long skirt, in a minute, but dresses are definitely out of the question.

My grandmother had me in church every Sunday and on Wednesday nights, too. I never participated in any church functions. I just sat there and watched the choir members fight for a solo, the drummer sweat, and the congregation catch the holy ghost. It was one big show with a commercial here and there if you asked me, and not only that, but there was a cover charge. And if someone didn't pay his or her full admission price the first go round, the collection plate came back again.

Although my grandmother and myself never said the words to each other we loved one another. It was one of those things that I could feel. And besides that, actions spoke louder than words.

"You was a beautiful young girl when you first came here," Grandmother said as she sat down beside me on my bed. "But now you're a beautiful young woman. You know that's what that means now, don't you?"

"Yes, Grandmother," I replied. I knew the day would come when I'd get my period and I'd get *the talk*. But I always thought Reese would be the one giving it to me. But I think I almost preferred *the talk* coming from Grandmother. She didn't include a lot of extra bullshit. She was short and right to the point, as always. It made it a lot easier. All I had to do was sit there and listen.

I loved living with Grandmother. She never had one problem with me because I always did everything I was told to do and did what I was supposed to without being told. In return, she took excellent care of me. I never had to worry about no boogieman either because grandmother wasn't thinking about no man, no man except for her pastor and God.

"Them the only two men that are going to get my old tired behind into heaven," she would say. "So those the only two men I got anything to say to."

And Grandmother was sincere in her words. She was a fine older woman, too. She had managed to keep herself healthy and in great shape. Her skin wouldn't have known what a wrinkle was and she had long black pepper Indian hair with a little bit of salt. She was light brown, like Ray, and had wise brown eyes.

I used to see some of the older men in the church tip their hat to Grandmother and wink as she walked by. She would cut her eyes at them and toot her nose up right to the sky. I suppose that's where I got a lot of my attitude and my habits, like the habit of being tight with my money.

My grandmother wasn't no cheap woman. She had nice things, including a pink Cadillac to match her house. But she had to be the most economizing woman in the world. I remember once I tried to throw away a bottle of lotion. My grandmother raised Cain when she found that bottle in the bathroom garbage can. She stormed in my room with that same bottle I had thrown in the trash. Only now it was cut into two pieces. She had taken a knife and cut the bottle in half so that we could scoop out the remainder of the lotion with our hands.

"Waste not, want not," she would say to me. "Worry about what you want tomorrow after you have what you need today."

That's when I came to understand that making sure you had all the things you needed in life was priority. It was okay to treat yourself to some extra wants every now and then, but not until all your needs had been met.

Grandmother was a loving free-spirited woman, a lot like Reese. That's why I never did understand why those two never got along. But it wasn't for me to worry about now. I was getting along with grandmother just fine and I would continue doing so for the next few years, that was until that awful day after church.

The pastor had just finished preaching a sermon about not taking life for granted. About appreciating the people in your life today because tomorrow wasn't promised.

We had just walked out of the church door when Grandmother was going down the steps and her feet came from underneath her. She landed at the bottom of the steps flat on her side. She couldn't move. The ambulance was called and Grandmother was rushed to the hospital. They let the pastor ride with her, and Sister Betty, one of the nurses at the church, drove me to the hospital right behind them.

We waited for about two hours before the doctors came out to tell us that Grandmother had broken her hip. I was sad, but relieved. I didn't know what I would have done without her, but I would soon find out.

After my grandmother broke her hip she went downhill from that point on. We even ended up having to hire a nurse to care for her in the home. But Grandmother was still the same free-spirited woman I had grown to love before she broke her hip and took ill. So I didn't worry much about her. Although she spent most of her day in bed, she still appeared healthy and lovely to me.

Then one day I came home from school and there were a dozen cars or so parked at the house. I recognized the majority of them as being the same cars from the church parking lot.

Sister Betty was sitting on the porch swing along with Ms. Susie from church. Sister Betty was fanning Ms. Susie. When she looked up and saw me her fanning motions stopped. She stood up and watched me approach the porch.

"Hi, Sister Betty," I said in a melancholy tone. "Is everything all right?"

"Oh, dear child," she said, running down the steps and throwing her arms around me. "Oh, dear child, Sister Jones is gone. The Lord done took her a couple of hours ago."

"Well where did he take her and when is he bringing her back?" is what I wanted to say. But instead I just let Sister Betty hold me as I looked up to the sky.

God had done it again. What his vendetta was against me I had yet to know. All I knew was that he had done it to me again.

Inside I was crying. I was screaming, but on the outside I was emotionless. Some people thought I was just in shock. But I was mad. I was angry. I had visited God's house every week, sometimes twice and this is how he repaid me. My allowance wasn't shit, but yet I put ten percent of it in the offerings and this is how God repaid me. I spit on that church vowing to never step foot in one again.

At the same time I was angry with Grandmother as well. Not only was she the one who had dragged me to that tabernacle, but now she had abandoned me too.

At Grandmother's funeral folks were overly nice to me. They were hugging and kissing on me. They were asking me if there was anything I needed and several folks even invited me to come live with them.

During the service I stayed out on the church steps. I pretended to be too distraught with grief to go inside. But on the real, I wasn't stepping foot into that church again, not even to pay respect to my grandmother. I felt abandoned and I was angry. I felt betrayed by God for all those years I had spent worshipping him. How could he? If I was his child, then I was his blood. Blood wasn't supposed to do that to one another. God was no better than Reese is how I felt.

Finally, I had guidance and security, my grandmother, my dead father's mother. And now I didn't even have her. I was alone, again.

Soon enough I would find out why all those church folks were overly kind to me. They knew something that I didn't know. They knew that I was to inherit everything Grandmother owned. I was her only living kin and besides that, she had willed everything to me. I got the house, which was paid for in full. I got the Cadillac, which had been paid for in cash right off the lot.

Evidently her husband, Granddaddy Jones, who had died about four years before I moved in, had worked for the railroad company. He had damn near left Grandmother her own little fortune. He had a one-hundred-thousand-dollar life insurance policy from the railroad that went to my grandmother. He also had another one-hundred-thousand-dollar life insurance policy from an independent insurance company, as well as stocks, bonds, and investments. Grandmother had sat on most of that by not spending any more than she needed to, even if she wanted to.

On top of what Grandfather had left her, she had her own one-hundred-thousand-dollar life insurance policy as well as some stocks and bonds of her own, all of which I inherited and would have sole possession of once I turned eighteen. At the time, my eighteenth birthday was four months away. So in short, I was paid!

When I turned eighteen I didn't go out on some wild spending spree either like most eighteen-year-olds would have done. Instead, I sat on it. I thought back to the day of not knowing if I was going to have food to eat. I couldn't spend today on bullshit what I might need for a pack of bologna and a loaf of bread tomorrow.

I remained living in my grandmother's house, doing nothing

pretty much, but still not spending any cash. The house had been bought and paid for years ago so all I had to worry with was utilities and annual property taxes. My grandmother's estate lawyer aided me in seeing that everything was taken care of.

Actually, sitting at home doing nothing was how I met Morgan. I think she was still in her first year of college. It was when she had that job selling magazine subscriptions. She came knocking on my door trying to sell me one.

"Thank you, but no thank you," I said to her. "I don't read."

"Shhh," she said, putting her index finger over her lips. "Your ancestors might hear you."

"What?" I asked with a confused look on my face.

"Some of your ancestors were beaten, hung, and murdered because of their hunger to learn to read. For you to say that you don't read is a calamity."

I was looking at her like she was crazy. Who in the hell did she think she was standing at my doorstep throwing words at me like calamity?

"Look, don't come to my home trying to make me feel bad just so you can make a nickel commission on a magazine sell," I snapped.

My insults didn't even get Morgan off my doorstep. As a matter of fact, for some reason she offered me a free magazine, saying that she would pay for it out of her commission check. I still refused the magazine but she wouldn't stop hounding me. Can you believe that dilly broad stood right there on my porch and started reading to me from an issue of *Vibe*? Hell, it didn't take long to get through. It only had a few articles. The majority of the pages were advertisements for hip-hop clothing and kicks.

I guess you could say that was the beginning of Morgan's and my friendship and her fascination for reading to me. Morgan started just dropping by my house on a regular as if she was an invited guest. I was always there when she came a knocking.

"Why are you always home?" Morgan finally got the courage to ask me. "Don't you work or anything?"

She was looking at me like I was some drug kingpin, or like I was dating one. How else could I afford to live in a house and drive a car?

I usually never gave a fuck about what anyone thought, but for some reason I didn't want her thinking those things about me. So that's when I shared with Morgan a little about my coming up. She was moved by all that I had gone through as a child. She told me that I should write a book about it. She told me that if I went out and got the computer, that she would dictate my story so that's exactly what I did.

Morgan would come over every weekend. We would laugh and talk. I would tell her a little bit of my story and she would type it. We dreamt that maybe some day some big producer would even take my book and turn it into a movie. But I thought only John Singleton could bring it to life. I wanted the girl that played Nick Cannon's love interest in *Drum Line* to play me in the movie. She also played the bitchy female pirate in the *Pirates of the Caribbean*. Morgan said that that girl and I could pass for twins if I wasn't so much lighter.

Eventually our excitement died down. We got sidetracked and ended up just hanging out and doing stuff together. We've been doing everything together ever since.

I was so blessed that day Morgan showed up on my doorstep. I suppose I needed a friend in my life. Everyone needs at least one friend. And with a friend like Morgan, someone so genuinely caring and loving, one friend is all I'll ever need.

6. Double Date

It was early Friday morning and the last day of the month. I had to renew my driver's license so Morgan was going to open up the store for me. My tags had officially expired four days ago on my birthday, but you know how black folk is. We always wait around until the last minute to handle that matter. Waiting in the DMV line was like waiting in the food stamp line (before they came out with those food stamp cards of course). I just wanted to get it over with.

I usually go to the one on the east side of Columbus where the Suga Shop is, but I live up north off of Karl Road, so this time I decided to go to the one on Morse Road instead. When I walked in I was glad to see that only five people were ahead of me. Who could have ever guessed that it would take those slow ass jiggaboos an hour to get through only three people?

Fortunately for me I had on my indigo Levis and they were huggin' the hell out of my size ten hips. There was a male clerk, a female clerk, and some old woman, who looked like the cafeteria lady, in the back working the camera.

I had caught the male clerk's eye when I walked through the door. I had him wishing that he was my thong. I just happened to look up and he was staring right at me. He signaled me to come up to his counter even though I still had two people ahead of me.

I crept on up to the counter, trying to be inconspicuous. He wasn't bad looking and was cool as hell too. If he hadn't been hounding me so hard with his eyes, I would have thought that he had a little sugar in his tank because of the slight femininity about him. Although he very well could have been a down-low brotha.

Once at the counter, he waited on me like it wasn't nothing. He didn't even try to hit on me. He just handled my business in a professional manner. I was having trouble with my eye exam, trying to read those small ass letters. I just told him that I wore glasses but had left them at home. He let me slide. After that, I was sure he was going to try to hit me up for the digits, but he didn't. He simply told me to have a good day and went on to the next customer.

See, I like brothas like that. He gave a sistah her space. He gave me the opportunity to make a move if I was feeling his vibe. I wasn't, but I'm grateful that he knocked twenty minutes off of my wait time.

After getting my new license, I headed to the Suga Shop.

"Hey, Morgan," I said, entering the store from the back storage room.

"Hey, girl," Morgan replied in her normal jolly tone. "Look who's back."

I looked up and saw Jazzy and York standing at the latte counter where Morgan had prepared them each a French vanilla cappuccino.

She was at the filing cabinet getting the $66.97 that Jazzy had left a couple of weeks back.

"What's up, sexy?" York said with a lucky in love smile on his face. "I like you in those jeans."

He was irritating as hell . . . but yet there was something about him that was just so cute. He was kind of like Dwayne Wayne on the comedy *A Different World.* At first you think, *hey, who is this woman hounding nerd* and then you think, *damn he ain't half bad and he's kind of sexy.*

"Thank you," I replied. "What's up yourself?"

"Oh, I can't call it, ma," he said, gazing into my eyes.

"Hey," I said, nodding at Jazzy who was standing there chewing on a coffee stir straw. He was silent, as always. I liked a man who only talked when he had something to say and didn't just run his mouth for the hell of it.

Morgan handed Jazzy the envelope with his change in it. "Oh, good lookin' out," he said, putting the money in his pocket.

"I was beginning to think that was my tip," I joked. "Since you never came back for it."

"Hey," he said. "Just like Mase, I'm back now."

Why in the hell was Jazzy so fine? And why in the hell was Morgan diggin' on him? I can't lie. There wasn't really anything wrong with York. I could perhaps see myself diggin' him a little bit, but I could see myself diggin' Jazzy a little bit more. He had the "it" factor. He had that little something extra that York, or any other brotha I had ever met for that matter, didn't have.

By just looking at him I could tell that he was confident in who he was and how he got there, kind of like me. Maybe that's why I was feeling him so much. He reminded me so much of myself.

Just as soon as I sensed an attraction between us, I should have stuck my claws in him. Pride will make you miss a calling. That's for sure. Now I would have the "what if" factor fucking with my head. What if I had just stepped to him?

"Jazzy, York and I were just talking about that new movie out staring Lisa Raye and Khalil Kain," Morgan said. "You know the one, *The Root of All Evil.*"

"Yeah," I said. "It's not even out yet."

"It starts today," Morgan said quickly.

"Yeah, the little lady here told us that somebody just celebrated their twenty-seventh birthday," York said. "Happy birthday, love."

"Thank you," I said, batting my eyes.

"Yeah, happy birthday," Jazzy said, smiling and cocky.

"Well, York thought it would be nice if we all went out to the movies and maybe got something to eat afterwards to celebrate your birthday since you haven't done anything for it," Morgan said, excited as if it were her own birthday treat.

"I had to work," I said, reminding Morgan. "I couldn't do anything. And I was dog tired by the time the store closed. You remember how busy it was in here."

"A hardworking woman like yourself needs a night out on the town every now and then," York said. "It's all the better now that we have a cause to celebrate."

"So, Harlem, what do you say?" Morgan said in a tone that was desperately pleading for me to say yes.

"Why not?" I said.

"Good," York said.

"Then I guess it's a date," Jazzy said, looking at me, nodding his head.

Morgan cleared her throat and said, "A double date that is."

Jazzy looked at Morgan and smiled. He gave her a wink. "Yeah, that's what I meant. A double date."

"Let me come pick you up," York said to me. "Where do you live?"

"That's all right," I replied. "We can meet y'all." I wasn't trying to let this fool know where I lived so that he can do unannounced dropbys like the bugaboo he looked like he had the potential of being.

"Oh, so it's like that?" York said with an attitude. I could tell his feelings were hurt so I contemplated my initial concerns.

"You know what?" I said in a sexy tone. "You look harmless enough. You can come scoop me at 15007 Sandal Wood."

"You can kill two birds with one stone," Morgan added. "I'll drive to her house and we'll both be waiting there for you two."

"Sounds like a winner," York said. "How does eight o'clock sound?"

"I don't close up the store until then," I replied. "How about nine-thirty?"

"That can be arranged." York winked. "I'll check on what time the movie starts."

"Okay," Morgan said, rubbing her hands together. She couldn't wait to get a piece of Jazzy.

"Then we'll see you two tonight," York said as he and Jazzy began to walk away.

"Oh yeah," Jazzy said, stopping in his tracks. "How much do we owe y'all for the coffee?"

"It's on me," I said, looking into Jazzy's hypnotizing eyes.

"Thank you," Jazzy said as him and York headed out of the door. Before getting all the way out of the door he turned around and said to me, "I owe you one."

Morgan and I watched York and Jazzy clear the corner. We were both in a daze.

It was at that very moment that I had made it up in my mind that I had to have him. Despite how Morgan might have felt about him. I had to have me some Jazzy.

York and Jazzy arrived at my house at 9:30 P.M. sharp. Jazzy was driving. He pulled up in front of my house in a Black Range Rover with spinners. He hadn't struck me as one of them flashy type of dudes. I can usually call it, but I guess I was wrong this time. But I had to give him credit. His whip was hot to def.

Before they could even park I had called Morgan out of the bathroom so that we could head out of the door. No need in them coming into my castle trying to get comfy. Then before you know it they'll be talking about, "Let's just skip the movie and hang out here." Jazzy could barely throw his shit in park before Morgan and I were out the door.

"Oh, y'all ready?" York said as he stepped out of the passenger side.

"We stay ready," I said as I locked the front door. "That way we never have to get ready."

York stood outside of the car until Morgan and I made it down the driveway. He then moved aside and allowed Morgan to sit in the front seat. Once she was nice and settled he closed the door behind her, then opened the back door for me.

"You're looking lovely," York said as he took my hand and assisted me into the back of the vehicle. I had on a long Tommy Hilfiger denim skirt with a black TH blouse that laced down the front.

"Thank you," I replied. "I'm diggin' that Roccawear getup you playing as well."

York was hurtin' that hookup. He could have been a model for the label. He wasn't a tall guy, probably my exact height. His bowlegs made him look a little shorter though. But without a doubt, he was easy on the eyes.

"The movie starts at 10:05 P.M. at the Lenox so let's ride," York said to Jazzy.

"Yo, York, why don't you blaze one?" Jazzy said, throwing his ride in drive. "It'll make the ride much smoother."

York rolled a blunt as we drove to the theater. I puff puffed the magic dragon and caught an instant buzz. I wasn't a regular weed smoker. I mean, I didn't go out and spend my money on the shit, but I would suck on somebody else's in a heartbeat.

We made it to the theater at about 9:55 P.M. With ten minutes to spare we got some popcorn, soda, and Milk Duds. The movie was excellent. It had my mind twisted. I was all caught up. I assumed everyone else felt the same because we didn't say shit to one another while in there. But I guess going to the movies really isn't something you should do on a first date since you can't talk or anything. I guess that's why I never have a problem going to the movies solo. Morgan thinks I'm crazy for just picking up and going to the movies by myself, but I figure it doesn't matter if you go to the movies alone or with five people. You can't talk in the damn theater nohow, so what's it matter? But nonetheless, we all enjoyed each other's presence.

After the movie let out we decided to go grab some food. On the way to eat we chatted a little bit.

"So what do you do for a living?" I asked York. It didn't make sense for me to wonder about whether or not this boy sold drugs for a living. I figured I wouldn't even fuck around with it, but to just come straight out and ask him.

"Huh?" he said, caught off guard.

"I said what do you do for a living?" I repeated. "And don't tell me construction or that you paint houses for your uncle. Keep that shit real."

Morgan and Jazzy both chuckled.

"You know The Golden Shower over there near Windsor?" York asked me.

"That car wash?" I asked.

"Yeah. Well, I run that. I'm the general manager."

"Um hm," I said with perhaps slight disbelief.

"What?" York said.

"Nothing. I just said um hm. How long you been working there?"

"For about a year now," York replied. "I was out of town for the longest, but I moved back to Columbus about a year and a half ago. I worked at Foot Locker for a minute and a couple of other crab ass places before getting put on at the car wash."

"You were out of town, huh?" I asked, maybe with a hint of disbelief in my tone.

"Yeah," York replied firmly.

"Well, I know how guys like to say they were out of town or in the army when they've really been locked up. You're not one of those guys are you?"

York looked at Morgan like *is your friend serious?* Then he looked back at me.

"I bet when you were a little girl you told all the other kids that there wasn't a Santa Claus didn't you?" York said.

Jazzy and Morgan cracked up laughing.

"So what do you do, Jazzy?" I said, turning the million dollar question to him now.

"Oh, me," Jazzy said like it wasn't nothing. "I sell drugs."

Then he looked at me through the rear view mirror as to say "nigga what?"

He had this cockiness to him that was down right sexy. I wasn't mad at him though. I would have had the same attitude in his position. There ain't nothing arrogant about the truth. But even so, I was riding around in a tricked out SUV with a dope boy. The police could have pulled us over any minute and hauled all of our asses off to jail.

"You ain't got shit up in this truck or nothing do you," I asked. Fuck that. Fine or not, I'm too cute for jail. Bitches would be fighting each other trying to bump coochies with me.

Jazzy sucked his teeth and looked at me in the rearview mirror. "I'm not going to even believe that you asked me that. You don't bite your tongue, huh?"

"Nope," I said. "And please believe that I did just ask you that. Can I get an answer?"

"What you gon' do if I say yes?" Jazzy asked me. "Get out of the truck?"

"You got any shit up in here that might land my ass in jail or not?" I said with a slight attitude.

"I wouldn't even do that to you," Jazzy said sincerely. "But even more so, I wouldn't even do that to myself. I'm better than that."

This nigga kept it real. I could feed off of his energy forever. I just wanted to be in his presence, vibin' off of what he had to offer. And to answer his question, no, I would not have gotten out of the truck. Maybe Jazzy was my crack rock, making me not give a fuck about things that I once might have.

Jazzy busted a right into the driveway of this spot called Salaam's. It was a nice little hang out owned by some Africans. It was a place where we could grab something to eat at as well as get some drinks.

When we entered the restaurant, there was a male host wearing African garb standing at the door.

"Hello, and welcome to Salaam's," the host said with an accent. "Name of your party please?"

"Brown," Jazzy said.

"Yes, Brown," the man said, scrolling down his reservations list. "Here you are right here. Let me grab some menus, then follow me right this way."

The host led us to a booth in the back of the restaurant. There was a nice crowd going on. It just happened to be open mic night so there were poets and rappers to entertain us while we got our grub on.

We each ordered a round of drinks and then the waiter came over to take our orders.

"Go ahead when you're ready," the waiter said.

"Let's let the birthday girl order first," York said, winking at me. "Go ahead, Harlem."

I stared at the menu for a minute before Morgan jumped in.

"Hey, Harlem," she said. "They've got grilled salmon. And you know how much we love salmon."

"Yeah, I'll take that," I said.

"What sides would you like?" the waiter asked.

"Hmm," I said. I could tell he was getting impatient with me.

"You can have mashed potatoes, salad, string beans—" the waiter said.

"I'll take the potatoes and salad," I said cutting him off.

He gladly moved on to take everyone else's order, then headed to the kitchen to turn in our request to the chef.

"Hey, Harlem, why don't you go up there and free style?" Morgan joked. "You know how you like to rhyme."

"You be flowing too?" York asked me. "Damn, you're every woman. Brains, beauty, and you can flow. Take your ass on up there girl."

"Yeah, let me see what you working with," Jazzy added with an underlying stimulating tone.

Was he speaking a language that only I could hear? Why wasn't anyone else picking up on the way he talked to me? Looked at me? Or maybe it was just me reading more into his words and his looks than were actually there.

Nonetheless, I felt as though I was being challenged by Jazzy to get up on stage and rock the mic, so I went on and signed the list to perform. There were a ton of names on that paper so I knew that by the time my name was called we would be long gone and I wouldn't have to get up there and embarrass myself. But to my surprise they got to my name sooner than I thought. When they called my name to come to the stage I was a little tipsy from the Long Island I had sucked down. But at the same time the liquor must have given me courage because I stepped to the mic like what.

Just off the top of my head I started rappin'. I didn't even know where the words were coming from, but the crowd was feeling it. They especially liked the line when I said, "I'm not a flashy chick. I'm a classy chick. I make any high rollin' broad feel like a trashy chick."

I got a standing ovation by the time I got off the stage. York was so proud of me. He was standing up doing the Arsenio Hall barking thing and throwing his fist in the air. I know it was just a little spot in a little corner of Columbus, Ohio, but I felt like a big star.

The owner was so impressed with my performance and how hyped I had gotten the crowd that he gave our table a round of drinks on the house. After sipping on the free drinks, it was time to call it a night.

Jazzy pulled up in front of my house at about 2:15 A.M. Just as I figured he would, no sooner than he put the car in park York said, "Can I come in and use your bathroom?"

Why did guys do that obvious shit? They might as well say, can I come in and see for myself if there's any chance of me getting laid tonight?

"Yeah, me too," Jazzy added.

Men, I thought to myself before saying, "Of course. Come on in."

York and Jazzy followed Morgan and me up to my porch. York held the screen for me while I unlocked the door.

"There's a bathroom straight down the hall to your left and one straight up the steps," I said as I turned on the hallway lamp.

York headed to the bathroom down the hall while Jazzy went upstairs.

"I'll show you where it's at," Morgan, the hoe, said, hurrying after him.

That bitch ain't hardly slick. I looked at her and gave her the naughty girl laugh. Just as soon as they were out of sight, my laughter died a quick death. That green-eyed monster had set in. York was cool, but my chemistry was stronger with Jazzy. I felt bad about the feelings I was having because of Morgan. In all of our years of friendship we had never been attracted to the same type of man. I usually hated the type of guys she ended up with. They were usually disrespecting assholes. Maybe Jazzy would turn out to be that same type of guy. I could be sweatin' this for nothing.

Morgan hadn't really *talked about* talked about Jazzy as if he could be the one. Morgan loved playing with bad boys. I should have just told her from jump that I wanted Jazzy and she could take York. She probably would have been down. But Jazzy had a sistah biting her tongue. Even though he wasn't showing any type of major interest in Morgan, I would have hated to get shot down by him. He surely wasn't another DC, who would have disrespected Morgan right in her face and tried to get at me. I could say that much about Jazzy. Usually I go for a man who knows what he wants anyway. And if Jazzy wants me, then sooner or later, he was going to have to speak up. And when he did, I would be there listening.

My jealously quickly dissolved as I thought about Morgan's MO. Morgan was good for a few kisses and a good feel, but I didn't see Jazzy taking it any further than that with her. She hadn't quite graduated with her Ghetto Education Degree and I was sure that a man like Jazzy definitely needed a ghetto princess by his side.

"I like how you decorated your bathroom," York said as he came down the hallway and joined me in the living room. "That old school black and white theme is tight, especially that drawing of Al Pacino as Scarface."

"Thank you," I said. "But my favorite is the one of Muhammad Ali, even though it took me a while to be able to piss in front of the champ."

"Yeah," York laughed. "I had to make sure Billie Holiday wasn't looking at me when I handled my business."

We both laughed. It was a sweet moment. I wasn't used to that so I had to change the mood.

"Did you find my house okay when you guys came to pick us up?" I asked.

"We found it fine," York said. "When Jazzy and I drove up to this pink house we wasn't sure exactly what the inside was going to look like. It looked like a big Barbie house or something. But it's tight up in here. Besides, I figured if it looked like a Barbie dream house, then perhaps a dream girl lived here."

"Thanks," I said, blushing.

York and I walked over to my couch and just sat there. He allowed his eyes to scroll the living room a little bit, checking out my nice things.

"Can I offer you anything?" I asked, pointing towards the kitchen.

York had this serious look on his face as he drew in closer to me.

"I'll take you," he said. He put his hand on my waist while he looked into my eyes for a reaction. He didn't know if touching me meant that I would marshmallow up or if he would have to brace himself for a blow.

"I can't, baby," I said softly, looking dead into his hungry eyes as I removed his hand from my waist. "It's that time of the month, bu."

"Are you bleeding heavy?" York asked undeterred.

"Excuse me?" I asked, pulling my head back and looking at him in surprise.

"Is it the beginning of your cycle or the end? Are you bleeding *bleeding* or is it at the end with that brown rusty lookin' stuff?"

This fool was dead serious. I couldn't help but bust out laughing.

"What's so funny?" he asked. "I'm serious as a muthafuck."

"You, man," I said, getting up off the couch. "You are what's funny. Look, do you want a drink or have you had enough for the night?"

"What? Why you trippin'?" York said, standing up following me into the kitchen. "I'm keeping it real."

I turned to him, now serious. "Look," I said, moving in close to him. "It's only the second day of my cycle. I'm a heavy bleeder. It's nasty down there. So unless you that grimy ass nigga who don't give a fuck, now isn't the time to get intimate."

I walked away and went to the refrigerator to grab us each a Mike's Hard Cranberry Lemonade. When I closed the refrigerator door, York was standing right there with a questionable look on his face.

"What now?" I asked.

He paused then grabbed me by the face and planted a heavy French kiss on me.

"I'm that grimy ass nigga," he said as he continued to kiss me.

I sat the bottles down and did what any sistah in her right mind would. I kissed him back. Shit, his tongue action was on point. After tonguin' him down and getting his dick nice and hard I replied, "Well, I ain't that grimy ass bitch. Now let's go drink up."

York and I headed back into the living room and sat down on the couch. No sooner than we sat down we heard a loud moan.

"Ohh, baby, don't stop," we heard Morgan shout from the guest bedroom. "Do it faster!"

Jazzy was good at taking orders because suddenly we heard the headboard banging up against the wall. Seconds later he shouted, "Oh, shit! Goddamn, I'm about to cum! I'm cummin'!"

Morgan was definitely getting her socks knocked off by Jazzy. I looked over at York and he had a crooked smile on his face, nodding his head up and down. It was a smile that said "that's my boy up there hittin' that."

I can't even explain the feeling that came over me. I want to say

I felt jealous, but I couldn't be jealous of my girl getting hers, could I? I suppose hearing her and Jazzy upstairs getting down squashed any ideas I had about getting with him myself. I had been so certain that he was diggin' me on the low the same way I was diggin' him.

Hearing those two screwing fucked up my buzz and the moment. I hated that it was York sitting next to me and not Jazzy. And I knew that Jazzy was a straight up baller and yet I was still drawn to him. I couldn't explain it. That had been Morgan's type of thing, not mine.

"You look as though your mind is a million miles away," York said, interrupting my thoughts.

"Oh, no, I'm cool. I'm just tired," I said, letting out a fake yawn.

"Oh, the I'm tired line," York said, twisting up his lips. "It's cool, ma. I'm not going to try to push up on you. You said no and I respect that. We can still chill."

"Nah," I said, getting up. "I really am tired. You can wait here until your boy finishes dirtying up my guest sheets, but I'm going to bed."

"Damn. Aren't you even going to finish your drink?" York asked.

"Nah. I'm good," I replied as I headed down the hall to my bedroom.

As I entered the bedroom and slammed the door behind me I heard York call, "Damn! Well, can't you at least show a brotha a titty or something?"

I laughed as I began to take off my clothes and change into my pajamas. York wasn't such a bad guy. Maybe I could really learn to like him.

7. Ballin' Out of Control

This was the third time in one month that FedEx had brought a delivery to my store that wasn't part of my inventory. Instead, they were personal gifts addressed to me. The first package was a pair of 18-carat gold gypsy hoop earrings. The second package was a gold bangle with three diamond chips, and now the third, a gold nameplate necklace with my name. The H in the nameplate had sparkling diamonds embedded in it. Each package was compliments of York.

I guess this was his way of wooing me. But I thought he could read into me better than that. I thought he could tell that I wasn't a woman who was impressed by material things. I mean, hell yeah I like the little name-brand things that I own, but I wasn't no gold digger like he had probably become accustomed to and had paid dearly for their time. I'm a different breed. I don't care about being able to brag to my girlfriends about how some dude got my hair *did* for me. I prefer to boast about what I was able to do for my damn self. Any material shit that catches my eye, I'm able to afford with or without a man.

"That is beautiful," Morgan said, leaning over my shoulder to admire it. "Another gift from York?"

I nodded yes.

"Damn, looks like I picked the wrong one to holler at. York is showing you mad love. How much money does one make running a car wash?"

Even though I wasn't into it, I had to admit that York's gifts were getting better and better each time. At least the brotha had good taste in gifts.

"And he don't even own the car wash," Morgan continued, staring in awe at the piece of jewelry. "He just runs the joint. Hell, Jazzy be ballin' out of control and he don't buy me shit like that. Probably because he's loaning all of his money to York to buy shit to impress you with."

"Jazzy don't buy you shit period," I reminded Morgan. "You still don't know how to work your hands right. Besides, Jazzy doesn't come across to me as the type who would give his money away."

"Just as long as he keeps laying the pipe, I'm good," Morgan said, winking. "But I'd still like to know just how did you get York to buy you all these gifts? You can tell me, girl. Did you swallow?"

Morgan laughed because she knew better. I had never been the type to trick or treat a muthafuka. I ain't even on that hoe shit.

"I didn't do anything," I said. "I mean yeah, I did let him do a sixty-eight on me real quick in the car that day last week when you and Jazzy ran into the gas station. But damn. I still owe him one and yet he still keeps giving gifts to me."

Morgan couldn't help but laugh. "You ain't gave him that plus one to make it an even sixty-nine yet?"

"I like York. I really do. I just can't bring myself to go all the way with him like that."

"But he's fine, girl. And he really really likes you. It ain't your panties he's after. He's proven that. Girl, he wants to be your man. And besides that, he done spent all his car wash tips on you. He deserves some pussy."

Morgan took the nameplate from my hand to observe it more closely.

"I just feel like he's sneaky and I'm not trying to get caught up," I said.

"Sneaky how?" Morgan asked. "You think he's seeing other women?"

"Hell, I know he's seeing other women. He's a man without a ring," I said, smacking my lips. "I'm not worried about that. I just think he's doing more than running that car wash. I think he's hustling out of that car wash. And you know I ain't never fucked around with no hustlers before. You know the saying: Wherever hustlers go, trouble follows. But you know me. I can hold my own, so it ain't even solely the fact that he's a hustler. I don't mind keepin' a nigga at arm's length. But if he is, in fact, slingin' rocks, that would make him a liar. Niggas that lie in the beginning will be lying in the end. I just don't have time for those type of games."

"But why would he lie about what he does? He rolls with Jazzy. Jazzy didn't have a problem coming right out and saying that he's a baller. If York was, I don't see why he wouldn't have just said it either. Jazzy probably just looks out for him, that's all. Besides, if he was a big balla, we would have heard of him before now."

"We hadn't heard of Jazzy before," I replied.

"I guess you're right about that." Morgan sighed. "But still, why would he lie? Y'all grown."

Morgan was right. Jazzy didn't have a problem coming right out and saying that he was a street pharmacist. Unfortunately it was shit like that that attracted me to him . . . honesty.

"York knows that I'm a no-nonsense bitch. I got it going on. To him, I don't seem like the type who would be fuckin' with somebody who slings drugs. And another thing, which you hit right on the money, him and Jazzy are tight. Odds are, both them cats are cut from the same cloth."

"Then if that's all that's keeping you from getting your rocks knocked, then just ask him," Morgan said, handing me back the necklace. "I've never known you to bite your tongue. Maybe you're into York just a little bit more than you think. Otherwise, just ask him straight up. What have you got to lose?"

Morgan was right. Why did I give a fuck what that fool did for a living? He was just somebody I enjoyed kickin' it with. I thought about what she said as I looked down at the lovely piece of jewelry. A month's worth of tips at the car wash couldn't have paid for this. I wasn't about to be one of them dumb broads who know they fuckin' with a dope boy but doesn't want to ask because they don't want to know so they can just keep cashing in on the blood money of the lost souls of the community. I wasn't going to be one of those type of broads. I needed to know what I might be getting myself into. Like I said, I needed to know if I needed to keep York at arm's length. Perhaps it was time I put in a call to York and try to get him to show me his hand. If I did decide to kick it with him on the regular, it was my right to know what cards he was holdin' in the game of life. That way, I could decide whether or not I wanted to play.

I can't remember the last time I invited a man to hang out at my house. I'm sure I had a date or two that might have picked me up, but none who stayed long enough to case the entire joint. York would probably be the first.

After my conversation with Morgan I decided to call York up and invite him over for a nightcap. I chilled some Hypnotiq and bought some Sprite and cranberry juice so that I could mix us up some Supermans. I had lit two candles on the living room table, but decided to blow them out. I didn't want to send off the wrong signal. This wasn't no bootie call.

I heard a car pull up in my driveway. I ran to the window and saw York's Gold Infiniti pull up.

"I know this fool ain't parking in my driveway," I said to myself. I thought every man knew that he wasn't supposed to park in a woman's driveway if he wasn't her husband. That shit sends off jezebel signals to the neighbors, especially if he plans on spending the night and leaving early in the morning. I guess I shouldn't be too ticked off since I didn't plan on him being at my house any more than a couple of hours. But that was definitely something I would have to school him on for future reference.

I hurried over to my couch, which was part of a three-piece chocolate suede living room set. I straightened up the chocolate pillows with gold fringes. The fringes matched the gold buttons going down the seams of the couch. I straightened out the corner of the white furry rug that was underneath my glass coffee table that I had kicked up when I walked over to straighten up the pillows. By then York was knocking at my door.

"Who is it?" I called for GP (general purposes).

"The big bad, wolf," York joked with that annoying, but cute, sense of humor he had.

I flattened out the long knitted gray poncho I was wearing. I pulled it down just right so that my left shoulder was showing. Can a girl tease a fella at least? Give him something to maybe look forward to? I sucked in my stomach and positioned the black DKNY jeans I was wearing. I had simply thrown on some black straw flip-flops for comfort. I thought the house slippers that I really wanted to wear was just a tad bit too ghetto.

I opened the door and York was standing there with his arms folded and a devilish grin.

"Come in," I said, opening the screen door for him.

"You look nice," he said, kissing me on the cheek and then handing me a bottle of Moet.

"Thank you," I said, taking it. "You've got expensive taste for a guy who works at a car wash."

"What's that supposed to mean?" he said in a defensive tone.

"Nothing," I said, walking over to the couch and sitting down. "Join me."

I patted a place for York to sit by me. He licked his lips, came out of his bowleg stance, walked over, and sat down next to me.

"I hope you like Supermans," I said as I removed the Hypnotiq from the ice bucket.

"What the hell is a Superman?" he asked.

"It's just Hypnotiq mixed with Sprite and cranberry juice," I said as I proceeded to mix the drinks. I put a couple of ice cubes from the ice bucket in our glasses then handed York one as I took my own.

"Let's toast," I said, holding my glass up.

"To what?" York asked, tilting his head.

"To the truth," I clinked his glass then took a swallow. He looked at me momentarily then took a swallow from his glass.

"This is good," he said. "I never had Hypnotiq before. I couldn't see myself drinking something that's blue."

"It tastes like Alizé," I said.

"That's a girl's drink."

"It is not," I laughed. "Why do guys always say that?"

"So what's up with that toast?" York said as if he couldn't wait to get to the bottom of his being there. "First you call me up out of the blue and then you invite me over, which was a shock to me, seeing as how you haven't used my cell number since I gave it to you. Then you make this toast to the truth. Come on, ma. What's on your mind?"

"Well, since you asked," I said, cutting to the chase. "I invited you here for two reasons. First of all, I felt that I needed to do a little somethin' somethin' for you for all of the lovely gifts you've been sending me. They are lovely, York, and I really appreciate them."

"I like sending you gifts," he said, taking another sip of his drink. "So you don't have to thank me, Harlem. I knew from the moment that I met you that you were a woman with exquisite taste."

York looked around and I could tell, once again, that he was very impressed with my home. I guess the one good thing I could say about York was that at least he wasn't intimidated by me. Once I told the few guys that I had gone out with where I lived, they started feeling inferior to me. They couldn't figure out how a young single woman like myself had managed to buy a one hundred ninety-five thousand dollar home in Woodward Park. For some reason a brotha gets intimidated by a woman who has more hustle than he does. But York had a different look in his eyes. He had that look that Morgan would have had. That "how can I be down" look. Teach me how to get what you got. I liked that about him.

I never bothered telling most of the guys I kicked it with that I had inherited the house. Hell, right now it's worth one hundred ninety-five thousand dollars, but when my grandparents moved in, they only paid half of that for this home. But nonetheless, I was impressed at how impressed York was with it . . . with me.

"I'm glad you like my home," I said to York. "Morgan did most of the decorating."

"You and Morgan tight like the fist on the afro pic, huh?"

"Yeah," I replied, taking a sip. "Kind of like you and Jazzy I suppose."

"Yeah, that's my boy," York said with a smile. "He put me on in the game for real."

"Excuse me?" I said. I think I caught this brotha slippin'. Now I wouldn't have to ask him what he really did for a living. He had just damn near told on himself. And he knew it too as he gulped down the last few swallows of his drink.

"Why don't you make me another one?" he said, handing his glass to me.

I rolled my eyes, took the glass, and sat it down on the table.

"Why don't you tell me what you meant by Jazzy put you on in the game?"

"What I meant by that is that Jazzy owns the car wash. Hell, he owns three or four," York stuttered as he recognized the "I'm not buying what you're selling" look on my face. "He put me on with a job. I told you that I was working some nickel and dime jobs when I first came back to town."

"I bet they were some nickel and dime jobs all right," I said. He was probably a tennis-shoe hustler at first, earned rank, then got upgraded. "Can I tell you something about myself, York?"

That was a question that didn't really require an answer so I continued. "You might as well be cellophane because I see right through you. It bothers me if a muthafucka steals from me, cheats on me, or even talks about me like a dirty dog. But what I hate most is for a muthafucka to lie to me. You feel me? Now I may be some dumb, but I ain't plumb dumb, so don't ever underestimate my intelligence."

York sighed then shook his head. "All right. Fuck it! I guess I'm busted," he said, throwing his hands up in surrender. "I don't know what to say. Fuck it. I sling. I gotta eat, you know?"

Hearing him say it after the fact, after I gave him a chance to come clean, didn't move me. I rolled my tongue against my jaw. I wasn't surprised. Just disappointed that he had lied to me. I suspected he was a baller all along, but I had to give the brotha the benefit of the doubt. Now, I knew the truth. Now I knew what I had to do.

"So do you want me to leave?" he asked. "You hate for muthafuckas to lie to you and I guess right about now I'm a lying muthafucka." York sipped the one tiny drop that was left in his glass as if he wasn't even fazed. No *sorry for lying to you* or nothing.

"I want to know why you lied?" I asked sincerely. "Jazzy didn't have a problem telling the truth when I asked him."

"So you wanna fuck Jazzy or something?" York snapped. "What do you care whether or not that nigga lies to you or tells you the truth? Don't be comparing me to no other man."

I had to think quick. "I don't like people around me that I have to guess twice about," I said.

"I mean come on, Harlem. It's not that serious," he said standing up. "And if you really want to get technical, I didn't really lie to you. You asked me what I did for a living and I told you that I was

the general manager at the car wash. Well, I am. You didn't ask me
if I did anything else."

Just as I suspected, one of them slick bastards. "Oh, so you one
of them brothas that like to lie by omission?"

"It ain't that serious, ma," York said, shaking his head.

"Maybe not to you because it's a lifestyle you've chosen to be a
part of. I haven't chosen it and I think it's unfair of you to force it
on me without giving me a choice. Allow me to fuck up my own
life, thank you very much."

"Ain't nobody forcing shit on you. I ain't asking you to hit the
block or asking can I use your crib to store my shit."

"You're being here, sitting up in my living room, living the
lifestyle that you live is forcing it on me. I know how jealous cats
are. For all I know a hater could have followed you over here and is
outside loading up his gat fixin' to spray my house this very second. That's the type of shit I'm talking about. That's the type of
shit a bitch need to be prepared for. Let a bitch know if she has to
install security cameras to see who's coming and going. What
makes you so certain I want that type of shit around me? How
could you even want it around yourself?"

"Look, I'm wrong," York said, throwing his hands up. "I'm
dead wrong."

I looked at him standing there with that puppy dog, now can I
have some pussy, look on his face. I proceeded to fix him another
Superman. He came back over and sat down next to me as I dropped
the ice cubes in his drink.

"Here you go," I said, handing him the drink. "But once you're
finished with it you need to go, York."

He took the drink with a smile. "It's all good. I fucked up. I didn't
keep it real with you from the jump, so I can't even be mad at you,

ma. I know the saying, bullshitters in the beginning, bullshitters in the end. It ain't even like that though, for real, ma. But it's cool. It's been real."

He took a sip of his drink then sat it down.

"But just to let you know that we still cool, and I'm still feeling you regardless, I'm going to give you this anyway," York said, pulling a Kay Jewelers box from his pocket. "I got this for you today at the mall. I still want you to have it even though you just basically told me to kick mud." He laid it on my lap.

Of course I opened it. I'm a woman with a Kay Jewelers box on her lap. I was curious.

My mouth dropped when I saw a platinum triple band staring at me. I was speechless. I hadn't even given this man the ill nah na and he was still showering me with lovely gifts.

"I always buy you a piece of jewelry because I'm a firm believer that jewelry isn't something a person should buy for themselves. It's something they should receive as a gift."

I just sat there admiring the stunning beauty of the ring.

"You don't like it?" York asked.

"No, it's not that. It's just that it's sooo gorgeous," I said, taking it out of the box.

"You might have to get it sized if it doesn't fit," York said.

"Did you really believe that I was going to think that you only worked at a car wash after buying me something like this?" I chuckled.

"I don't know what I thought you were going to believe," York said. "Most chicks don't ask, they just take. They usually know the deal, but don't want to speak on it and confirm their suspicions. Broads don't want to be an accessory before the fact."

"I'm not most chicks," I said, putting the ring back into the box.

I reached over to the glass end table and grabbed the plastic bag I had sitting on it. I opened the bag and dropped the Kay Jeweler's box down in it along with all of the other gifts York had given me. I handed him the bag.

"What's this?" he said, taking it then looking inside of it. "Why are you giving everything back? I said I still want you to have this stuff. What's the matter? You don't like a man spending money on you? Are you that independent of a broad?"

Now he was trying to piss me off. Well, guess what? It was working.

"I don't have a problem with a man spending money on me. I guess I just have a problem with a man who spends money so easily."

"Why?" York asked. "Don't you feel like you deserve nice things?"

"I know I deserve nice things," I said in a matter-of-fact tone. "It's just that men who spend their money easy usually make easy money. They don't know the true value, so it's easy come easy go. It's temporary bliss, not long term."

York grinned and sat his glass down on the coffee table.

"I'm not one of those broads with the ching ching mentality that you are used to. You don't have to buy me jewelry and designer purses, get my nails done and shit. Buy my ass a savings bonds or something. See, I'm on some other shit than these Columbus scavengers. I'm on a five-year plan, baby. And I'm going to work for mine. I don't want it from some nigga who can make me check my shit in the minute I don't want to suck his dick."

"Oh, so now I'm some nigga?" York said offended.

"Baby, you're not hearing me," I said, finishing off my drink and putting it down next to his. I turned to face him and I liked what I saw. I saw a sincere man who was genuinely attentive to my words. I paused, caught myself from zoning, then continued.

"I'm not saying that. But what I am saying is that if you wanted to kick it with me, cool. But you don't have to buy my time. If I feel you deserve it, then it's yours for free. You feeling that you had to buy me shit in order to get some of my time makes me wonder what kind of woman you think I am."

"You know it ain't even like that," York said. "I mean look at you, Harlem. You ain't one of these little chicken heads running around. You think I can't see that? You run your own business. You own your own home. You got a nice whip, clothes and shit. You're like some ghetto princess or some shit," York snickered. "I came up hard. You don't know how hard, man."

York clenched his teeth. He closed his eyes as if he had been hit hard by a hurtful memory. He balled his fist and took a deep breath.

"There were times when I didn't even know where my next meal was coming from," he said. "My moms, God knows she did the best she could, killed herself when I was only eight years old. She got tired of the ass whippings my daddy plagued her with night after night. After she died it was just my little sister and me left to be raised with the man who forced my mom to put a gun to her head. All he was worried about was drinking, running with his homies, and women. Oh yeah, and Charge, he was my dad's black Labrador Retriever. Do you know there would be days when my sister and I didn't have a damn thing to eat and we would sit and watch Charge eat Dog Chow out of his bowl? My sister and I used to joke about eating the dog food. Then one summer day our belly's ached with hunger pains that were so bad, that it wasn't a joke anymore. I'll never forget me and my sister sitting there eating a plate of dog food."

York closed his lips tight and I could see a tear well up in his eye. I could see the pain on his face. I had had that look in my own eyes a time or two.

"Can you believe it?" York said. "The man made sure the fuckin' dog had food and not his own children." York paused again. He ran his hand down his eyes to wipe away the tears before they could fall. "Well, Jazzy helped me find a cure for those hunger pains. Slingin' rocks settled both my sister's and my hunger pains. I guess Jazzy is what you could say was the big man on campus. I met him one day out at The Classic. He was in town on business from Atlanta. I was struggling, trying to get in the game here. So I asked one of my boys, who knew one of the dudes he was with that night, to get permission for me to holler at him. Jazzy okayed a conversation with me. I stepped to him and let him know how I was livin' and how I wanted to start livin'. He did his research, then let me roll back to the ATL with him and his boys. He put me up in a house to run. At first he just let me hold an eight ball or two to see what I could do with it. I proved loyal and to be a hard worker. I kept moving up rank until he put me in charge of one of his car washes there. That's where mad weight gets moved. I set it off. I mean I was booming in the ATL, then my sister, who stayed here in Columbus, got herself into a little trouble and I had to leave the life and come back to see about her. Then we found ourselves struggling again. Back in the ATL the police started sniffing up Jazzy's ass so he decided to uproot shop, with me being here and him knowing how well I had proved myself in Atlanta, he decided to come to Columbus and set up shop."

York guzzled down his drink.

"I don't want to hear anymore, York," I said. "The less I know, the better."

"You just don't understand how it is for a brotha from the projects, Harlem."

"Oh, I see," I said, clearing my throat. "So you're pretty much saying don't blame me for being in the game, blame my circumstances."

"I knew your stuck up yellow ass wouldn't understand shit about street life and why muthafuckas choose it," York said, standing up. "So a brotha has to do what he has to do to make a come up in life. Don't knock the hustle."

"That's bullshit, York, and you know it," I said angrily. "People survive those streets every day and I'm living proof. Don't get it twisted. I'll never knock the hustle. Hell, every muthafuckin' thing in life is a hustle."

York looked at me and laughed as if I was joking.

"Oh, you survived the streets, huh?" He looked around admiring my African artwork, the mask, the paintings, the drums. He rubbed his hand on my brown sued couch and tapped the lampshade to my crystal lamp. "Yeah, it's clear you came from the streets."

"You have no idea where the fuck I've come from," I said, jumping up off of the couch. "I, too, know what it's like not to know where your next meal is going to come from or if there's even going to be a next meal. I've fought my mother, the system and grown ass men. My fingernails are still buried in the brick walls I've had to climb over, muthafucka, so don't you dare try to come at me with that condescending attitude. Yeah, the picture looks pretty now, but you should have seen it before it hit the canvas."

York could see that he had done it now. I was pissed. My bottom lip was trembling and I was fighting tears of anger. He walked over to me.

"I didn't know that about you," York said. "I'm sorry. I'm sorry for whatever you had to go through to get what you got. I didn't know."

"You didn't ask. All you did was perceive me as some material-ist bitch and try to buy me. Yeah, I got some nice things, but I don't make purchases to impress or buy any muthafucka."

"I've never tried to buy you, Harlem. I bought you those things because I wanted you to have them. Girl, when I look at your mean ass, I get chills. I know you probably use that attitude to scare peo-ple off, but it only made me want to get to know you better. I'm from the streets. I didn't know how to say that shit so I used gifts as my words. You can't fault a brotha for trying. I mean, it's not like you're the easiest person in the world to get next to," York said, putting his hands on my face. "To get close to. To talk to."

York ran his hand down the side of my face. I closed my eyes. His touch was so soft. He kissed me softly.

"Can I?" he asked under his breath as he kissed me again. "Can I get next to you, Harlem?" He kissed me again, this time slipping his tongue in and out. "Can I get inside of you?"

I began to suck on his tongue. The Hypnotiq tasted that much better.

"Can I?" he asked again, this time waiting for an answer as my tongue tried to seek out his, but he wouldn't give it to me until I responded.

What was I doing? What was happening? Everything was back-firing it seemed. The minute I got the answer that I didn't want to hear, York was supposed to be out of sight, out of mind. I wasn't supposed to end up feeling this way. I wasn't supposed to end up understanding.

"Can I, baby?" he asked again, in a whisper.

I closed my eyes. "Yes," I said breathing heavily. "Yes."

He gave me his tongue. I grabbed the back of his head and tongue fucked him hard. He eased his hands down to my belly button and began unsnapping my pants. I felt the warmth of his hand find its way down to my pleasure dome.

"Oooh," I spoke in a weak and fragile voice. I hadn't been touched like this ever.

"You all right?" York said, looking at me.

"Umm hmm," I replied. "I like the way you touch me."

York began kissing me and stroking my clit with his fingers. He had to be proud of how wet he had gotten me. My wetness was turning him on more and more. Finally he slid my pants down to my ankles and watched me step out of them. He looked up at me, licked his lips, then got up and sat down on the couch.

"Take it all off for me," he said in the most sensual tone.

I've never been one to be shy, but this boy had me blushing like a schoolgirl. However, my pussy wanted beat up tonight, so I figured the quicker I got my clothes off the sooner I could get fucked, so I quickly pulled my shirt over my head and went for the bra snap.

"Slow down, baby," York said as he undid his pants, pulled his dick out and began stroking it. Now that shit turned me on.

Slowly I began unsnapping my bra, not taking my eyes off of that big ass pipe he was packing. Damn, I wish I hadn't looked at it until after I let him fuck me. Now I was a little tense at letting something so huge enter my body. I had only been with about three men my entire life, and I didn't have any kids, so my pussy was petite.

I guess York could sense my uneasiness because he whispered, "Don't worry, I'm not going to hurt you. I'm going to make you feel good."

I got my bra and panties off and I don't know how it got there, but the next thing I knew his dick was in my mouth. I was on my knees, between his thighs, going up and down on his rod like I was bobbin' for apples. And I swear it tasted like a red candy coated one from the Ohio State Fair.

"Ohhh. Ohhh," York groaned as he grabbed the back of my head. Any other man would have gotten cut for that shit, but I was feeling the moment so I let him get away with it. Besides, he wasn't aggressive with it. He just pretty much had his hand on the back of my head allowing it to go up and down with the motion of my head.

As he pre-ejaculated I slurped up the sweet lava. He was delicious. I couldn't believe I was doing this, and loving it. I cupped his nuts and began massaging them as I inhaled as much of his dick as I possibly could. I locked his dick in my mouth and sucked hard. He began to tremble. That's when I stopped. Now a little pre-ejaculation I didn't mind, but I wasn't about to let him cum in my mouth.

I stood up and York stood up with me. He took off his shoes, his pants and his underwear then he sat back down on the couch with his dick pointing straight at me, like come here, bitch. I guess that was my signal to climb up on it, so that's exactly what I did.

I put one of my knees on each side of him and came down slowly. I began to tremble with fear as only the tip of that fat ass dick entered me.

I throttled on it, covering the tip with my pussy juices.

"You don't have to put it all in if you don't want to," York whispered as he rubbed his hands down my ass. The look in his eye was so sincere that I melted. I melted right down on his rock hard dick.

"I want all of it in me," I said, going up and down, each time allowing more and more of him inside of me. "I want you deep inside of me, York."

Before I knew it he had filled me up and I was going wild on his shit. Thank goodness his shit was double jointed because I worked the hell out of that dick. I was on the pill, just to stay regular, but I didn't know where that boy's dick had been to be riding it raw like I was doing. But in all honesty, I don't know if a condom would have even fit on his dick. I think that boy would have even given a Magnum a run for its money. *Harlem,* I said to myself, *What the fuck are you doing?*

"Turn that ass around," York said as he humped me back.

It was feeling so good that I didn't want to stop so I just kept fucking him.

"Turn it around," he repeated.

Without removing his dick from inside me, I spun around on that muthafucka and started working it backwards. He took off his shirt and got fully comfortable. York used his fingers to play with my clit as he pumped from behind.

"Ohhh," I moaned. "Ohhh, York." I looked down and could see my cream dripping down his dick. Watching my pussy eat his dick alive turned me on even more.

"You like that, baby? I know you like that," he said.

He was wrong. I didn't like it. I loved it. I began to rock faster and faster and he shoved himself into me harder and harder. Our bodies were making such a ruckus as they abused one another.

"Can I cum in you?" he whispered. "Are you on the pill?"

At that very moment, my own advice went right out of the window. I looked at York. Is this the man I wanted to father my child? Fuck it! This was the nigga I wanted to make me cum. It be like that sometimes. I guess now I knew how shit happens. But at least I am on the pill.

"Cum in me, baby," I said on the verge of climaxing. "I'm cummin' with you. Oh, God, I'm cummin' with you."

"Oh, shit, baby," he said, sitting up against me. I could feel his six pack on my bare back. We were both sticky and sweaty.

"Oh shit," he repeated. "Oh shit," he said as he started nutting inside of me.

I could feel his dick jerking and spitting inside of me. He had my titties bouncing and my hair flying out of control he was fucking me so hard. He was fucking me so good that I exploded with him. I swear it felt like he jerked inside of me for two minutes straight as my juices poured down his dick and onto his balls.

He trembled. Ten seconds would go by and he would tremble again.

After a moment of huffing and puffing I leaned back on him to rest. Then I thought about my suede couch and prayed that we hadn't stained it.

I felt brand new. York had taken my body places it had never been. For the first time in my life I felt like a woman. I looked over at York while he laid there with his eyes closed, noticing a tattoo of a gun shooting the word "BANG" on his chest. Oh, what had I gotten myself into? Now that I had given him a sample of the ill nah na, that fool wasn't going nowhere. And with how good he fucked me, I didn't know if I wanted him to go anywhere. Hell, maybe a thug in my life was exactly what the doctor had ordered.

York and I started spending time with each other on the regular. We did something almost every weekend. This past weekend we went skating. I hadn't been roller skating in ages. I didn't even know if I could still stand up in skates, but York was a pro.

He was pearling around the rink like nobody's business. I told him that I could see right now that he was going to be the old man rolling around the skating rink with a white towel to wipe off his sweat. He laughed and agreed that he probably would be.

After skating we stopped off at Wendy's and grabbed a burger and some fries. Then York took me home, walking me into my house.

That date felt like a real one. I thought that York was feeling the same way until he said, "I want to start taking you to really nice places, like the Bahamas and trips to Jamaica."

"That sounds good, but I like the places we go," I said. "If you want to start taking me to some new nice places, take me to the zoo, a play, or take me to the museum or something."

That really threw York for a loop. I kept trying to tell him that I wasn't one of them chicks he had to buy a set of Louis Vuitton luggage for and travel around the world. I can find pleasure in simple shit.

"Where have you been all of my life?" York asked, playfully. "You are the perfect girl. You're not a chick who drives around in a Ford Escort, but wants a man who's driving a Mercedes. That's what I'm feeling. But I wish I was feeling you right about now."

York knew how to fuck up a romantic moment with sex talk. But once again I was on my period, so I had to decline. But that didn't stop York. He begged for me to let him hit it, even if it was that time of the month.

"Why are you always trying to fuck me when I'm on my period?" I asked him in an agitated tone.

"Because someone once told me that a soldier is not a real soldier unless he's fought in a bloody war," York replied, staring deep into my eyes.

I thought I was slick. But some of the slickest shit ever came out of his mouth. The slicker his tongue, the wetter my clit.

"You are so nasty," I said, screwing up my mug.

"So is that a yes?" he asked, waiting patiently for a response.

"You know what?" I said, finally giving in to his request. "I just might be willing to draft your ass."

I led York to my bedroom and we did what some couples do. We had sex while I was on the rag. I laid a dark blue towel down over my Ralph Lauren Hennessy Paisley gold sheets and we went to work. I had never had sex on my period before. The thought alone had always grossed me out, but York's soft touch made me forget just what time of the month it was. He laid me down and did me up just right. And damn was it good.

Afterwards he lay cuddled behind me in my bed. I laid there staring into the dark, loving the way he made me feel, but hating how he made his living. These brothas and their goddamn complex occupations. I know getting out the game ain't easy, but maybe with enough convincing on my part, York could try.

Even if I didn't see myself spending the rest of my life with York, I was becoming more and more fond of him each day. Nobody ever won the game called life. I didn't ever want to see York end up dead or in jail. So when I felt the time was right I told myself that I was going to talk to him about changing his way of life. It just never seemed to be the right time.

"I can't believe her!" I shouted as I looked at the store clock. It was already a quarter past ten and Morgan hadn't shown up yet.

I had already called her cell phone and her home phone a dozen times, leaving messages, but I guess it didn't hurt to try one mo' gen'. I dialed Morgan's home number and there was still no answer. I dialed her cell number and there was still no answer. I angrily hung up the phone.

"She's probably laying up with that damn Jazzy," I said as I slammed the phone down.

A customer came into the store so I had to wait on her. She had her hair in rollers so I knew she was coming over from one of the salons. She needed change for a hundred dollar bill and tried to buy a single bag of potato chips. I wasn't about to let her take all of my change for no lousy bag of chips, especially without Morgan being there so that I could run to the bank and get more. I made her spend more money. It was either that, or her stylist was going to get one hell of a tip.

After the customer left, I tried calling Morgan again, then I thought to call York to see if he could get in touch with Jazzy to see if Morgan was perhaps with him. When I called York, he and Jazzy were at the car wash together so there went that theory. That's when I started to worry.

Never ever in life had I closed down my store during business hours, but this day would have to be the exception. I had to see what was up with my girl. I decided that if Morgan wasn't in the store by noon, that I was going to put an out to lunch sign up and close down. At 12:05 P.M. that's exactly what I did.

Morgan lived in a condo all the way out in the New Albany suburbs so it took me about forty-five minutes to get to her house in traffic. When I pulled up to her condo, all of her blinds were closed, but her car was under her carport. Immediately my heartbeat picked up.

I walked up to her door and knocked. There was no answer. I knocked again, and harder this time. Still there was no answer.

Perhaps she was in the shower or something. I knocked one more time then I used my key to her house to let myself in.

"Morgan," I called as I entered. "Don't shoot. It's me, Harlem."

There was no response.

"Morgan," I said again, almost in a singing tone.

As I made my way to her bedroom I could see that the bedroom door was cracked. I could see that Morgan was lying across the bed, but I could only see her feet.

"Morgan," I said, but she didn't respond. I opened the door and saw her lying there.

"Morgan," I said. "What's wrong?"

Her face was buried in a pillow and she was crying. I didn't know what to think.

"What happened? Did someone hurt you? Are they still in the house?" I frantically asked.

Morgan lifted her head up and replied, "No."

Her eyes were bloodshot red like she had been crying for hours. She had a wad of tissue in her hand and a couple of wads on the floor.

"Then what's wrong?" I said, walking over to her and sitting down next to her on the bed.

She sat up and tried to speak, but she couldn't get the words out for crying so hard. Finally she blurted out, "My dad is cheating on my mom." Then she fell into my arms.

Ain't this about a bitch? is all I could think. Here I thought I was about to walk up in here and find her stankin' and she's locked up in her house crying over her father's infidelity. But I'm not all mean. I know when a friend needs a listening ear so I obliged her.

"How do you know that? Tell me what happened," I said in a concerned tone.

Morgan gathered her composure and began to speak.

"Last night Jazzy and I went to the Mariott Courtyard for dinner. You know they have the best crab cakes in the world and I had a taste for some," Morgan said, wiping her eyes.

Yeah, yeah, I thought. Just get to the story.

"After we finished eating I got up to go to the bathroom. I noticed a man that looked like my father dining alone on the other side of the restaurant. He appeared to be dining alone anyway. But then I remembered my mother telling me that my father was out of town on business. So I started second-guessing what I was seeing. I was only getting a side profile, but I knew my own father when I saw him. So I decided to head over to his table. Well, before I got there a woman, who was coming from the direction of the ladies room, walked up to him and put her hand on his shoulder. She leaned over and kissed him on the lips and sat down. Harlem, the woman wasn't my mother."

"I'm so sorry, Morgan," I said, rubbing her leg. "What did he say when he saw you?"

"He didn't," Morgan said. "I stopped in my tracks. I thought, okay, maybe she's a client, a friendly client. Okay, a very friendly client. But then I saw my father place his hand on top of hers. Their waiter brought them their meal receipt and then they left. Only they didn't leave out of the public exit. They headed towards the guest elevators."

Morgan busted out crying again. I was even like whoa. I couldn't believe her pops was playing on her moms like that. I kind of looked up to the relationship he had with his wife myself, so I know Morgan was devastated. I felt like I did when I found out that Reverend Jesse Jackson had cheated on his wife, Bill Cosby on his, former President Clinton on his, and Michael Jordan on his.

"I felt like such a fool," Morgan said. "I had to pretend with Jazzy like nothing had happened. No way could I say, thanks for dinner and by the way, let me take you upstairs in the hotel so that you can meet my father who is probably fucking his mistress's brains out."

I snickered under my breath. Morgan began to cry again.

"But Jazzy could tell that something was wrong with me because I barely said two words for the remainder of dinner. After dinner we went back to my house and I was in a funk. We were lying there in my bed watching television and I just burst out crying. I thought Jazzy was going to think that I was nuts. He kept asking me what was wrong and all I could do was cry. I told him that I didn't want to talk about it. He respected that and didn't ask me again. He just stayed there with me the entire night, holding me as I laid there and cried on his chest. I cried myself to sleep. This morning when I woke up, he was gone, but those were here."

Morgan pointed to her nightstand. There was the most beautiful bouquet of roses I had ever seen.

"The only other man who has ever given my flowers is my daddy," Morgan cried.

Believe it or not, because I couldn't believe it my damn self, but I was happy that Jazzy had been there for my girl. Now there was yet another side of him I was curious to explore.

"So what are you going to do?" I asked. Hell, if she was going to tell her mother, I wanted to be there with popcorn and a bullet-proof vest.

"I don't know," Morgan said. "How does a child tell her mother that her husband is cheating on her?"

"People do it all of the time on the Jerry Springer show," I said. "And usually it's the daughter who is cheating with the husband."

Morgan looked up at me and chuckled. Of course her laughter soon turned to tears.

"Oh, Harlem, what am I supposed to do?" Morgan cried. "I love them both so much. If I tell my mother it will hurt her. If I tell my mother it will hurt my father that I told my mother. I don't want to hurt either of my parents. What would you do?"

"Well you know me," I said, sucking my teeth. "I would have marched right on over to that table when I saw my father in the first place. I would have treated that tramp like the home wrecker she was and given my father, right then and there, the ultimatum of him telling my mother or me telling her."

"If you were my mother would you want to know?" Morgan asked me.

I thought momentarily and then I replied, "No. I think all women say they want to know, but do they really? Do they really want to know the one thing that could turn their life upside down? I personally don't think so, but would I rather know than not know if I was carrying around the suspicions? Yes."

Morgan wiped her eyes then looked up at me.

"Morgan, you have to understand, what's done in the dark always comes to light. Your mother will find out eventually. How she finds out is the question."

Morgan sighed, took a deep breath, then said, "Looks like I'm going to have to tell her."

Morgan drove to her mother's house later on that evening. I offered to go with her for moral support, or just in case she tried to wimp out, but she felt that it was something she needed to do alone.

She had called her mother at work from my house to make sure that her schedule was clear. She knew that her father wouldn't be home, because he was supposedly still going to be out of town for one more night. Even so, things didn't go as Morgan had planned. When Morgan left her mother's house she came straight back to mine. I couldn't believe my ears as she told me how everything went down.

When Morgan arrived at her parent's house, her mother had asked the maid to prepare a light snack of cheese, crackers, salami, grapes, and tea for them. Morgan had no appetite whatsoever, though. She wished she could have just told her mother over the phone. She didn't want to witness the hurt and pain her mother was about to endure. But I convinced her that telling her in person was better.

"Morgan, I was so glad when you called and said that you were going to stop by," her mother said as she entered the house, kissing her on the cheek. "Darling, I've missed you. I'm always busy at the office and you're always busy with Harlem at the store. What's she been up to anyway?"

"Same old, same old," Morgan said. "Just working."

"Has she gotten herself a boyfriend yet?"

"She's working on it," Morgan said. "You know Harlem."

"Yes, yes. She's a feisty one isn't she? I think only a man willing to wear the skirt could handle that Harlem. I like that about her though, you know?"

"Mom, I didn't come here to talk about Harlem," Morgan snapped.

"Well," her mother said, surprised at Morgan's attitude. "Is mommy's little girl jealous? Come now, sit and let's talk about you."

Morgan's mother sat down on the sofa and picked up a cracker from the tray on the coffee table. She patted her hand in the spot next to her for Morgan to join her.

Her mother was so happy that Morgan didn't know if she could go though with telling her what she had come to tell her. Morgan feared that afterwards she would never see her mother happy again. After all, her parents had been married for twenty-eight years and were together five years prior to marriage. She could only imagine how devastated her mother was going to be.

"So tell me what's been going on with you?" Morgan's mother asked her. "Are you seeing anyone special? And by special I don't mean the boys who rode the short bus to school like you used to bring around."

"Oh, mom," Morgan said with a forced smile. Then she realized that this was the perfect time to ease into the subject matter. She took a deep breath and proceeded. "As a matter of fact, I am seeing someone. We had dinner last night."

"Oh really? Where did he take you? What did you eat? Do tell mommy all about it."

"He took me to the Mariott," Morgan said.

"A hotel, dear?" her mother said with disapproval as she picked up her cup of tea. "That's the last place I'd expect a man to take my daughter for dinner.

Here it goes, Morgan thought to herself. Once again she took a deep breath and paused. But she knew if she didn't just go ahead and tell her mother now, that she might not ever tell her. And like I had told her, what's done in the dark always comes to light. Eventually Morgan's mother would find out. How would she feel knowing that her own daughter knew all along?

"Then we must think alike," Morgan said. "Because when I saw daddy there having dinner, that's the same thing I thought. This is the last place I'd expect my father to take my mother for dinner. But then I realized that the woman he was with wasn't you."

Morgan's mother paused for a moment. She sipped some tea and then placed the cup back on the table.

"Oh," she said, appearing surprised, but not too affected by Morgan's discovery.

"Oh," Morgan repeated her mother. "I just told you that your husband was with another woman, mom, in a hotel, when he lied to you and told you that he was going to be out of town. All you have to say is oh?"

Morgan's mother paused and took a deep breath then asked, "What did this woman who your father was with look like?"

"Well, she was about my height," Morgan said, squinting her eyes, trying to recall the woman's features. "She looked to be in her late thirties. She had a medium brown complexion."

"Was her hair cut in a bob style and did she have bangs?" Morgan's mother asked.

"Yes. Do you know this woman, mom?"

"Loraine. She's the receptionist at our office. She's the third receptionist in four years. If your father gets any sloppier you'll end up having to come work for us, sweetheart," she said with a feeble attempt to laugh it off.

Morgan was too through at this point. She stood up and walked over to the mantel and looked at the family portrait of her mother, her father, and herself.

"What are you saying, mom?" Morgan said with a puzzled look on her face. "Am I hearing what I think I'm hearing? Do you mean to tell me that you knew that daddy was fooling around with this woman?"

"A woman always knows, dear," her mother replied. "Knowing and acknowledging it is two different things though."

Morgan expected her mother to fall out in tears. She thought that there was a chance her mother would start screaming for a divorce even. None of this was happening. Morgan had prepared herself to comfort her distressed mother. She hadn't prepared herself for this type of nonchalant reaction. All of a sudden Morgan was starting to feel like the only one who had been played in this game.

"Mother, I'm getting really confused here," Morgan said, holding her forehead and sitting down on the couch. "Please explain to me what is going on."

Taking a deep breath her mother proceeded with her monologue. "Your father and I have what we call an unspoken arrangement," her mother said. "I suppose you could say that we have one of those open relationships. Isn't that what you kids call it? But anyway, we decided a long time ago that we needed to make a change in our relationship if we were going to be able to live with one another for the rest of our lives. Don't get me wrong. Daddy and I have love for each other. And we both love you dearly. As a matter of fact, we did this for you." She put her hand on Morgan's shoulder.

"That's sick!" Morgan shouted as she pushed her mother's hands off of her. "The entire situation is just plain sick!"

"Now you watch it young lady," her mother said, pointing her finger at Morgan. "Grown or not, I am still your mother and you will still show me some respect."

"Respect?" Morgan said. "But you don't even respect yourself. What kind of woman allows her husband to go gallivanting around local hotels with the office help? Oh, but I guess it's okay if she's getting her groove on with the, who Mother? Who is it for you, the mail guy?"

Morgan had never even received a spanking as a child. Not even when she cut up her mother's Armani pantsuit to make clothes for her baby dolls. But now for the first time in her life, her mother would give her a taste of corporal punishment.

Her mother struck her so hard across the face that Morgan saw stars. She was in pure disbelief.

"You will not disrespect me like that!" Morgan's mother yelled. "As hard as your father and I have worked to make sure that you had everything you asked for, you will not talk down to us. We did what we had to do to keep our relationship, both business and personal, intact. You don't know how lucky you were, do you? How many people your age do you know who grew up with both biological parents? How many of them are still together? Your father and I did everything we could to see to it that you were raised in a two parent home so that you would grow up to seek stability in your own life."

"But it was all a façade," Morgan said. "That changes everything that I believed in what you and daddy had."

"Life is a façade, dear," Morgan's mother said, walking over to a vase where she pulled the silk flowers out if it and grabbed a pack of cigarettes. "As long as you remember that one little bit of information, that life itself is a façade, then you'll go a long way." She lifted the vase and retrieved a pack of matches from underneath it. "Besides, all of your father's indiscretions, as well as my own, were nothing more than flighty affairs. It's not like they were actual relationships. They were physical, not mental. There's a difference, you know, between having an affair outside of your marriage and having a relationship."

Morgan's mother lit the cigarette and took a puff. She closed her eyes and exhaled. She smiled. It felt good to exhale. She had been inhaling a lie for years for her daughter's sake and now, finally, she could exhale.

"What are you doing?" Morgan asked. "You stopped smoking years ago."

"Yeah, but then I started up again," she replied.

"When?" Morgan asked.

"Years ago. Actually very shortly after I stopped smoking in the first place. That was around the time I realized that your father had stopped loving me. Or should I say, wasn't *in love* with me anymore?"

Morgan watched her mother try to cover up the hurt she was truly feeling inside by puffing away everything she loved and believed in as a little girl. Just like the rings of smoke her mother was shooting out of her mouth, everything Morgan ever knew to be true about her family was going up in smoke.

8. Not in a Million Years

I don't know how I let York talk me into going out to a club tonight. I haven't been to a club since that shit went down with DC at the Second Wind. But supposedly, the club where York was taking me was a drama-free environment. It's this spot called Club 504 in the Arena District of downtown Columbus. In other words, it's in an area where the diehard Buckeye fans hang out, white people. But it was mostly frequented by blacks.

It was called Club 504 because 504 is the address. An older black gentleman who knew how to run a respectable business had bought out this particular club. He didn't even have to put up a dress code sign. One just knew when stopping off in there to dress classy. It was pretty much a twenty-five and older crowd so I figured I could work with it.

I had just taken out the choker rhinestone necklace from my grandmother's jewelry box and put it around my neck when I heard York pull up. I could hear the bass in his car-stereo system. It had never sounded that loud before. He must have been geeking himself up to go out.

As York knocked on the door, I grabbed the little silver chain link evening purse that matched the dress that I was wearing, then I answered it.

When I opened the door I could see how beautiful I was in York's eyes. His mouth dropped open and his eyes got hungry, like he hadn't eaten in weeks and was about to sop me up with a biscuit.

I must admit, I was looking quite ravishing. Morgan talked me into buying this little silver one shoulder dress from Lazarus. It was knitted, like a chain link fence, and fringes hung down at the bottom. And can you believe it? The dress was cut well above my knee. It was far from a churchgoing dress. I had on some three inch strappy slide-ins that I planned on leaving on while I fucked York tonight.

The rhinestone necklace I was wearing had a matching bracelet that I used as an anklet and of course the matching teardrop earrings were so necessary. I wasn't wearing a ponytail that night. I had talked the owner of Scizzors Hair Salon, Terri Deal, to stay late and do my hair. She obliged me and I tipped her fifteen dollars for doing so. Not to mention she laid my hair out.

She had given me a spiral curl roller set. She had put three soft and fluffy corn rolls in the front and on the top of my head to keep my hair out of my face. She had permed it up nicely so it was definitely bouncing and behaving. And as always, the cosmetics were flawless. Tonight, instead of just clear lip gloss, I had on a sandy sable colored lip gloss. There were no words to describe my appearance that night. I think that was the best I had looked in my entire life. Something about York brought out the woman in me that loved to be a woman.

"You are my muthafucka," York said as he looked me up and down, nodding his head.

"Does that mean I look nice?" I said.

"Baby, you look better than nice," York said, shaking his head in disbelief. "I hope a brotha ain't got to fight to prove his love tonight."

"You are stupid, boy," I said, blushing.

"You ready to go, babe?"

"I stay ready," I said with a wink.

York kissed me on the lips softy, as not to mess up my lip color, and we headed to the club.

"You can find me at the club," York sang along to 50 Cent's party anthem.

The DJ had been rocking all night long. He offered a nice mixture of hip-hop and R&B, and when he played slow jams, they were old school.

York and I had only been up in the spot for about an hour. Although the DJ was regulating, we hadn't danced yet. We were too busy getting our drink on. Then finally the DJ played The Notorious BIG's "Give Me One More Chance" remix, and York and I both had to hit the floor on that one.

York helped me slide out of the oval VIP booth we had been hugging all night. He then escorted me to the dance floor like we were the only somma bitches in the club.

York had a nice black silk like hookup on that shimmered when he walked. The shimmer complemented my outfit. We looked like a black Romeo and Juliet stepping to the dance floor.

This was the first time I had been out of the booth the entire night so this was the first time most of the people in there were getting a good look at me. The fellas were hawking and the females

were hating. There was one female in particular eyeballing the hell
out of me. And why she was hating was beyond me. She looked
way better than I did, if you like that exotic look.

I could tell that she was mixed with something. Black and Asian
maybe. Her Oriental type grade of hair was hot curled into the
cutest feathered style and her body would have given Tyra Banks a
run for her money. She was playing this simple but becoming black
slip dress, but her shoes were what set it off. They were black and
swirled up her leg right below her calves. She had the type of
skin tone that didn't need makeup. It was a light manually tanned
bronze. So she was good with just the eyeliner and lipstick she had
on. I suppose it was the attitude she was displaying that took away
from her beauty.

Oh well, I felt like one in a million and my attitude reflected it. I
graciously walked onto the dance floor and the men all paused. I
started giving York a little bit of my smooth mellow swing. You
know, that smooth Midwest shit. I stood in one spot, swaying my
hips and snapping my fingers. Sometimes I gave a little shoulder. I
wasn't into none of that grab your knees pussy poppin' shit. I was
too old for that. There was nothing more simple than a broad damn
near pushing thirty out poppin' her pussy and getting low, especially
when you knew that she had two kids at home.

York was eating it up. He couldn't dance for watching me. And
he wasn't alone. Every now and then I'd glare off into the crowd to
see who was seeing me. If I saw a halfway decent guy showing me
love with a stare, I'd put a little more into my hips simply because
he was watching.

After our crank went off, York and I had started to head back
to the table. But then the DJ decided to switch up the slow-jam
pattern he had been following all night. Instead of playing an old

school song, like "In Between the Sheets," he played Maxwell's "Fortunate." York and I couldn't resist our first slow dance together.

I honestly felt like Cinderella. I put my hands around York's waist and he put his arms over my shoulder. We looked into each other's eyes as we grooved. York started lip-synching the words to me. It was pure magic. But just like anything else in my life that was going too much like right, there was a little voodoo right around the corner.

After the slow song went off York and I went back over to our table. To my surprise someone was sitting there. It was the chick who had been mean mugging me all night, the black and Asian mami.

York and I both stopped and looked at her like she was crazy.

"Oh, pardon me," she said, staring dead into York's eyes. "Was this seat taken?"

I thought to myself, *Now this is a bold ass bitch. I just might like her.*

"Zondra, what are you doing?" York questioned her. "You know damn well this seat is taken."

She licked her lips and started sliding out of the booth.

"My bad," she said to York as she brushed by him. She made sure that at least her nipples grazed him.

I was looking too good to get jealous. If this bitch thought she could jack me for him, then I say let her ass go for it.

"Sorry about that," York said to me as Zondra walked away. But she didn't go far. "I used to know her."

How dare he give me that DJ Quick quote? I wasn't stupid. I knew exactly what *used to know* her meant. It meant that he used to fuck her.

Once York and I got situated back in the booth we looked up and there she was, damn near giving us a striptease as she danced to the song that was playing. This chick had issues. That was evident.

"Why don't you go ahead and take her out to the car and hit her off a little somethin' somethin'? That way she can leave us the fuck alone and allow us to enjoy the rest of our night," I said to York. And I was dead serious. I was so sincere.

York shook his head and sighed. This Zondra was really getting under his skin.

"Yo, Zondra," he said, telling her to come here with his finger.

She smiled and looked at me like, yeah, bitch, I can still get at your man.

"Yes, baby?" Zondra said to York as she approached the table.

I saw her look to her left and smile an *I told you so* smile. When I looked over there was a group of three chicks giving each other high fives and thumbs up to Zondra. Looks as though she had bet those broads that she could still get with York if she wanted to. Even if it meant getting him from me to do it.

"Come here," York said softly, licking his lips.

Zondra looked at me and rolled her eyes. She slid in the booth next to York and put her hand on his chest.

"Talk to me, Daddy," she said.

"I saw you dancing over there," York said to her.

"You know I was dancing for you," Zondra said, now rubbing his chest. She looked back over to her girls to make sure that they were catching all of this. "I know how you used to like for me to dance for you."

I knew that York was a man who knew how to handle his business so I chilled and let him handle his.

"Did I look hot?" Zondra asked.

"Yeah, you did," York said, grabbing Zondra's wrist from his chest. I could tell that he wanted to break the muthafucker. Zondra was in shock and in pain as York gripped her wrist tightly and began yelling at her through gritted teeth.

"Yeah, you looked hot," he said to her. "You looked a hot mess. Not only that, but you were disrespecting my girl right here. Ain't a hoe up in here got enough class to be even trying to disrespect her. Now you need to get the fuck up out of here and go enjoy the rest of your night and let me enjoy the rest of mine with my lady. If you don't, I'm going to give her permission to go down in her purse, pull out a tube of ghetto, and beat your ass."

I started laughing. Zondra was humiliated. She managed to snatch her wrist away from York and storm out of the booth.

"When you knew her," I said to York, "you must have left one hell of an impression."

"It wasn't even like that," York said, putting his head down. "She's a bum. She's a nobody."

"Well, obviously she doesn't feel that way about you," I said. "But never mind all of that. I need to go to the ladies room."

York got up and helped me out of the booth. I kissed him on the lips and headed to the bathroom.

As I approached I heard the typical chitchat of a clique of females dogging out and calling one another bitches. Little did I know that this particular clique was referring to me.

"That hoe can't whoop me," I heard Zondra say. But all conversation came to a halt when they looked up and saw me standing there.

The three girls Zondra was with nodded, signaling Zondra to just let it slide and walk away. Zondra obliged and followed her three friends towards the door.

I couldn't let her slide that easy, however. I didn't want to get with her or anything like that. I was looking too good to scrap, but I did want to fuck with her head.

"Hey, you," I said to Zondra in a freaky tone. "Don't walk away, girl. After the way you been looking at me all night now you gon' try to play me?"

"Excuse me?" Zondra said, stopping in her tracks and twisting up her face. There were other women in the bathroom and at the sink washing their hands and touching up their makeup. They were all in the business. Zondra was so embarrassed.

"Come on," I said, looking deeply into her eyes and taking her hand in mine. "Don't be scurred. You still wanna get at York? That's cool. We can do that, ma. We can go on back to my place for a nightcap. We can drink doubles and sleep triple, if you know what I'm saying."

Zondra was appalled and I was in hysterics on the inside, trying my damnedest to keep a straight face on the outside. The other women in the bathroom, as well as her girlfriends, were completely glued to the situation at hand.

"Look, it ain't even that type of party," Zondra said in a panic, trying to get away from me as soon as she could. But I still had a hold of her hand.

"Don't front on me now, sweetheart," I said, licking my lips. "Every time I looked up, your eyes were burning a hole through me. And then that table dance you gave me. Damn. If I had a dick it would have been as hard as a rock."

Zondra managed to snatch her hand away from me. Everyone was looking at her waiting on her response. Hell, I think a couple of them wanted to come watch if the shit did go down.

"I was just messing around out there," Zondra pleaded. "I play like that all of the time with York. Ask my girlfriends. I mean not my *girlfriends* girlfriends. My girls, lady friends, girls that are just friends."

Zondra was a babbling fool. I had turned that tables real nice on her trick ass.

"You and York just enjoy the rest of your night. Without me. Okay?" Zondra said as she started backing up out of the door. "And it was nice meeting you."

Zondra was gone. I had the win. I took a deep breath and smiled. When I turned around to head into the bathroom stall I noticed that chicks were staring at me. I felt as though I owed them one last line so I decided to give them what they were waiting for.

"Can you believe that?" I said, putting my hands on my hips. "Another clit teaser. That little cunt. Oh well. You win some and you lose some."

I threw my hands up and entered the stall.

After I told York about my little incident with Zondra in the bathroom, we laughed for hours. That's when I realized that I never laughed so much in my life than when I was with York. He had definitely grown on me. And I liked how he felt.

York started taking me to all those places I had suggested he take me in lieu of extravagant excursions. He took me to the zoo and we even went to see Tyler Perry's play *Why Did I Get Married?* But one place he hadn't taken me was to his house, and it was a fine time I find out why.

York and I had just left Mitchell's Steak House in downtown Columbus. It was the best steak house in the city, hands down. It was pricey, but you got the best cut of meat and the best service in town. And on top of that, they didn't treat us funny because we had brown skin.

Jazzy and Morgan were supposed to join us for dinner, but at the last minute, Jazzy backed out. He had backed out on his last couple of dates with Morgan. Morgan said it was just because he was so busy keeping the car washes in check. At least that's what she tried to convince herself of. The life of being a hustler's wifey was starting to show its face to her. But nonetheless, York and I went on and enjoyed our steaks without them.

I felt like Fat Bastard from *Austin Powers* after eating our meal. I'm not one of those women who leave a quarter of their meal just so that they don't appear greedy. I ate every last bite. I was absolutely stuffed. I could hardly walk to the car.

Before dinner we had visited the Columbus Museum of Art. Before we went in, York had pulled a bottle of wine out from a little cooler case that was on his back seat. He was trying to romance me with some ol' *Jason's Lyric* shit. Only he had forgotten to bring the glasses with him so we had to drink it from the bottle and off of each other's tongue.

York was trying hard to do things for me to show me that he was really starting to care for me, without going over the top. He convinced me to take all the gifts back that he had given me. I agreed under one stipulation: I told him that he had to accept a gift from me. He agreed, but he knew me better than to think that I was going to go out and buy some extravagant gift for him. He knew that I was going to come up with something slick. Well I did, and tonight was the night that I was going to give it to him.

I was excited. It was really nice. I wouldn't say that what I got him was extravagant, but it did cost me a nice penny having it cus-tomized. I would say it was more special than anything.

"You all right?" York said as I moaned and groaned all the way to the car. Damn, why was the valet parking full? Of all nights I was struggling to make it to the car.

"Yes," I replied. "I'm just so stuffed that I can hardly walk. I feel like I'm going to bust out of these pants.

"Unbutton them," York said.

"What you know about that?" I said, smiling at York.

"I know a lot about women," he said, winking as he opened the car door for me.

"Oh yeah?" I said.

"Yeah." He kissed me on the lips and closed the door after I had settled in.

York wanted to go to some spot called The Flames. That was his hang out. It was a motorcycle club, a nice little chill spot, but I was dead tired. So I told him to drop me off at home and go on without me.

On the drive home is when I decided to give him the gift I had gotten for him. Him driving while I gave it to him made it easier on me. I wasn't used to mushy moments and I didn't want to have to start getting used to them.

"You know how I told you that I was going to keep all the gifts you bought me if you let me get you something?" I asked York.

"Yes," he said.

"Well, here's that something," I said, handing him a box. It just so happened that that the light turned red and the car was stopped. He took the box and opened it. His mouth dropped as he took it out of the box and held it up.

"Harlem," York said, shaking his head. He was speechless.

Morgan and I had taken the personalized nameplate that he had gotten me to my jeweler, None Other Goldsmiths. I had them add the words "Knew York" to the plate. I gave them some scrap gold to use from old chains and bracelets that I had crimped up and ruined. They did an excellent job.

"You and I both have come a long way," I said looking into York's eyes. "And I'm certain our struggles aren't over yet. I plan on maybe finishing that book I started about my life some day and sharing my struggles with the world. But no matter how my story ends, when people do get to read about me, I want them to know, and I want you to always remember, that Harlem knew York. You've truly been one of the better parts of my life."

I swear to God if that car behind us hadn't have blown its horn, York would have started crying. Hell, maybe me, too, for that matter. Instead, York gripped the plate in his hand and drove off.

Neither of us knew what to say after that priceless moment. We were both too emotional to even speak, so we didn't until we got to my house.

"You sure you don't want to go to The Flames with me?" York asked as he pulled up in my driveway.

"I'm positive," I replied. "You go on and have a good time."

"Well, do you want me to come in?"

"Did I ask you to come in?" I said. "No offense, but why do guys do that? Just fuckin' ask if you can come in."

"You are a mean ass bitch," York said, shaking his head at me.

"And you love every inch of this mean ass," I said, rolling my eyes. "Besides, why don't you ask me over to your house sometime? Why does a brotha always want to chill up over the female's house? You got a baby's mama or something you hiding?"

"Hell, no," York was quick to say. "You know I ain't got no kids. My sister and I share a house. I thought I told you that. We don't ever bring our dates home. We respect one another like that."

"Oh, so I'm just a date?" I inquired with an attitude.

York looked down at the Harlem Knew York plate. Then he looked up at me. He took my hand into his.

"You are more than a date fo sho," he said, then he leaned over and kissed me.

"Then prove it," I said.

"Oh, I will," he said, licking his lips.

"I'm going to hold you to that," I said in a sexy kind of tone. "So are you going to invite me over one day?"

"Yes, Harlem. I'm going to invite you over."

"I can hardly wait."

I gave him a peck on the cheek then got out of the car. As I walked up to my front door to unlock it York rolled down his window.

"And, yo, Harlem!" he shouted.

"What?"

"When you do come over make sure you wear that little cream off the shoulder top of yours."

"My poncho?" I asked.

"Yeah, yeah."

"Why?" I asked with a puzzled look on my face.

"Because it goes perfect with the carpet on my bedroom floor." York smiled a huge grin, backed up out of my driveway, and then drove away.

I smiled as I watched his rear lights fade out of my view. I surprised myself with York. I had feelings for him that I couldn't have predicted I would have. Not in a million years. I would find myself thinking about him and wondering as to the next time we would see each other. Before I knew it, I was thinking less and less about Jazzy. But it wouldn't be long before all that changed.

Finally York was taking me to his house. I always had a feeling that someone lived with him, his sister perhaps, but he never mentioned it and I never asked. York's a lot like me in a sense. Don't ask, don't tell. Not big on conversation. I was just relieved that his sister is a blood sister and not a play sister, someone he's close to.

I was curious to meet her because York was so private and protective of her ever since they were children that he rarely discussed her. Hell, I didn't even know her name. There was a time when I didn't even want to know more about York. I just thought we'd kick it and be done with it already.

York and I had just left Applebees and were on our way to his house when he decided that he needed to make a pit stop.

"I need to stop off over at the car wash on Fifth for a second," York said. "I got to holler at Jazzy for a minute."

"Cool," I said as we headed to the car wash.

When we pulled up we parked in front of the car wash. There were some nice ass rides parked amongst our car. There was a Suburban inside being detailed.

York put the car in park then reached underneath his seat. He pulled out a brown paper bag. I clowned.

"I know the fuck you didn't have me riding up in this muthatfucka while you holdin'," I lashed out at York. "I can't believe this shit! What are you, Jazzy's mule or some shit? You hold his dope for him? If you want to put yourself out there like that, then that's on you. You are a grown ass man and I dig you for you, not what you do. I can't make you change your occupation, but all I asked was that you don't put me in no fucked up situations. I don't think that was asking too much. So take me the fuck home now! As a matter of fact, I'll walk."

I went to open the car door and York grabbed me by the arm.

"Will you hold the fuck up please?" he said as he opened the bag. He pulled out a stack of green, pine tree car freshners. "It's for our *real* customers at the car wash. We give them away free with every service."

I slumped down in my seat feeling like boo-boo. I was so damn embarrassed that it wasn't funny. Not to me anyway, but York began to laugh.

"When will you learn that I love you, girl?" York said. "I would never do anything like that to you, ma. So don't trip on me like that ever again. Have some faith in ya boy, all right?"

I put my head down and put my hand over my face. I shook my head in shame. York put his hand on mine and pulled it off of my face. I looked at him and he winked at me.

"Come on, let's go," he said, opening his door then walking around to open mine for me.

As I watched him walk around the car his words came back to me. At that moment I realized that that boy had just said that he loved me. He said that he loved me. I now knew, firsthand, how a girl could slip up and fall in love with a hustler.

I smiled as York opened the door for me and we headed into the building.

"Yo, what up, blood?" York said to this dude who was wiping down the wheels on the Suburban.

"I ain't into nothing," the guy responded, then he eyeballed me up and down. "Nothing that you about to get into anyway."

"Is Jazzy back there in the office?" York asked him.

"Yeah, he back there," the guy replied.

"All right then man," York said, walking over to give him some pound. "I'll holler at you later."

York took me by the hand and led me back to Jazzy's office. The door was slightly cracked and we could hear voices.

"Yo, Jay," York said, slowly pushing the door open. "Oh, my bad, man."

"Oh, it's cool," Jazzy said, waving York inside his office. "Come on in."

York and I entered the office and when Jazzy saw me, at first he had this *oh shit* look on his face. But his *I'm that nigga* grin shortly followed.

"Harlem World, what's up?" Jazzy said, pulling a cigar out from his desk drawer then placing it between the corner of his mouth to chew on.

I rolled my eyes at him and turned my attention to the broad that was standing up over him, buttoning up her blouse. It was Zondra, ole girl from the club. Needless to say, I didn't respond to his salutation. But Jazzy could have cared less as he sat there looking like a man whore. I hadn't thought much about him with the exception of when I saw the roses he had given Morgan. He had been out of sight and out of mind. Now here he was, all up in my face, with Zondra no less.

I really didn't care much about Zondra being York's ex. At the club York wasn't giving her any action, so I wasn't all that pressed about the broad. But obviously Jazzy felt that she was well worth the time of day, so now I'm slightly pressed. I'm not gonna be bumpin' into this bitch too many more times.

"Hey, New York," Zondra said to York, with a mischievous grin on her face.

"What's up, Zondra?" York said in a dry tone. I could tell by the look on his face that he was just as displeased as Jazzy being with Zondra as I was.

"You'll call me later, Jazzy?" Zondra said as she put her hand to her ear like it was a phone.

"Later," Jazzy said.

Zondra brushed by York and was staring him right in his face. It was as if she wanted to say, "Sorry about your loss, but your boy fucks me better than you do." York had his head down. He couldn't even look at her.

As Zondra brushed by me I decided to fuck her head up one last time. I winked at her and bit my bottom lip in a sexy motion. She was disgusted. She twisted her face up, rolled her eyes, smacked her lips, and headed out of the door.

I knew that hoe was probably spreading all kinds of rumors about Harlem the dyke. But I didn't give a fuck. I didn't run the streets like that. I didn't care what muthatfuckas thought about me.

All I knew, though, was that at that particular time and moment, I did not want to be there, in that room, with York and Jazzy. Crazy emotions started developing. It felt too damn awkward.

"Look, baby," I said to York, "I'm going to go wait in the car. You two handle whatever business you need to handle. I'm out."

I turned and walked out of the office. I wasn't three steps out of the door before I heard Jazzy say, "Yo, Harlem. Tell Morgan I said hey."

I stopped in my tracks. I closed my eyes and took several deep breaths. I stormed back into Jazzy's office, walked right up in front of his desk and tipped the son of a bitch over on him. Well, at least that's what I visualized myself doing while my eyes were closed. But instead I took a few more deep breaths, opened my eyes, and then went back out to the car to wait patiently for York.

As I sat in the car, I tried to make myself understand why I had true feelings for York, and enjoyed being with him, but for some reason a part of me was still craving Jazzy. I wondered if there were other women out there like me going through this same type of emotional roller coaster, being with one man while thinking about another. It felt sick having my mind controlled by a situation such as that.

When York walked out of the car wash about five minutes later, I got warm inside just watching his fine ass pimp over to the car. See, that's the emotional roller coaster I'm talking about. One minute I'm all over him, wanting every inch of him inside me, and the next minute, once he is inside me, I'm closing my eyes wishing it was Jazzy. I felt like two different people. Like Zane's novel, I was starting to get *nervous*.

"Did I take too long?" he asked.

"No, you're good."

We then proceeded to drive off to his house, which wasn't far from the car wash.

"Damn it!" I said.

"What?" York asked as he turned onto his street.

"I left my purse at the fuckin' Applebees," I said, just realizing my purse was gone as I went to look for it so that I could touch up my makeup before meeting his sister.

"We're at my house now," York said, pulling into the driveway. "Let's just call the restaurant. I'm sure our waitress or the bus boy got it."

"I only had about fifty dollars in it, but my personal shit," I said. "Who wants to go through the trouble of canceling credit cards and getting a new driver's license and shit?"

York pulled out his cell phone and called up the restaurant. He relayed to them what my purse looked like and who our waitress was. Fortunately, the waitress had found my purse and turned it in.

"We'll be there shortly to pick it up," York said, hanging up the phone. "See there, baby. I told you everything was going to be all right. Now give daddy some suga."

I smiled then turned to kiss York. His lips were puckered. He looked like a little boy waiting on his first kiss.

"I need to say something to you first," I said to York.

"What's wrong?" he asked.

"Oh, nothing is wrong," I began to fumble. "It's about something you said to me in the car before we went into the car wash. I need to say something back to you now."

I closed my eyes and gathered myself. It wasn't going to be an easy feat getting those three words out of my mouth. But I did have love for York. No matter how fucked up my head was about things, I still had love for him. I cleared my throat, but before I could even speak, my car door was flung open and I was pulled out of the car by my little cream off the shoulder top.

"What the fuck are you doing at my house, bitch? And what the fuck are you doing with my brother?" a female voice yelled at me.

I didn't know what the hell was going on. I jumped to my feet and standing there before me was Yvette. Talk about six degrees of separation. Of all the guys I decide to get it with on a steady basis and finally open up my heart to, it's her brother.

Yvette was in a boxing stance. She had her fist raised like she was ready to brawl, and she had the nerve to have on a little denim dress. Her ghetto ass cocked that son of a bitch above her hips, thong showing, and was seriously ready to rumble with me.

She looked a sight. And on top of that, she hadn't even shaved her nasty ass panty line. Hair was hanging all out the cracks of her thong. And she really wasn't that bad looking of a broad. Her body was bangin'. I can't even hate. That hoe had been doing some Pilates or something. She was about my complexion, maybe a shade or two darker, but her features weren't pretty, they were just okay.

I knew I was going to have to fight this crazy bitch. I twisted my ponytail into a bun while York questioned his sister's actions.

"Yvette, what are you doing?" York said, rushing to my side to see if I was okay.

That pissed Yvette off even more, to see her brother come running to the beautiful damsel in distress.

Before I knew it, Yvette came charging at me again. This time I stuck my foot up just in the nick of time so that the heel of my shoe stuck her right in her thigh.

"Ugh," she gasped as she looked down at her injury. My heel had punctured her thigh good. Now she was infuriated. "Fuckin' rat bitch!" she yelled, charging at me once again. York tried to get in between us and spread us apart, but Yvette managed to swing her arm around him and hit me in my ear. After that, I wanted that ass. Oooh, I could taste it.

"Stop it, Yvette!" York said, none the wiser as to why his sister was going off on me.

"That's her!" Yvette said, pointing at me as tears of anger welled up in her eyes. "That's the bitch I was telling you about who got me put out of my house back in the day. This is that bitch that caused me all that trouble that landed us flat broke again."

I stood there speechless, breathing heavily. I was trying to keep my guard up just in case Yvette came at me again. In the midst of doing so I looked over at York, whose mouth had dropped open. He couldn't believe what his sister was telling him and he wanted me to tell him that it wasn't true, that I wasn't that bitch. My failed vocabulary was my admission of guilt.

"Is that true, Harlem?" York said, hoping that my answer would be negative. I kept quiet.

York had no idea that I was the girl Yvette had accused over the years of dropping the dime on her to Uncle Sam. All she ever referred to me as was that bitch, so York never thought twice about it. He never suspected that I was his sister's worst enemy.

"See, I told you. That's why she ain't saying shit. She knows she's wrong," Yvette said, jumping up and down and pacing. Spit had capped up in the crack of her mouth she was so angry. She looked like a pit bull with rabies.

She had her hair microbraided straight back. If she came at me again it was my plan to take her down by her hair and punch the fuck out of her face.

"I knew it was you," Yvette continued on with her rage. "I knew it was you who dropped the dime on me. When I looked out the door and saw you sitting in my brother's car I said 'oh, hell no!' "

Yvette was pumping herself up again. I didn't know what to do. I wanted to fight her for stretching out my top, but I didn't want to have to stand there and fight York's sister. But just in case I had to get down, I lifted my foot up so that I could start taking off my shoes. I didn't want to get caught slippin', literally.

I didn't even get a chance to touch my shoe before Yvette was charging at me again. Once again, York got in between us, but this time I was able to grab her hair and take her down. Just when I was going to stomp that bitch in the fuckin' throat with the heel of my shoe, York snatched me roughly, and pushed me into his car. I landed hard against the side mirror on the passenger side.

I could tell by the look on his face that he didn't mean to push me that hard. He just couldn't stand to let this chick fight play out.

I quickly gained my composure and stood straight up. I felt like someone had cracked me across the back with a crowbar. I shook off the pain and focused on Yvette. My fists were balled and I was ready to get down. But I looked over at York and the torn look that was on his face. I didn't want to cause him more confusion than he was already dealing with at the moment. I knew I could take Yvette, though. And as bad as I had wanted to get off in that ass, I put my fist away and turned to York and said, "York, can you just take me home please?"

York put his head down, jingled his key and started walking to his car. But it wasn't a half of a second before Yvette stopped him right in his tracks.

"You better let that bitch walk," Yvette said with every ounce of hate she had in her.

York looked at me like what to do.

I decided to let him off the hook easy.

"Don't even worry about it," I said sincerely. "I'm not about to have you choose between a lady friend and your sister because I know what my choice would be."

I turned and began walking. I didn't really plan on walking all the way home. I suspected that York would get his sister situated, clear his head, and come after me. That way I could explain to him how it all went down back in the day. That I didn't just out of the blue drop a dime on Yvette, but that she had done some scandalous shit to me. But can you believe that muthafucka let me walk? And I had on some three inch Mary Jane pumps.

"Fuck it!" I said to myself. I figured I'd go to a pay phone and call a taxi. I had walked several blocks before I came to a pay phone.

That's when I realized that I didn't even have a goddamn quarter. My purse was at the restaurant. I tried calling Morgan collect but she had a block on her phone. Last year she had been kicking it with this guy named Bounce who ended up going to jail. After receiving a two hundred fifty-three dollar phone bill, she got a block on her phone real quick. I guess she forgot to call the phone company and remove the block. Some good that was doing my ass right about now.

It took me an hour and twenty minutes to walk back to that restaurant to retrieve my purse. My dogs were barking. My feet were probably covered in blisters. All the way to the restaurant I just knew that every car that passed me by was going to be York. I thought that he would at least tend to his sister for a minute and then come see about me. But he didn't.

From Applebee's I called a cab to take me home. Even on the cab ride home I kept saying to myself that there better be at least fifty messages from York on my phone when I get home. Surprisingly there wasn't a one message from him. I guess he was treating me the same way he treated his money. Easy come, easy go.

Today was a new day and I wasn't even going to sweat over what went down with York, his sister, and me yesterday. I ain't even going to lie, though. I waited all night long hoping that my phone would ring and it would be his number in my caller ID box. But it wasn't. The only phone number that showed up was Morgan's. I didn't feel like discussing the situation with her just yet. It would make for great conversation at work over a cup of latte.

I tried telling myself that I really didn't care if York ever dialed my number again. But who was I kidding? Although my initial preference would have been to kick it with Jazzy, York wasn't second best by far. He had managed to creep all up in my heart, but not my head. I wasn't going to lose any sleep or weight over the loss of kicking it with him. I had lost far more in my life than to trip off of this situation.

As I drove into work I still couldn't believe that he hadn't even left a message on my cell phone. Maybe he thought I was pissed by having to walk. Perhaps he just wanted to let things die down before he came at me. I was trying so hard to give him the benefit of the doubt. But the longer he took coming at me, I started to doubt what the benefits of ever having him in my life were.

"I tried calling you all last night," Morgan said when she arrived in the store about fifteen minutes after me. "Your phone just rang and rang and then went into voice mail."

"Yeah, well," I said in a nonchalant tone. I guess I was still lightweight mad at Morgan for not having taken that block off of her phone.

"I tried calling your cell phone too," Morgan said in this nagging tone.

I started pretending to straighten up candy boxes to keep busy. That didn't shut Morgan up though.

"Jazzy told me about what happened. About Yvette and all. Can you believe of all the people in the world to start dating, you pick her brother?"

"I would have never believed it in a million years if a psychic had told me," I replied.

"So how do you feel?" Morgan asked sincerely.

I paused. I hadn't really decided on how I truly felt about the matter. I know a lot of my thoughts and feelings were simply out of anger. As I stood there pondering Morgan's question, the bell on the door rang. We had a customer.

"Good morning, Miss Jones," Morgan said as Reese entered the store.

Today was not the day for Reese to come in trying to bum shit. Morgan knew that and that's exactly why she played the chipper store clerk, trying to keep Reese out of my path.

"Well, hello, Morgan," Reese said, teeth just a shining. It was striking how she still managed to maintain her oral hygiene. How did she do it? I had to admit, crackhead or not, her smile was definitely a Colgate smile.

"What can I do you for today, Ms. Jones?"

"It's chilly this morning," Reese said, rubbing her arms. I was surprised that dust didn't float off of her dirty ass. "How about a cup of coffee? A large cup. And I'll take it black."

"Coming right up!" Morgan said, glad to prepare it.

I hated how nice Morgan was being to Reese. That woman was the cause of my childhood being all fucked up. I wanted Morgan to hate her just as much as I did. Hell, I wanted the whole world to hate her and all unfit mothers who were just like her.

As Morgan prepared Reese's coffee I tried not to look up at her, but when I did, she was staring right at me. Damn.

"Hey, baby girl," Reese said. Oh, you know I ignored her ass. She put her head down. I knew it saddened her that her own daughter didn't have two words to say to her. I could see how much it was hurting her, but instead of feeling sorry for her, I could only feel victorious. The same way I had to walk around for years with my head down is how I wanted her to live the rest of her life. I never wanted that bitch to have a reason to hold her head up high. Never!

"Here you go, Ms. Jones," Morgan said. "It's nice and hot."

"Thank you, baby. How much do I owe you?"

"It's ninety-nine cents," Morgan said.

Reese took out a few one dollar bills, laid one of them on the counter, and pushed it towards Morgan. That's all I wanted to see was that she was paying her way up in my store. But I knew Morgan well enough to know that just as soon as I turned my back, she would push the dollar right back to Reese.

"Thanks, Morgan," Reese said, winking at her. "You have a good day. You too, Harlem."

Reese was back out into the chilly morning.

"So how are things going with your mom and dad?" I asked Morgan, turning the focus of conversation on her so that we wouldn't have to discuss my situation with York.

"Well, it seems as though now that the cat is out of the bag, my father is contemplating divorce," Morgan said. "Can you believe it? For all these years my mom and dad weren't necessarily hiding their indiscretions from one another, they were hiding them from me?"

"Still, I say you need to count your blessings that you had parents willing to sacrifice their own happiness for yours," I said. "Remember that book turned movie, *The Root of All Evil?* Remember what that mother did for her child? Now that's a sacrifice. I could see your mother doing something like that for you."

Morgan leaned against the counter and started to cry. She hated the lie that her parents had been living for her sake, but at the same time she was so moved.

I just watched Morgan let it all out. She didn't need me running over to her giving her a shoulder to cry on. She needed to stand up and let all that shit go.

"They say that they love each other," Morgan sniffed. "And I really believe that they do. I really do. I just don't understand this so-called arrangement thing. My mother told me that she and my father haven't slept together in over three years."

"You've got to be kidding me," I said.

"Nope. Dad's been staying in the guestroom. And just to think, I had no idea. I've been so caught up in trying to find the man of my dreams so that I could end up like my parents, that I neglected to even notice what was going on with them."

Morgan just stood there weeping. I really did feel for her. I had watched her go through men trying to find daddy. All of the time she had been on this search to find a man just like her father, little had she known that all along her father was just like every other man.

9. One Night Man

It was Sunday afternoon and I decided to go scope out the competition. What I mean by that is that I wanted to go see what was what in the big-chain bookstores. My store is closed on Sundays so every so often I like to go check out other bookstores such as Waldenbooks and Barnes and Noble. Of course the Suga Shop can't compare to the inventory they hold, but I like to stay as updated as possible so that I can provide my community with the best service that I can. I don't half step like some of these other African American bookstores. If my sign says that I'm open from eight in the morning until eight in the evening, then you best believe my store is up and running during those times.

My store was actually featured in the Columbus Dispatch and awarded the Small Business Golden Quality Service Award. It was also noted to be one of the most profitable female-owned businesses in the city.

I'm fixated on being the best at anything I do. Morgan says I'm fixated on keeping busy so that I don't have time to allow people in my life, but that's not true. I just want to stay focused and stack my loot. By the time I'm thirty-five I want to be set for life.

I decided that the first store I would hit up was Barnes and Noble at the Easton Town Center Shopping Village. They had a nice African American section going on, but they didn't support the self-published authors as much as I did. As a matter of fact, if it weren't for the self-published authors, my store might have never even gotten off the ground.

When I was working on writing a book about my life I joined a writing group called The Literary World. Most of the time I never even opened any of the emails that came through. I would always forward them to Morgan and get her insight. Morgan found it astounding how many authors were putting their own work out instead of shopping their manuscripts to major publishing houses. They discussed the woes of trying to get major chains to carry their titles. That's when I decided to take my money and invest it in a bookstore to support the struggling authors. Who knew? I just might be one of them someday.

I had Morgan send an email stating that any author could send me up to twenty copies of each of their titles on a sixty percent (author) and forty percent (store) consignment basis. In a matter of weeks I received over a hundred titles. I pushed the author's titles as if I had written the books myself. The authors had also sent me posters, bookmarks, postcards, magnet, calendars and other neat promotional items for their work. That way when a customer bought a book, they received a bag full of freebies also. I didn't see them giving any of their customers a bag full of freebies at Barnes and Noble.

I hadn't been in the African American book section more than five minutes when a nice looking gentleman approached me.

He was wearing a nice pair of black slacks, a long sleeve white dress shirt, and a silver and black tie. He had a name button on his shirt that read Traci.

"Can I help you find something in particular?" he said with a warm smile. His smile said wonders for him. I was never into that animal instinct attraction, but his handsome smile sent chills down my spine and to my clit. At that moment, when he spoke to me, I would have never guessed in a million years that this would be the man I would spend the night with.

"I'm fine," I replied to him. "But thanks anyway, Traci."

This peculiar look came across his face. "Have we met before?" Traci asked.

"That line went out with fat colored shoe strings," I said. "No, but seriously, your name is on your button there."

He looked down at his name badge that I was pointing to.

"Oh, that's right," he said, feeling a wee bit stupid.

"That's okay," I said. "If we'd had met before, you would have remembered."

I turned my back to him and started running my finger down the spines of the books like I was really interested in them.

"Well, if you need anything, be sure to ask for me. Traci," he said, pulling out one of his business cards from his pocket and handing it to me.

"I will," I replied, taking it and putting it into my purse. I then proceeded back to looking at the books. I could feel him standing there for a minute. He turned to walk away and just when I thought he was going to punk out and not make a move on me he said, "Hey. I'm off in a few minutes. Do you want to wait around and maybe we can walk over to the Shark Bar for a drink? I would like it very much if you did."

I knew he was dealing with that same animalistic attraction that I was dealing with. I had never felt like this before, just instantly attracted to someone. I didn't know how to feel and thangs. My mind went blank.

Sexy, sexy was the only thing that came to mind when this man spoke his verbal invitation to me. Why had I not ever seen him before? Maybe I had seen him before, just never noticed him. It seemed as though lately I was starting to notice a lot of things in life that I had never noticed before.

"How long is a few minutes?" I asked. "Patience is not my virtue."

"About fifteen," he said.

He could tell I wasn't feeling the fifteen minute wait thing by my facial expression.

"Make it five minutes," he said.

I smiled. I waited. He was ready to go in four minutes.

"I've disobeyed my mother's number one rule that she taught me growing up," Traci said as we walked over to the Shark Bar. It was only about a three minute walk from Barnes and Noble, definitely walking distance.

"What do you mean?" I asked him.

"My mother always told me never to talk to strangers and yet here I am going to have a drink with one."

"Oh, forgive me," I said, smiling. "Harlem. My name is Harlem."

"That's a unique name," he said.

"I'm a unique person."

"I guessed that," he said, giving me a sexy look.

I was loving how this man was making me feel. He was so attentive. I could feel him looking at me as I looked straight ahead. He'd grab my hand and assist me every time we went up or down a curb. Walking next to him I felt like the only woman in the world.

When we entered the Shark Bar an Alicia Keys song was playing. It was a nice little crowd going on for it to be a late Sunday afternoon. I think that was my first time being there so I did what I always do when I go to an unfamiliar spot. I looked for the second exit and the ladies room. Once I peeped those out, I was good to go.

Traci and I sat down and chatted over drinks for about an hour. He told me a little bit about himself and how he got into the book business. I told him a little bit about myself, including how I got into the book business. Off the bat we already had a great deal in common, our careers.

"Will you excuse me while I go to the bathroom?" I said.

"Sure," he replied, standing up to excuse me from the table.

I got up from the table and shimmied away. I was hoping he was watching my ass switch in the Gloria Vanderbelt jeans I had pulled out from the back of my closet and thrown on.

Okay, I was diggin' this cat's entire steelo. I was all out of character. The more feminine side of me was definitely making a cameo. Something inside of me told me that Traci was going to be something special.

I used the restroom and reapplied a coat of lip gloss over my lips. I then headed out back to join Traci.

Perhaps I was too caught up in the idea of Traci watchin' my ass switch on the way to the bathroom, that I hadn't noticed going in what I noticed coming out. Sitting right there at a table with two other dudes was York and Jazzy. Of all the places for them to be and of all the days to be there.

I put it on everything that I could hear my fuckin' heart beating. I hadn't talked to York in two weeks. I wasn't about to step to his ass. Both York and Jazzy noticed me noticing them, but I kept right on steppin' as if they weren't even there. York had the boo-boo face when I just walked on by.

As I approached the table, Traci stood up to greet my return. Then we both sat back down.

"I ordered you another Long Island while you were gone," Traci said with all kinds of bass up in his vocals.

"Thank you," I replied.

See, that's what I'm talking about in a brotha. A man who doesn't ask a woman if she wants something, he just goes on and gets it. There is nothing more attractive than a man who knows what a woman wants.

Traci and I sat and talked while sipping on our alcoholic beverages. Both Traci and I were driving separate so we both had to cut ourselves off. But even after doing so, we still hung out and talked for another hour after that before deciding to call it a night. By then it was going on eight o'clock.

When the waitress brought over our bill she laid it down on the table and checked again to make sure that we didn't need anything else. When both Traci and I declined anything else, the waitress walked away.

As Traci reached down in his pocket for his wallet I interjected.

"I got this," I said, picking up the bill.

I could tell by the look on Traci's face that he was highly impressed. I pulled my credit card out. I didn't have enough cash on me to cover the bill because I hadn't planned on needing any that day.

I gave our waitress eye contact, letting her know that I was ready for her to come pick up our bill. She came over and took my credit card along with the bill. After running the card she came back for me to sign the receipt. She had been a pretty decent waitress so I tipped her twenty percent. Traci was impressed even more as he watched me fill in the tip line. No sooner than the waitress walked away, I felt a presence standing over me. That last Long Island had a sistah buzzing. I had forgotten all about York being there until I looked up and saw him standing over me.

"Harlem, can I talk to you for a minute?" York asked in a low tone.

Oh, Lord. The bitch in him was about to show her face.

"York, this is not the time or the place," I said with a straight face as if I wasn't fazed, knowing I was embarrassed as fuck. York was standing there like he was my deranged, crazy baby daddy. Poor Traci didn't know what to think. He just sat there looking at me like, it's your move and you better make the right one. "So, no, we can't talk," I added. "Maybe some other time."

"I think we should talk now," York said, trying to put some bass in his voice.

"We've had two weeks to talk and you want to talk now?" I said, sucking my teeth. I then looked up at Traci and said, "Baby, let's go."

I know. I know. I didn't have to call him baby like that in front of York. But that's what bitches do and I was in straight bitch mode.

"Oh, so it's like that?" York said, looking Traci up and down.

"Harlem, if you want to talk to him I don't mind," Traci said. "I can step aside for a minute, but not to worry, I'll be back."

"Man, she don't need your permission to talk to me," York said to Traci, flexin' his chest. "Who is this suit anyway?"

"I don't want to talk to him," I said to Traci in a calm tone. "But thank you for being understanding. Now if you don't mind, I'm ready to go."

"Fuck that!" York shouted. "How you gonna play me, Harlem? You actin' like I ain't nobody, like we wasn't nothing. Look, let's just talk."

Now York was really starting to get soft on me. I liked that he was letting his guard down. That thug mentality will only get a brotha so far in a relationship. A woman needs to know that a man is sensitive and has feelings. A woman needs to know that even thugs cry. But for York, it was too little, too late.

"Look, York," I said, standing up. "You made it clear where I stand with you. You made it clear when you let me walk my ass home. You made it clearer when you didn't even call to make sure that I made it home okay. For all you know I could be laying dead in a ditch somewhere."

"I knew you were okay," York said. "Jazzy talks to Morgan. I knew you were okay."

"Well, it's nice to know that you two aren't cut from the same cloth after all. I'm glad to know that Jazzy *talks* to Morgan."

By now Jazzy had stepped over to the table as well. He wanted to make sure that his boy didn't require backup.

"Come on, man," Jazzy said, looking down his nose at me. "There's plenty more where that came from."

"That's where you're wrong," I said to Jazzy, licking my lips. "I'm one of a kind. God stopped with me because he got tired of showing off."

Jazzy was biting his jaw. He looked over at Traci to size him up. His facial expression was more displeasing with my being in there with Traci than York's was.

"Then I guess it's our loss," Jazzy said, looking dead at me in my eyes.

"Our loss?" I questioned him. Even York had to look at him on that one.

"York's loss rather," he corrected himself. Jazzy and I just stood there staring at one another. All of a sudden it didn't even seem like it was about York and me anymore. It seemed like it was about Jazzy and me.

"Come on, man," Jazzy said to York, tugging him by the arm.

Traci stood up and asked me, "So are you ready to go?"

"I am, thank you," I said, reaching my hand out to Traci. He took it into his, gazing into my eyes and me gazing into his. He then led me out of the Shark Bar. I left York standing there with his face splattered all over the floor.

"Where are you parked?" Traci asked me as we exited the Shark Bar.

"I'm parked over by Panneria Bread," I replied.

"I'm parked in the garage," Traci said, thinking for a moment. "I don't want you walking by yourself. Just walk with me to my car and I'll drive you to yours."

"That sounds good," I said, taking Traci by the arm, hoping that York and his boys got a view of that.

Traci walked me to his car and then drove me back to mine. He was such a gentleman. I liked the fact that he wasn't turned off or intimidated by York's little tantrum, but instead, kicked right into protection gear.

"Thank you so much," I said, taking my seat belt off to get out of Traci's car. I surprised myself when I leaned in and kissed him.

"Let me go home with you," Traci whispered. "I mean, let me

just follow you home. I'm really worried about you. I just want to make sure that that fool isn't waiting on you when you get there or anything."

"Sure," I said with a smile.

Traci proceeded to follow me home. I looked up in my rearview mirror every now and then to make sure he was keeping up with my wild Mustang. A smile came across my face every time I saw him back there.

We pulled up at my house about ten minutes later. I opened the garage door and pulled my car inside. I walked back out to Traci, who was pulled over to the curb in front of my house, so that I could thank him and tell him goodnight. Besides that, he hadn't even asked me for my information, my phone number or nothing. I had to give him one last opportunity.

As I approached his car, Traci rolled down his window.

"You straight?" he asked me.

"Yeah. I think I'll be fine."

"You don't sound so sure," Traci said, grabbing my hand.

His touch was melting. This didn't make no sense how this man had me sprung out the gate.

"Let me stay the night," Traci asked, looking into my eyes. "I'll sleep on the couch. It would just make me feel so much better."

"I don't even know you," I said with a smile. "You could be a serial killer for all I know."

"And yet you let me follow me home," Traci said.

I put my head down and smiled.

"You got any girlfriends?" Traci asked out of the blue.

"Huh?" I said.

"Do you have any girlfriends, female friends, partners, buddies?"

"Yeah," I said with a chuckle.

"Here then," Traci said, handing me his cell phone. He then he pulled out his wallet and handed me his driver's license. "Call one of your girls and tell her you're with me. Give her my name and information from my driver's license and my license plate number. Now would a serial killer allow you to do that?"

I smiled and proceeded to use his phone to dial Morgan's number.

"See, my cell phone number will even show up on her caller ID," Traci said. But I had dialed Morgan's home phone and it didn't have caller ID.

"Hey, Morgan," I said when she answered her phone.

"Hey, you," she said in a perky tone.

"Get a pen and take down this information," I said.

"Hold on." I heard her scrambling for writing material. "Okay. Go ahead."

I proceeded to give her Traci's name, address, social security number, and license plate number. I told her that he is who I was with so if anything happened to me, to give the police his information. Traci laughed when I said that. I hung up with Morgan and handed Traci his phone and drivers license back.

"So is it cool for me to stay the night?" he asked with puppy-dog eyes.

"It's cool," I said, running my tongue across my teeth.

What was I doing? I kept asking myself as Traci rolled up his window and prepared to join me in my house.

Traci followed me into the house and made his way over to the living room couch. He kicked off his shoes and laid down as if he was the man of the house.

I stood over him with my hands on my hips.

"I have a guestroom you can sleep in, you know," I said.

"Where is it?" Traci asked.

"Upstairs."

Traci sat up on the couch and asked, "Now how am I supposed to protect you from all the way up there?" He winked then laid back down.

I smiled and walked away to go get him a blanket. *Thank goodness this fool didn't have a process in his hair,* I thought as I walked away. He definitely would have had to sleep in the guestroom then. I couldn't chance him getting activator all over my suede couch.

I went and got Traci a sheet to lay on and a blanket to cover up with.

"Thanks again for staying, but you really don't have to," I said. "I'm sure I'll be just fine."

"I want to," he said. "And you're welcome."

I turned off the light and headed to my bedroom.

I got undressed and slipped on a Varsity Sports sleep shirt that I had gotten from Kohl's department store. I tucked myself into bed and I must say, even though I never thought for one moment that York would come over to my house and do something stupid, I felt safe knowing that Traci was out there. I felt safe until the middle of the night when my phone rang.

The ringing phone ripped me from my sleep. I got that stomach turning feeling that one gets when their phone rings in the middle of the night.

"Hello," I said, lightweight frantic. There was no sound on the other end of the phone. I had been getting hang up calls at the store every now and then, but this was the first time I had received one at my home.

"Bitch, you keep fuckin' around and you're dead," the caller said in a muffled crank-calling voice. "Don't think for one minute that I forgot about your ass."

I couldn't tell whether the caller was a male or female, but the voice had me sitting straight up in my bed.

"What?" I asked. "Who is this?"

"You heard me, bitch. I'm watching you so you're fucked now," the caller said right before hanging up.

I hung up the phone and pulled my nightstand drawer out.

"Fuck!" I said to myself. I had left my 9-millimeter in my glove box. Some good it was going to do me out there. It was a fine time I invest in two guns for sure. That was definitely on my things to do list.

I got out of bed and put on my house shoes. I needed to go out to my car and get my piece just in case the caller wasn't a prank, but meant business.

As I walked down the hall into the living room, the sleeping body on my couch startled me. I had forgotten all about Traci being there. I sighed and thought to myself, *Hell, I don't need to go outside and get my piece. I have a piece laying right here on my couch.*

I walked over to the couch and saw that Traci was sleeping sound like a baby. He appeared to be sleeping hard. I don't know if he would have even been awakened by an intruder because he looked to be sleeping so deep.

I sat down on the suede chair. I curled my feet up under my bottom and watched Traci's chest go up and down as he slept. I had never watched a man sleep before. I felt safe sitting there watching him. After a few minutes I had forgotten all about the harassing phone call. I closed my eyes and took a deep breath. When I opened them Traci was staring dead at me. I jumped. He scared me to death. I wasn't expecting him to be awake.

"You all right?" he asked concerned.

"Yeah," I replied, catching my breath.

He stared at me for a moment with his luscious eyes. I stared back with mine.

"Come here, girl," he said, stretching out with a yawn.

I stood up and walked over to him like a shy little girl. I just stood over him waiting for his next command.

"Come here," he said, patting his chest for me to lay down on it.

I followed his instructions and climbed upon his soft body. It felt so good laying there. I placed my head on his chest. He put his hand on the back of my head and began rubbing my hair. I looked up at him. He moved his head forward and placed his lips on mine.

I indulged on his lips and then his tongue. We found ourselves in a long deep passionate kiss. Breathing heavily I sucked on his tongue like it was a popsicle. He grabbed me by my head and pulled me into him as he stuck his tongue out as far as he could for me to suck on. I could feel his dick poking my pussy through my sleep shirt like a dagger. It felt huge, like it would definitely fill my pussy up and give it pleasure.

Thump thump. Thump thump, my clit beat as we continued to tongue fuck. After a couple of minutes we ended the kiss. Traci looked into my eyes, kissed me on the forehead and whispered, "Goodnight."

That was the most romantic episode I had ever found myself in. I laid my head back on his chest and kept my eyes open until I felt his dick go down. He didn't push the kiss any further and Lord knows he could have. My britches were soaking wet. But instead we just laid there and slept the night away . . . together.

When morning came Traci got up and headed home. I offered to cook him breakfast, but he said that he had to go because he was going to be late for work. I too needed to get up and get my damn self ready for work. But I was willing to be late in order to return the favor of him staying the night with me. Besides, Monday's were the slowest days with most of the salons and barbershops being closed.

I got showered and dressed and headed into work. I knew of all days, Morgan was going to be at the store right on time to get the 411 on the mystery man.

Just as I had expected, when I pulled up behind the bookstore, there was Morgan's car. She had opened the store. The minute I walked in she was standing behind the counter with two cups of latte.

"All right hoe," she said. "Who's this Traci and can he fuck?"

"Well, damn," I said. "What would you say if you knew how to speak your mind?"

"Come on, Harlem," Morgan begged. "Every since you called me last night, I've been aching to get the 411. What happened? Who is he?"

I decided to appease Morgan's curiosity and fill her in on the details of how I met Traci and the scene York made in the Shark Bar. Morgan was hanging onto my every word as if I was recounting a soap opera.

"Harlem, girl," Morgan said as she put her hand on my forehead. "You got the fever."

"What are you talking about?" I said, pushing her hand off of my forehead.

"I ain't never seen you talk about someone like that before. Your eyes are all lit up and shit. Are you sure you didn't fuck him?"

"No," I said.

"He didn't eat you out or nothing? No sixty eight and you owe him one?"

"Girl, no," I said.

"But you just glowing and shit," Morgan said. "I mean, I'm glad to see you like this. It makes me happy for you, girl."

Morgan hugged me.

"Thank you," I said, putting my head down to blush.

"And this man has got you blushing, too. Okay, when are you two hooking up again?"

"Oh shit!" I said. "I didn't give him my number."

"You're kidding me, right?" Morgan said.

"Damn. I wish I was. Fuck!" I sighed.

"Calm down," Morgan said. "It's not like you don't know where he works."

"You're right," I said with a sigh of relief.

"So call him," Morgan suggested.

"No," I said. "I'm not going to call him. You know I don't call guys."

"Well, he sure can't call you so it looks like you two won't be talking again."

I thought about Morgan's words. If ever I wanted to see a man again it was Traci. I went and dug Traci's business card out of my purse. I stared at it for a moment. Morgan came and stood over my shoulder and looked down at the card.

"So call him already," she said. "Don't be scurred."

I looked up at the store clock. It was only eight-fifteen.

"Don't you think it's too early?" I asked Morgan.

"No," Morgan said. "And besides, just call his cell phone. Leave a message, if anything, thanking him for looking after you. And that gives you an opportunity to leave your number so that he can contact you from now on."

Morgan made helluv sense so I decided to follow her advice and dial Traci's cell phone number.

"Hello," a woman's voice answered.

I swallowed hard. I was for sure caught off guard with a female answering the phone. Perhaps I had dialed the wrong number. I'm sure I had, but I still replied.

"Hello," I said.

"Yes," she said in a pleasant tone.

"I was calling for Traci," I said. "But I think I have the wrong number."

"Oh, you have the right phone number. This is Traci's wife. He's in the shower right now getting ready to go into work," the woman said. "Are you one of the women from a book club or something? Are you calling to set up a signing or club meeting at Traci's store?"

I guess that was the excuse Traci told his wife just in case one of his women on the side called him.

"Uh, yes," I replied. "But, I can call back later. As a matter of fact, tell him that Harlem called and she's canceling her meeting indefinitely. Thank you so much."

I quickly hung up the phone and just sat there. My heart sank deep into my chest. It didn't want to be seen by my other organs. I was just that humiliated.

"What's wrong?" Morgan asked.

"Oh, nothing," I said.

"Well, what did he say?"

"He didn't say anything." I paused. "But his wife said enough."

Morgan didn't know what to say to comfort me. The brand new Harlem with the glow that she would have loved to get used to was gone just as quickly as she had came. The old Harlem was back. And she was here to stay. Never again would I let my guard down. Something told me that God had something to do with this let-down just like all of the others.

Morgan put her chin on my shoulder and kissed me on the cheek.

"Sorry, Harlem," Morgan said, pouting her lips. "And just think, York saw you leave with him last night. You know how his mind is playing tricks on him, eating away at his male ego. The vision of you sucking Traci's dick probably tormented him all night. And for what? A married man whose dick you never even got to see, let alone suck."

I forced out a fake laugh. "Yeah, York probably took his Kanye West CD out of his stereo and put in Eamon's CD, the song 'F*ck It' on repeat."

"Well, like the song says, if you do decide to throw out all the gifts he gave you, can you throw them my way?" Morgan smiled and winked as a customer entered the store. She went over and tended to them.

I just sat there thinking about the fool I was by being the stubborn bitch I am and not hearing York out and not giving him a chance to hear me out. Then I started thinking about the fool I almost was by getting caught up with a married man. If it ain't a hustler it's a married man. I thought Traci was going to be something special. I guess he would simply go down in my book as being a one-night man.

After work one night Morgan invited me to her house to watch the season premier of *Soul Food* on Showtime. I stopped at Roosters

and got some chicken wings, seasoned wedges, and side salads
while Morgan stopped at the bank and made our daily deposit.

We weren't five minutes into the show when her phone rang.

"Hello," Morgan said. "Oh, hey, you."

Her tone changed. It got much more perky and sensual. I knew
it was a guy on the other end.

"Sitting here in the living room with my girl watching *Soul
Food*," Morgan answered his inquiries. "Sure, come on. Okay. I'll
see you in a bit."

Morgan hung up the phone and sat there looking like the cat
that ate the canary. I couldn't believe she had just invited someone
over and we were supposed to be chillin' together.

I didn't even make it easy for her to tell me by asking her who
that was on the phone. I pretended not to have heard her side of
the conversation at all. Then a full five minutes later, as if she had
just hung up the phone, she said, "Jazzy's going to stop through."

"Oh, then I guess I better get going," I said with an attitude.

"Now, Harlem, you know you don't have to leave."

"I'm not about to be a third wheel over here. I thought we were
supposed to chill and watch *Soul Food*."

"And that's what we're doing," Morgan said, copping an attitude
right along with me. "I don't know why you're mad at Jazzy. He
didn't do anything to you. It was his boy. You can't be mad at him
because of what York did and you can't expect me to cut Jazzy off
because of what York did either. We're not in high school, Harlem."

"Did I fuckin' say you had to cut Jazzy off?" I snapped. "No, I
didn't, now did I? So I don't know what the hell you're talking about.
But why you wouldn't want to cut him off is beyond me. As a matter of fact, you probably should have cut him off a long time ago.
He doesn't treat you any different than any other guy you've ever

been involved with, only you're too dumb to see it. You throw yourself at men then expect them to expect more out of you than pussy. You act like men are slot machines. You think you're going to pull down on a lever and it's going to say 'you hit the jackpot,' Morgan?"

Morgan looked at me with hurt in her eyes. She was in just as much shock hearing those words come out of my mouth as I was for allowing them to come out of my mouth. Instantly, I wanted to apologize. I needed to apologize, but before I could, Morgan retaliated.

"You are my girl, Harlem. Nothing is going to ever change that. Right now I know that you're pissed. I know you're hurt by the way things turned out between you and York. You express yourself with anger. You always have. That's just who you are and I've accepted that about you. But to hear those words come out of my best friend's mouth is just something I never expected. You basically called me a stupid hoe. I can only wonder how long you've felt that way about me."

"Come on Morgan, in so many words, I've always told you that," I said in an attempt to be caring, but once again not thinking about how I was wording shit.

"You are fucking unbelievable," Morgan said, throwing her hands up. "I am not some stupid hoe. Maybe it does seem as though I'm looking for 'Mr. Right for me' in all the wrong places. I know I'm not going to find him in a club or in the streets. But who says that's what I want right now? I never said that. I'm young and free. And I like men. I like dating them and having fun. I know it seems as though I'm always attracted to the bad boy type who isn't right for me now, but who knows what the future holds? People change. I grew up in a home with two parents who I witnessed love and respect one another. You don't think I know how a man treats a woman he loves? Well, I do. But I'm not looking for love in every man I meet. 'Spite what you think, Harlem, I understand a little bit about the game. I might not have graduated yet, but I have been paying attention while in class."

I hate to say it, but Morgan's words went in one ear and out the other. I was still trippin' on the shit I had said to her. I couldn't believe I was snappin' off on her like that, and over a dude. I don't know what it was about that fuckin' Jazzy, but he had really gotten under my skin in a crazy kind of way. One minute I wanted him. One minute I hated him. The next minute I hated him because I wanted him. Just sick I tell you. I wanted to hate him every minute, and yet there was just this unspoken thing between us. I know there was. I could feel it. Poor Morgan was just getting caught up in the crossfire of my crazy emotions. In all truthfulness, I was mad at her. I was pissed at her because she had something that I wanted a taste of. And what does she do, she invites him over her house, while I'm there, to rub it in my face.

Morgan and I ended up watching the remainder of *Soul Food* without saying two words to one another. Every now and then, out of the corner of my eye, I could see her wiping her eyes. I knew that I had hurt her feelings, but at the same time I was telling the truth in a sense. Still, she was my friend and deserved better from me.

I made it up in my head that I was going to apologize after *Soul Food* went off. During the remainder of the show I gathered my thoughts so that I would know what to say to her and to say it right. But just as if it was perfect timing on his part, as the credits rolled, Jazzy knocked on the door.

Morgan jumped up to get the door. She could have cared less about the fight she and I had just had.

"Who it is?" Morgan asked through the door.

"Jazz," he said in baritone.

Morgan opened the door to let him in and the two embraced. I looked up and Jazzy caught me looking. Our eyes locked, then he began kissing Morgan open mouth while staring right at me.

Oooh, I hate him so much right now, I thought.

"Harlem's still here," Morgan said to Jazzy, clearing her throat.

"So I see," Jazzy said, walking over to me. "Harlem World, what's up, pimp?"

Why was this nigga trying to be funny? I rolled my eyes and got up from the floor.

"Hey, Morgan, I'm outty five thousand," I said. I would have to apologize later. No way was I about to hang around. "You two kids have fun."

"You don't have to go, Harlem," Morgan said sincerely, grabbing my hand.

I smiled at her. "Three's a crowd," I replied. I suppose that was apology enough. That's one thing I can say about Morgan and me, we never ever stayed mad at one another no matter what. That's true homies. That right there is nothing but love.

"Well, we can make it a foursome," Jazzy said. "All I have to do is call my boy York over."

"Not cool, Jazzy," Morgan whispered.

"I'll call you later, Morgan," I said.

"Damn!" Morgan said, stomping her foot. "I just thought of something. Hold up before you go, Harlem. I still have the bank deposit. My mom called me on my cell phone. I got to talking to her and I forgot to stop and drop it off. It's out in my car. I'll go get it."

Morgan exited her house, leaving Jazzy and me in her living room. I twisted my lips up, not saying a word to him. He wouldn't take his eyes off of me. He just stared at me with this evil grin on his face.

"That's fucked up how you played my boy, Harlem," Jazzy said to me in a serious tone.

"Your boy played himself," I said. "So he and I kicked it a couple of times, and I don't see no wedding ring on my finger. When that muthafucka sent me hiking in stilettos, he played me. So I guess one good play deserves another. Hate the game, not the player, playboy."

Jazzy shook his head and smiled. "I know your kind, Harlem," he said, looking into my eyes. "You gon' play hard all your life?"

I looked at him like he was crazy.

"Don't look at me like you don't know what I'm talking about," he said, moving in closer. "You sit around waiting for people to cross you don't you? So that you have a reason not to let them in. Not to let them in there." Jazzy pointed to my heart, slightly touching my breast. My insides quivered.

"York might not see it. Morgan might not see it. Hell, your own mama might not even see it. But I see it." Jazzy ran his finger up my chest to my shoulder, where my ponytail was resting. He tugged on it softly. I bit down on my lip. "Yeah, I see right through you, Harlem World. And you know it too."

Jazzy was all up in my space by now, reading me like a mystery novel. He was bound and determined to figure me out.

"You see right through me, huh?" I asked, staring right back into his eyes.

He nodded his head yes as he licked his lips.

"Then I guess that makes you muthafuckin' Superman, huh?" I said sharply, not backing down.

Jazzy tilted his head, ran his tongue inside his jaw, and backed out of my space. Me and my big ass mouth. Damn, how I wanted him in my space. To be that close to him was amazing.

"You really think you hot shit don't you?" Jazzy said, shaking his head.

"Obviously I got your boy thinking it for me," I said, coming hard in the paint.

"You just need to be more careful of who you hurt," Jazzy said. "You really need to be careful. Shit always comes back to you. That's life."

"Is that a threat?" I asked.

"No. It's just some good old-fashion advice," Jazzy said.

"Well, I don't need any advice, especially from someone like you," I said, turning my nose up at him and rolling my eyes.

"Oh, you think you better than me?" Jazzy said, laughing. "Everybody gets broke down, Harlem."

"Let me guess," I said, hands on hips. "And you want to be the one to break me down?"

Jazzy just stood there staring at me for a moment. I can't even begin to explain the look in his eyes. Oooh, he was killing me softly. When I couldn't take him staring down my insides, picking my soul apart with his eyes, I looked down to the floor. He quickly lifted my head by my chin. He held his hand there, forcing me to look at him.

"Furthest thing from the truth," Jazzy said in a soft whisper, now easing his way back into my space. "How long you gonna play this game, Harlem? You can't win. You ain't as up on your game as you think you are. If you were, then you would have seen that wedding ring on playboy's finger you were out with at the Shark Bar. Or had you noticed it? I don't know. Maybe you did. You down with OPP, Harlem?"

My eyes widened.

"See," Jazzy said, now nose to nose with me. "I know you think you're this strong invincible woman who has everything under control. But, baby girl, you can be just as blind as the next. It's amazing just how much you can miss when you blink your eyes."

I swallowed hard then harshly pushed his hand off of my chin. I did it as if I didn't want him touching me. But actually, I heard Morgan coming. I quickly backed up away from him.

"Here you go, Harlem," Morgan said, handing me the deposit bag.

I took the bag from her and allowed my normal hard attitude to resurface. Jazzy stood there lipping the words "you can't win" to me.

I rolled my eyes at him. "Hope you enjoy the rest of your night, Morgan," I said, grabbing my purse and heading out of the door.

I slammed the door behind me. Even on the other side of the door I could feel Jazzy. I closed my eyes and just stood there holding the doorknob as if I was clutching his manhood, massaging it, wishing it was inside of me. Wishing he was inside of me. But then I realized that he was already inside of me. He was in my head.

10. Penny for Your Thoughts

The next morning Morgan was late for work as usual. She had probably been up all night with Jazzy, therefore, she would probably be even extra late. The store hadn't been open five minutes when the first customer came through the door.

"Good morning," the girl said as she entered the store. She had big red rollers in her hair and a hair net tied around them. Even with a head full of rollers she looked cute, sportin' a powder blue FUBU jogging suit with matching kicks.

"Hey," I replied to her. For some reason I couldn't take my eyes off of her. No, I wasn't trying to be gay for a day. It was just that she looked so familiar. I just couldn't figure out where I knew her from.

After grabbing a six pack of Dolly Madison powered donuts she walked over to the latte bar. I made my way over there so that I could serve her.

"Can I get a medium coffee?" she asked while staring at the price sign. "Make that a large. You might as well for only twenty cents more."

I proceeded to fix her coffee. I could feel her staring at me as if she was trying to figure out where she knew me from as well.

"Harlem?" the girl suddenly said, with her big brown eyes wide open.

I looked at her. I knew her face but still couldn't place it.

"Your name is Harlem, right?" she asked.

"Yeah," I said, still puzzled trying to figure out who shorty was.

"It's me," she said, smiling as if I should know who she was by now.

I squinted my eyes, stared at her, and asked my brain to hurry up and figure out who this chick was. Then it came to me.

"Penny?" I said as my mouth dropped open. "Penny."

"Yeah, it's me," she said, reaching her arms out to hug me.

I was anything but the touchy, huggy type, but I made an exception. I didn't want to leave her hangin'. She pat my back as I hugged her. She sighed then I initiated the separation.

"How have you been?" I asked her as I put the lid on her coffee and handed it to her.

"Pretty good, considering," she said, shaking her head. She grabbed a couple packs of sugar. "I see you're doing pretty good yourself. Is this you?"

"Yep, this is my baby," I said proudly, looking around the store.

"Look at you. You got you a lil' shop going on and thangs. I had no idea this was you. Terri, next door, been doing my hair for a year now. I've been in here once before, I think, to get some change. But it was another girl in here."

"Yeah, that's my partner," I said, proud of my own self for doing so well.

"Well, good for you," Penny said, unzipping her purse and digging inside of it for her wallet. "How much do I owe you?"

The strangest feeling came over me. For some reason I felt like I owed Penny. After all, I left her in that house that night. I knew what her mother's boyfriend was doing to her and I left her there. And on top of that, I never even told anyone. I never sent help her way. That burden, that debt, I hadn't realized I was carrying until just now.

"You don't owe me anything," I said. "It's on the house. Anytime you're next door getting your hair done, stop in. It's on the house. As a matter of fact, just stop in just because."

"Thank you, Harlem," she smiled, zipping her purse back up. "Well, I guess I better go get back under that dryer before Terri has a fit. But it was good seeing you."

"You too," I said as Penny headed out the door. "Hey, Penny. How's your mom?"

Penny stopped dead in her tracks. She froze for a minute, then shook it off.

"She's doing good, to be locked down," Penny said, her mind wandering off.

"She's in jail?" I asked surprised. I couldn't imagine Miss Myla doing anything to land herself in jail. She was as sweet as cotton candy.

"Yeah, she got fifteen to twenty-five years for manslaughter," Penny said.

"Damn!" I couldn't help but say. Penny could tell by the look on my face that I was dying to know exactly who Miss Myla took out, so she saved me the trouble of asking.

"I know. Seems like forever," Penny said sadly. "But at least now the boogieman won't be able to bother anybody else's little girl."

A slight smile appeared on Penny's lips, then it was gone and so was she.

11. Sweet Gone Sour

Later on that night Jazzy came over to my house to apologize for
the way he had acted towards me at Morgan's house the day before. It was the middle of the night and I was caught so off guard
that I almost didn't hear him knocking. I couldn't imagine who
in the hell was at my door at two o'clock in the damn morning. I
have to say, though, that when I looked through the peephole and
saw that it was Jazzy, the time didn't matter.

Wearing nothing but a long T-shirt and my slippers, I opened the
door. I didn't even put on a housecoat. I guess a part of me wanted
Jazzy to see as much of my skin as he could. When I opened the
door he was standing there with this look on his face, it was a look
as if he already felt fully at fault for what was about to take place
between the two of us.

"Harlem World," he said as he gave off a slight smile. His arms
were folded and he was leaning against the doorframe.

"What are you doing here?" I asked, rubbing my eyes. I had to
make sure I was seeing shit clearly.

"I came to apologize for how I came at you yesterday," he said. "I couldn't stop thinking about you. On the real, Harlem. A nigga ain't stopped thinking about you since the day he laid eyes on you."

About goddamn time! He had finally gripped his sack and stepped to me like a man. I knew he wanted me. I could feel it. I just needed to hear him say it.

I decided to open the door wide, allowing him to enter my throne. After closing the door behind him, I turned to lock it. As soon as I turned around to face him he was standing right there up on me. We were nose to nose. I could feel his breath on my face.

Without further ado, he grabbed each side of my face with his hands and pulled me into his tongue. I sucked that son of a bitch dry too. Wasn't a drop of saliva in his mouth by the time I finished with it.

His tongue was thick like homemade taffy and just as sweet if not sweeter. I pulled on it with my teeth. Jazzy was somewhat of a roughneck so I knew he had to like it a little rough. I opened my eyes to watch him enjoy the pain of my teeth scraping down his tongue.

Next thing I knew his hands crawled from my facial cheeks to my ass cheeks. He rubbed and squeezed on them like he was picking out cantaloupe at the local supermarket. His heavy manly touch was so strong that I couldn't take it anymore. I wanted him inside of me. I wanted him to plunge in and out of me so deep that he caused my pussy to make air noises that whined out his name like the sound of the wind.

I unbuckled Jazzy's belt and unbuttoned his jeans. His pants fell to the floor. I couldn't resist grabbing hold of his black stallion. It was hard, pointed straight out. It curved to the left a little bit, but it was fat so I could work with it. A skinny curvy dick ain't nothing to play with. Them pointy crooked fuckers hurt. But Jazzy's was just right.

As I placed my tongue in his mouth ferociously, I pushed his boxers down with my hands. That was his welcome-home sign.

He quickly lifted my shirt, lifted me up around his waist, and then slammed my back into the door, almost violently. His fingers were dancing inside of me. Lucky for him I didn't have on panties so he had easy access, no drawz to push to the side. My pussy had been longing for him for oh so long. He couldn't fuck me soon enough.

He sucked and bit all over my neck as I moaned and groaned. All I wanted him to do was put it in. I had had enough of that foreplay shit. I was ready to fuck.

Jazzy placed his hands on my butt and spread my ass cheeks. I liked how he was handling his, teasing me and shit. Making me want him even more.

He scooted me up, as I had slid down a little. After positioning himself just right he was ready to run up in me. Right before he was about to place himself inside of me I woke up from out of my sleep.

I was laying there in my bed, sheets wet, hair wet, and pussy wet. I touched myself. My pussy was sticky too. That's when I realized that I had cum.

I sat up in my bed and thought for a minute. Was Jazzy really here and maybe I just thought that I was dreaming? That's just how real that wet dream felt. I mean it had me wanting to pick up the phone and call Morgan to apologize for fucking her dude.

I got up out of my bed and headed to the bathroom. I was in definite need of a shower. A cold one. My pussy was on fire and I needed something to put it out.

I walked over to the shower and turned the water on. I stepped in and then realized that I had to pee. Already wet from the shower water, I didn't feel like drying off to go sit on the toilet so I decided to just pee in the shower.

I got the water to just the right temperature and let it beat down on every curve of my body. It wasn't freezing cold, but it was cool. My hands flowed down my body with the water as I fantasized about the dream of being intimate with Jazzy that I had just had. In doing so my fingers found their way to my clit. With my index finger and my thumb I began plucking it like a guitar string. I twisted it, teasing every tantalizing nerve.

I pretended that my index finger was Jazzy's dick and I was grinding on it. I turned and placed my head against the shower wall for balance. I crossed my legs and squeezed them as tight as I could around my finger and began to slide my pussy up and down on it. The wall turned into Jazzy's chest as my head rested up against it. I fucked harder and harder until I began to quiver.

"Uhh, ahh" I screamed out. "Oh shit!" It felt good being alone in the shower, able to scream out in ecstasy as loud as I wanted without shame.

I felt so complete as my river of juices washed down my thigh and into the drain. What I wouldn't have given for that hand to be Jazzy's hand instead of mine. What I wouldn't have given for it to had been his dick.

After my shower I slipped into a nice black chemise. Hell, I was feeling sexy by then. Just like anybody else who busted two good nuts back to back, I slept like a baby for the rest of the night.

"Fuck! Fuck! Fuck!" I can't believe I can't find my car keys. I have searched high and low for those sons of bitches.

Morgan was out of town visiting her cousin in Milwaukee so I didn't even have the comfort of knowing that she was going to be able to open the store. It was already ten minutes to eight and the drive from my house to the store is at least fifteen minutes. I could kick myself for oversleeping.

I could see already that it was going to be a long day, and to add salt to a wound, I didn't even feel one hundred percent on point in my appearance. All I had time to do to get ready for work was splash my face with some water and run the toothbrush across my teeth for two minutes, short of my normal three minutes. I didn't have time to iron the outfit I had in mind to wear so I just threw on a lightweight wrinkled Fila jogging suit. Now if I could just find my keys I could be on my way.

After looking down into my purse a second time, I found the keys and headed out of the door.

When I arrived to unlock the store, I noticed that the back door in the storage room was slightly ajar. I grabbed my gun out of my glove box and walked through the door.

What I saw once I opened the door all of the way brought me down to my knees. I literally dropped. I closed my eyes and I stayed on the ground and took a few deep breaths. I was hoping that once I opened my eyes everything would be normal, that what I had just seen wasn't real. I opened my eyes again only to be confronted by the ugliest of reality.

Every box in the storage room had been ripped open. Books were thrown all over the place. Candy had been scattered all over and the coffee grounds had actually been dumped out of their packaging.

There were broken CDs on the floor and even my supply of register tape was tee peed all over the place. I let the horrible scene sink in then I prepared myself for what else was in store for me.

I walked into the store area and just fuckin' screamed.

Every book in the store was off the shelf. The shelves were tipped over and broken. The CDs had been opened or stomped on hard enough to crack the cases. Some loose pages from books and magazines, where they had been ripped out, were scattered. The candy was dumped on the floor, candy bars stomped, and the coffee and latte machines were smashed on the floor. The tables and chairs were nothing more than a pile of firewood.

The cash registers were cracked open, but I never kept money in the store overnight. I made deposits every night so I wasn't worried that any cash was missing. But from the looks of things, the intruder didn't have money on the mind. If they had, they would have stolen all they could and flipped it on the streets rather than destroy it.

I couldn't begin to add up the cost of the damage that had been done. Of course I had insurance, but the pain I was feeling of seeing my store destroyed was priceless. No amount of money could heal the pain.

I called the police and when they showed up they told me that they weren't even going to dust for fingerprints. I was told that there would be a high number of expected prints from customers, so it would be a waste of time.

I told them to at least do the cash registers because only Morgan and I would have touched them. They didn't hear me though. And they wonder why a muthafucka keeps their glock cocked to take matters into their own hands.

The police asked me if there was anyone who I thought might

want to do something like that to me and I told them no. Hours later, after I had gone home, someone did come to mind. A couple of someones, indeed.

I didn't call Morgan and tell her what had happened to the store. I didn't want to ruin her vacation with her cousin. And besides that, there was nothing she could have done about it. The damage was done. The store was ruined. I was forced to close it down.

When Morgan got back into town I drove out to her house to tell her in person what had happened. She was devastated and didn't even believe me. After I convinced her that I would never play such a cruel joke on her, she said that she wanted to drive out to the store so that she could see it for herself. So we hopped into her car and headed to the store.

When Morgan first walked into the back storage room, she pretty much had the same reaction that I had had, only I was there to catch her before her knees hit the ground.

"Why?" Morgan said as her eyes filled with tears.

I supported her by holding onto her arm, then she pulled away and continued into the storefront.

"Oh, Jesus!" she said, now with tears running down her face. "Harlem, my God! I can't believe this!"

Morgan looked around in horror. It was a nightmare. All the hard work she and I had put into the Suga Shop was no longer evident. Morgan saw this disaster as elbow grease, blood, sweat and tears, down the drain.

"Who do you think could have done something like this?" Morgan asked me as tears ran down her face.

"I don't know," I lied. Morgan could hear it in my voice that I had my suspicions. She knew damn well who I thought the culprit, or culprits, were.

"You think it was York, don't you?" Morgan said. I didn't reply. "And I know what else you're thinking too. Cut from the same cloth. You're thinking that Jazzy might have had a hand in it too."

I looked at Morgan and shrugged. She was waiting on a verbal reply from me.

"Morgan, I don't want to assume anything. But if it walks like a duck and it quacks like a duck."

"I can't believe this. I knew I should have stop fuckin' with his ass," Morgan said. "When you cut York loose, I should have done the same to him."

"If York was going to fuck up my store, he was going to do it whether you cut Jazzy off or not, so that has nothing to do with it. He just went out like a bitch is all."

"Well, it's better late than never," Morgan said, wiping her tears with her hands.

"What do you mean?" I asked.

"I can't wait to call him and give him a piece of my mind," Morgan said, digging down in her purse. "He's about to get cut the fuck off and then some. Son of a bitch."

Morgan whipped out her cell phone and called Jazzy. It rang and rang, but there was no answer. At first, when his voicemail picked up, she was going to hang up, but instead she decided to leave him a message.

"Hey, Jazzy, it's me, Morgan. You know," Morgan said as her voice went from calm into a complete lioness roar, "the one whose store you fucked up you son of a bitch! If you think that we don't know that you and your flunky are the ones responsible for tearing up the store then you must think we're idiots. We might never be able to prove it to the police, but you best believe we name-droppin'."

I snatched Morgan's phone out of her hand so damn fast. I angrily slammed down the flip.

"Bitch, are you crazy?" I fussed at Morgan. "Don't you ever threaten a muthafucka workin' the streets with the police. You trying to have your mama find you in the trunk of your damn car with your throat slit?"

"Fuck them, Harlem. Fuck them!" Morgan screamed. "Look what they did to us. Look what they did."

Morgan fell to her knees in tears. I shook my head.

"Look, Morgan, I know you're pissed. I'm pissed. This was the fuckin' beginning of my empire. But it's gone, babe. It's gone."

"How can you act like this, Harlem?" Morgan looked around the store and started crying again.

"God been fucking with me from the moment the doctor smacked me on the ass. I'm almost immune to this type of shit now."

"We sure can pick 'em, huh, Harlem? Especially me," Morgan said.

"This is not our fault," I assured her. "We didn't ask for this."

"But we knew their kind," Morgan said. "Thugs. And that was your golden rule, don't fuck with a dope boy or a thug. And what do we do? We fuck with niggas who are both."

"Look, there's nothing we can do about it," I said, looking around the store in disgust. "We'll just have to start over."

"Start over? But we worked so hard," Morgan said angrily. "We worked so hard to build this store up to what it is. What it was."

"And we'll do it again, Morgan, shit," I said. "This shit right here only makes me hungrier. Someone thought that they were going to shut us down. Well, they're wrong. They are only going to build us up that much stronger. You with me?"

Morgan shook her head.

"I don't know, Harlem," she said. "It was so much work. So much work down the fucking drain. Looking at this shit, I don't know if I have the energy to do it again. I don't know if I want to put my time into starting from fuckin' scratch."

"Then what do you plan on doing, Morgan?" I shouted at her. "Are you gonna run off with your college degree and go get a job in corporate America and leave me hanging? Or let me guess, you're going to go out and start selling magazines again."

"That's a great idea," Morgan said, wiping her tears.

"What? Sell magazines door to door?" I asked.

"No, you can get a degree too, Harlem. You could go back to school," Morgan said as if a lightbulb had just gone off in her head.

For a minute I thought her ass was going to break down and start singing "Tomorrow" from *Annie*.

"Oh, no you don't," I said to Morgan, throwing my hand up at her. "I'm not trying to hear that shit, Morgan, and you know it. I'm twenty-seven years old. Thirty is right around the corner. I can do what I need to do in life without going back to school."

"But you're only going to be able to go so far, Harlem," Morgan tried convincing me, but instead, her preaching was pissing me off. "The fact that you're pushing thirty is the number one reason why you do need to go back to school and get your education. How do you know that I'm always going to be here for you, Harlem? I mean look at you. You're running a bookstore and you can't even—"

"Fuck you!" I screamed to Morgan, cutting off her words. "Fuck you! You're not my fucking mother, Morgan. You're not my fucking mother. Do you hear me?"

I stormed into the back storage room then out of the store. Morgan remained inside the store shattered. She buried her head down in her hands.

"Damn it!" Morgan screamed at the top of her lungs. She was so hurt. I was hurt too, but I was tired. I was tired of trying to figure out God and why he hated me so much. I wanted to throw in the towel to life, but according to that psychic, I still had sixty-two years to go. Somehow I had to keep moving.

12. Wolves in Sheep's Clothing

With the Suga Shop being remodeled, Morgan and I had more time on our hands than ever. After we had it out that day in the store, we made up and decided that we were just going to move forward, reopen the store. The insurance company ended up giving me a check for seven hundred thousand dollars to do repairs. I had gotten an estimate from a well-known builder in the city. He was one of the best. His estimate is what the insurance company based the claim check on. But of course a business broad like myself paid Morgan's uncle and his crackhead crew two hundred fifty thousand in labor and materials to make the repairs. I still had to rebuild my inventory, but even then I had a few ends to splurge with. Morgan was still in somewhat of a funk, so I decided to take her and myself on a shopping spree. So all afternoon we spoiled ourselves rotten.

We rarely did girlfriend things such as go shopping, but with no men in our lives and no work, there was nothing left to do but play.

Summer was knocking on spring's door so it was time for new gear anyway. Morgan and I spent about four hours at the shopping center before calling it a day. By the time we finished shopping it was just starting to get dark outside.

"You are the best friend in the whole wide world," Morgan said, gazing down at her wrist, which was laced with a 3-carat diamond tennis bracelet that was set in sterling silver. Hell, sterling silver, platinum, white gold. I don't know what it was. It was all the same difference to me.

"Hey, someone once told me that a person should never have to buy jewelry for themselves," I said to Morgan, mocking York, of course. "Jewelry should be received as a gift. So that's my gift, from me to you Morgan Kleiningham."

I noticed tears forming in Morgan's eyes as I hit the button to pop the trunk. We couldn't get to my car fast enough with all of those bags we were carrying as a result of our shopping spree. I always parked my Mustang as far as I could away from other cars so that I didn't have to worry about any dings from the careless person parked beside me.

As Morgan and I stuffed our Victoria's Secret, Lazarus, Coach, and Foot Locker bags into the trunk of my car, a red Nissan Altima pulled up behind us.

"You ladies coming or going?" the passenger asked.

"That all depends," Morgan said in a flirtatious tone. Jazzy hadn't been out of her life but two months and she had already been on five dates, now working on number six.

I can't lie, though, the guy was looking rather edible. He was a light skin, good hair, gray eyed cutie pie. He was wearing a nice lightweight V-neck sweater and his sexy chest hairs were visible. He had sparkling diamond earrings in his ears, probably about

two carats each. I could just barely smell his cologne: Very Sexy
for men.

"We're going," I said, giving Morgan the back off look.

"Damn, I don't know if I want y'all to go now," the driver said.

I looked at him. Damn, he was fine too. They looked as though
they could have been brothers only the driver was a little darker
than the passenger was.

"Do y'all smoke?" the driver asked. "We got that sticky icky."
He winked.

I could tell Morgan was ready to put her lips on a blunt. But before she could respond, I did.

"Sorry, but we have to go," I said in a matter-of-fact, but
friendly tone.

"Speak for yourself," Morgan stated. "Where are you two fellas
headed?"

"The mall," they said as they both looked at each other chuckling. That was a stupid ass question of Morgan to ask.

"Of course you are," I said. "Now come on, Morgan. Let's let
these two fine gentlemen get their shop on."

"Y'all sure y'all don't want to go blaze one?" the driver asked.

"Nah, we good," I said. I headed towards the driver door, but
Morgan stayed put.

"Hold up," the passenger said, getting out of the car. "Let me at
least open the door for you, miss lady."

I guess chivalry wasn't dead. I paused and smiled. Hell, if a
brotha wanted to open the door for me, I was surely going to let
him. I hadn't had a door opened for me since York. Actually, I
hadn't even had a door opened for me before York.

When the passenger got out of the car he walked over by Morgan and looked at her with squinted eyes.

"Are you two related?" he asked.

"Yeah, right," I said, sucking my teeth. "Now you know we don't look a damn thing alike.

"Well, do you love her like a sister?" he asked.

I twisted my face, confused.

"Do you love her?" he asked calmly.

I giggled. I didn't know what he was getting at.

"Do you love her?" he said in a more stern voice. By this time his friend had gotten out of the driver's side and walked up behind me. Suddenly my stomach began to hurt. Chills came over me. You know that feeling you get when something just ain't right? Well, this was that feeling.

Keeping my eye on the driver without being too conspicuous, I didn't answer the question. My ignoring him only angered him more.

"You heard me, bitch," he said. "Do you love her?"

By now I could feel the driver's breath trickling down my neck. I could smell the Miller Genuine Draft on his breath. I tried to look behind me without turning my head. I looked up at Morgan and could see that the passenger now had a knife to her throat and all I remember him saying was, "Do you love her?"

Morgan had the fear of death in her eyes. This was happening all too fast.

"Yes," I replied, still trying to look behind me. Where was everybody? Why did I park so far from the mall? There was no one in sight to help us.

"Then if you love her you'll get your ass in the car without making a peep."

I looked up at the fish-gutting knife the passenger had to

Morgan's throat. It was pressed hard. I could tell she was in pain. I stood there frozen, unable to move.

"I said if you love her you'll get your ass in the car," he said, pressing the knife even tighter against Morgan's throat. I saw her blood begin to drip onto the blade of the knife.

The driver opened the back door of the car for me to get in. Trying to remain the cool ass bitch that I was, or at least thought I was, I smacked my lips and began to climb into the back seat slowly. I guess I was moving too slow because the driver grabbed me tightly by my hair and rammed me into the back seat where he joined me.

Still with the blade to Morgan's throat the passenger shoved Morgan into the front passenger seat.

"Think about jumping out and your friend is dead," he said, looking at Morgan then back at me. He winked at me. "But not until I fuck her first."

Both men began laughing.

Morgan sat in the front seat trembling. She was even too afraid to turn her head to look back at me. I could see a tear running down the left side of her face.

He walked around to the driver's side and got back into the car. He gunned the gas, looked over at Morgan and said, "Get ready for the ride of your life, sweetheart." Then he drove off.

"Keep your muthafuckin' heads down," the guy riding with me in the back seat yelled as I looked out of the window. I was trying to figure out where in the fuck they were taking us.

"Yo, Tiny," the driver said. "Give them one of those magazines to read so that their eyes don't wander."

"Good idea," Tiny said, scrambling for a couple of the magazines that were on the back seat floor.

Now I knew that this cat's name was Tiny. That wasn't telling me much, but if I lived through this ordeal, I'd surely find out who the fuck this Tiny was.

Tiny threw a magazine around at Morgan, slapping her in the face with it.

"Read it," the driver said to her. "Don't look up. Eyes down on the magazine, baby. Eyes down."

It was obvious they didn't want us to be able to figure out where they were taking us. They didn't want us looking up at street signs or anything. This only let me know that Morgan and I weren't their first victims, and we probably wouldn't be their last. Not unless I could help it.

Morgan grabbed the magazine. She turned back and looked at me. I'll never forget the look in her eyes. Never. Her eyes were telling me to do something to save us. Her eyes were asking me why I was letting this happen to us. I could read her mind. It said, "Harlem, you're supposed to be the baddest bitch. Protect us. Do something. Use those street skills and knowledge you're always bragging about having."

I felt like a punk because I couldn't do shit.

WHAM!

"Didn't I say keep your eyes on the book, bitch?" the driver said, slapping Morgan. I guess she had looked at me a little too long.

My blood boiled. I didn't give a fuck what those bastards planned on doing to me, but they were fuckin' with my girl, my best friend, my partna . . . my muthafuckin' ace. I wanted them to die. Never had I wished death upon anybody and truly meant it, but I wanted those two sons of bitches dead with every ounce of my soul and I wanted their blood on my hands.

We drove for about fifteen minutes before the car came to a stop. Morgan and I didn't dare look up from our magazines. Mine was an *Essence* magazine. I was flipping pages, but I wasn't reading. I was thinking about how in the fuck to escape from this nightmare. I turned my last page and there was some type of form to fill out. It was either a survey or a sweepstakes entry form. Someone named Amy Brown had completed it. At least that's what the handwritten words looked like anyway. An address was filled in also. It looked like 5734 Aqler Peak. I repeated what I thought I read to be the name and address fifty times over in my head until it was a permanent fixture in my memory. I assumed Amy was probably one of their girlfriends or something. I wonder if she had any idea what type of person she was sleeping with every night.

"It's show time," Tiny said, as he snatched the magazine out of my hand and threw it back on the floor. He opened the door, grabbed me by my hair and dragged me out of the car.

"Muthafucka, I would have walked out if you had just asked me to," I said angrily. This bastard had just gotten mud all over my brand new white Guess jeans. Even at a time like this, little shit like that was pissing me off.

"Oh, yours has a fly mouth," the driver said as he turned off the ignition, leaving the headlights on, and climbed over next to Morgan. He unlocked her door and pushed her out with him right behind her. Morgan fell to the dirty ground.

"Please don't hurt us," Morgan began to beg. She hadn't said one word during the entire drive, but now she feared for her life. We were in a wooded tree area that only God knew where. It wasn't looking good for Morgan and me.

"Don't beg these niggas for shit," I said, tightening my lips. "I'd rather die than beg these bitches for mercy." But Morgan wasn't on the same page as me as she continued begging.

"Please, we'll do anything. Just don't hurt us, please," Morgan began sobbing.

"Fuck," the driver said. "We've got us a cryer on our hands. The pussy ain't never good with a bitch weeping in your ear."

They both laughed. I grew angrier.

"Well, if you're going to fuck us then just do it," I said. "It shouldn't take but what, two minutes tops?" I looked down at their private areas inferring that they had small penises. I wanted to make them so mad at me that they hurt only me and not Morgan.

"Tell your girlfriend to shut up," the driver said, grabbing Morgan by her throat that was seeping blood from where she had been scratched with the knife.

"Please, Harlem," Morgan spoke through his chokehold. I looked away and he released Morgan.

I looked around but there was nothing but trees. I didn't know where we were. It was dark now, with the exception of the headlights from their car. There were just so many trees. The next thing I knew my face hit the ground. I had been thrown face down to the ground. I could feel my pants being pulled off of me. I lay there with my nails clawed to the ground. Then I saw the trees again. Tiny had turned me over. Before I knew it, he was inside of me. I couldn't believe it. As he rammed himself inside of me I just laid there. My thoughts turned to God. I asked Him why He was allowing this to happen. I asked Him why didn't He love me. I asked Him to make them stop, but He didn't.

"No, no!" I heard Morgan screaming.

I looked to my right and about six feet beside me was Morgan. She was lying on her stomach. She was butt naked and in pain. The driver was humping her violently.

"Oh, God, no!" Morgan screamed.

I could tell from her anguished scream that he just wasn't having sex with her from the back, but that he was sodomizing her. I could only imagine how painful that was for Morgan. I grew angrier. I was so mad at what was happening to Morgan that I never even realized that Tiny had already reached his climax by cumming inside of me. My thoughts were on Morgan. I wanted to save her, but I couldn't.

"Oh, shit, you got the bomb ass pussy," Tiny said as he laid his body on top of mine to rest. He was huffing and puffing in my ear. He sounded like a wild animal.

"You gon' love her pussy," Tiny said to his partner-in-crime as he lay there on top of me.

His partner was too busy humiliating my best friend to pay attention. He was ramming himself inside of her as hard as he could to cause her as much pain possible. He started making sounds like a bear. I knew he was about to cum. I wanted him to hurry up and cum so that he would leave her alone.

"Oh, shit," he said as he rammed himself in and out of Morgan. "Oh, fuck. Oh shit. Goddamn!"

He threw his head back and allowed his fluids to jerk inside of Morgan, then he pulled himself out of her and used his hand to squirt any remaining semen onto Morgan. She had stopped crying by now. She was in complete shock.

I closed my eyes in disgust. Any other person would have prayed to God right about now, but not me. I knew it would be in vain. When I opened my eyes, the driver was standing over Tiny and me. I immediately looked over to see what Morgan was doing. She was laying on the ground stiff.

"My turn to get in that ass now," he said as he stood over us. That was their signal to switch. Tiny got up off of me.

"You the bad ass bitch," the driver said, standing over my half naked body. "I can't wait for you to feel my wrath."

I looked up at him. I could tell by his movements and the sound of his hand slapping against his skin that he was stroking his dick. I imagined taking the knife he had in his hand and cutting it off. My thoughts ended with him turning me over onto my stomach. I felt his hands opening up my butt cheeks to enter. My eyes began to well up with tears. I bit down on my bottom lip and held them back.

Daddy always said that crying doesn't get you anywhere, I told myself over and over in my head. It wasn't time to cry. It was time to be smart. I never wanted to be fucked in the ass consensual, let alone unconsensual.

"Oh, you only like fuckin' in the ass?" I said to him in a snide tone. "You don't know how to please a real pussy, huh? What's the matter, you can't make a real woman cum?"

I knew that would anger him. I knew he would want to prove me wrong. Just like I expected he turned me back over, but unexpectedly he slashed me across the face with the knife. I felt as though my entire mug had been split open. I could feel the blood pouring down the right side of my face where he had cut me. It was stinging.

"You talk too fuckin' much," he said. "It's about time someone shuts you up once and for all. Guess who that someone is going to be?"

He entered me slow as if he was making love to me, staring into my eyes the entire time. He knew he was making me sick.

Slowly he entered me and began kissing on my neck. Then he forced his tongue into my mouth, when I wouldn't return the affection he began humping me harder and harder, but he was still moving slowly.

"I'm gonna fuck you all night, big mouth," he said as he started laughing. Then he grazed the wound on my face with his tongue. My blood covered his mouth. He was this wild beast on top of me doing his business. I closed my eyes so that no tears would even think about escaping. Of all the people in the world, I wasn't about to let this fucker make me cry.

As he continued ramming himself inside of me I looked over to Morgan where Tiny was giving her a hand job. I guess he couldn't get it back up after cumming in me, but he couldn't resist the sexual torture.

Morgan was moaning in agony. It looked as though Tiny was trying to ram his entire fist into her. I could feel her pain. I closed my eyes, but I could still see everything taking place in the light of their car headlights.

It felt like an hour had passed and he was still inside of me. I wanted it to be over. I did the only other thing I could think to do. I started humping him back. I started humping him back harder and harder. I had to hurry up and make him cum so that he would go away. I needed to see about Morgan.

"I knew you couldn't resist this dick," he said, getting excited. "I knew you couldn't. This is the best dick you've ever had. Say it, bitch!"

I wouldn't dare say that shit to him. Then he began choking me. His grip around my neck was so tight that I could hardly breathe.

"Say it!" he yelled.

"This is the best dick I've ever had," I obliged.

"Fuck me back, baby. That's right fuck me back," he said moaning.

I knew he was about to cum so I put my back into it, hips grinding and all.

"Oh, shit, bitch! Oh, shit you fuckin' bitch," he said as I felt him release himself inside of me. I wanted to scream. I wanted to die. Oh, God why?

"Lick it off," he said as he pulled himself out of me and placed his penis on my lips. "Lick it off for daddy."

I gave him a sexy look then opened my mouth wide. I bit down so hard. I was hoping to take a hunk right out of him, but I can't remember if I did or not. I was bludgeoned with his fist and knocked out. My eyes closed. I don't know if they'll ever open again. So this is what death feels like.

13. What Goes Up...

When I opened my eyes the first thing I saw was the ceiling of the hospital room. I could smell that hospital scent. I knew exactly where I was. I slowly lowered my eyes and sitting in a chair next to my bed, staring dead into my eyes, was Reese.

"Hey, baby girl," she said softly, standing up out of the chair and walking over to me.

"Reese?" I forced out in a groggy voice.

"Don't try to speak, baby girl. Just rest. It's okay. It's all over now."

I hurt so bad. I was in so much pain that it was unbelievable. I felt as though the devil was inside my body burning me from the inside out. My vagina was throbbing, my head ached, and my chest felt as though a ton of bricks was sitting on it. My face felt numb and had a stinging sensation.

I closed my eyes and took a deep breath. It hurt like hell to just breathe. I opened my eyes again and looked at Reese again. She looked different than crackhead Reese. She looked like she did when her and daddy were together. Her hair wasn't matted like how I had been used to seeing it. It was pulled back into a long curly ponytail and she had on a nice clean sweatsuit. Fruit of the Loom or something.

I could smell the lotion she was wearing. The eucalyptus that it contained completely covered the pissy smell I was used to her reeking of.

"What are you doing here?" I asked. And where's Morgan?"

"I'm here to see you, baby girl," Reese replied as she rubbed her hand down my hair. "You've been pretty much out of it for two days. I've been sitting here waiting for you to come fully to."

"You've been here for two days?" I asked with a look of disbelief on my face.

"Umm hmm," Reese said proudly. "A nice nurse gave me toiletries and even bought me these clothes and tennis shoes."

Reese lifted her leg to show me the pair of white tennis shoes she had on. The weren't Nike or anything, but they were clean.

Reese continued, "She got them from the Dollar General store, but I ain't complaining. Hell, I ain't looked this good in years."

Reese laughed. She could tell that I wasn't in a laughing mood so hers quickly faded. "I washed my hair and one of the other nurses did it for me when she got off duty. She put some stuff in it called Wet and Wavy. It brings out the natural curl of my hair. Do you like it?" Reese said, taking her hand to pat her ponytail.

I turned my head away from her without answering.

"Anyway, like I said," Reese continued as she walked back over to the chair and sat down. "I ain't left this hospital since I found out you was here."

"You mean to tell me that you ain't left out of this building for not even five minutes?" I said. Reese knew what I was getting at.

"I ain't thought about no drugs, Harlem," Reese said sincerely. "You was on my mind, baby girl. That's when I realized that crack ain't nothing but a mind drug. I was too scared and worried about you to even think twice about it. I swear it, baby girl. Now I ain't gonna lie and say that I didn't want none, that if someone handed me a pipe right now that I wouldn't smoke it. But right now, the situation is what it is. I'm only worried about you, not getting high."

"Well as you can see," I said, trying to scoot up into a more comfortable position, only there was no such thing as comfort with the shape I was in, "I'm much better now, so you can go back to doing what you do. I mean now that I won't be on your mind and all anymore. You're free to go do you."

Reese sighed. I had succeeded at hurting her feelings and at making her two days of being clean seem like nothing.

"I ain't going back to that life, Harlem," Reese said as her eyes welled up with tears. "I know it sounds like all talk right now, but I mean it. I almost lost you and all I would have been able to have as a memory is you cussing me for coming into your store begging because of a crack habit. I'm not going to miss out on the life of another one of my babies because of no crack, Harlem. I mean it. You've got to believe me. I know God is going to get us through this. I'm gonna get some help and beat this thing."

I clenched my teeth together hard. I wanted to feel for Reese and to believe her and to believe in her. I really did, but it was so hard to believe in anything right now, especially God.

"I know actions speak louder than words so I guess I'm just going to have to show you," Reese said. "I'm doing this for you, Harlem. But most importantly, I'm doing this for me. I can't live like this any more. Doing the things I do for a drug."

Reese put her head down in shame. I could see her tears planting dark wet spots on her light gray sweatpants.

That was my mother sitting there. I wanted so badly to reach out and hold her. I wanted to forgive her, but I felt as though she deserved my hate.

"Knock, knock," a male voice said.

I looked over to the door and York was standing there with a huge bouquet of mixed flowers. It had to be about two feet long.

"Can I come in?" York said in a hesitant tone.

I nodded yes and he entered. Behind him was Jazzy. Jazzy didn't even want to look at me. His head was hanging, and if I wasn't mistaken, it looked as though he had been crying.

"Hey, love," York said, laying the flowers across my stomach.

My face must have been fucked up because he looked at me and shook his head, then buried his face in his hand.

"It's all right," Jazzy said, walking over to comfort his friend by putting his hand on his shoulder.

"Hi, Jazzy," I said, taking my attention off of York. That fool was about to make me cry and you know how I am about crying in front of people, about crying period.

"Harlem World," Jazzy replied.

"Jazzy you said?" Reese stood up. She had been indiscreetly just sitting there staring at him.

"Yes, ma'am," Jazzy replied.

"You're Peanut's boy, right?" Reese said to Jazzy.

"Yes ma'am," Jazzy said, shocked. No one called his father Peanut anymore. He knew Reese and his pops must have gone way back for her to still be calling him by his old Columbus street name.

"I uhh, thought he lived in Atlanta now. He ain't back is he?" Reese asked.

"He does live in Atlanta now," Jazzy said, smiling, happy to meet one of his dad's peoples from back in the day. "How do you know him?"

"Well, uhh, I don't *know him* know him. You know what I mean?" Reese said, acting peculiar. I noticed how from that point on, Reese couldn't take her eyes off of Jazzy.

"I'm sorry about all of this," York said as he walked closer to me. "You don't have to be sorry," I moaned as I tried to move my aching body. "You didn't do it. You weren't there."

I finally just decided to grin and bear the pain by pulling my body up. I felt like every bone in my body cracked.

York caught on to how I exaggerated the part about him not being there. I knew it wasn't his fault, but something inside of me wanted him to feel guilty. I wanted him to think that if he hadn't played me that day by making me walk home because of an old beef with his sister, that perhaps we all would had been together somewhere on a double date. Then Morgan and I wouldn't have even been in a position to get caught up with those psychos.

"Don't, Harlem," York said.

"Don't what?" I asked.

"Don't make me feel any worse than I already do. I wasn't there for you—to protect you—and it's eating me up inside," York said with every sincere bone in his body.

York placed his hands in a triangle position over his nose and mouth. He closed his eyes and took a deep breath. When he opened his eyes he had the same look of disgust with my disfigured face as he had when he first entered the hospital room.

I touched my face and could feel a knot on the side of my head. I hoped to God I didn't look like Tom Cruise in *Vanilla Sky.*

"I never wanted to see you hurt, Harlem, in spite of everything,"

York said. "But seeing you at the Shark Bar with ol' dude did something to me, man. I just lost it."

"Yeah, I could tell just how much you lost it by the way my store looked," I said.

"What?" York said, taking offense. "So you do really think that I did that to your store?"

Trying to tame the flame that everyone could feel warming up the room, Reese jumped in and attempted to change the subject.

"Those are some lovely flowers," she said in regards to the bouquet of flowers Jazzy had in his hands. I hadn't even noticed them.

"Oh yeah, they were for Morgan," Jazzy said, putting his head down and pausing. "But I guess you can have them, Harlem."

Jazzy walked over and handed me the flowers. He couldn't look at me as he held back tears. I could tell that it was hard for both Jazzy and York to fight back tears. They weren't about to let us see them cry although we could tell they already had been. But I didn't blame them. That's when people see you as weak and you feel weak. I never wanted to put myself in that type of vulnerable state.

"Well, I guess we better get going, huh, York?" Jazzy said, taping him on the arm.

"Uh, yeah, man, yeah," York said, clearing his throat. "You take care, Harlem. All right?"

"Yeah. You too," I said as the two men headed out of the door. "I'll be sure to give these flowers to Morgan for you since that's who you bought them for in the first place."

Jazzy looked at me strangely. Just then two detectives, escorted by a nurse, showed up in the doorway. York and Jazzy exited and the new guest entered.

"Harlem," the nurse said. "These two officers would like to talk with you about what happened to you and your friend. Do you think you can talk with them?"

I nodded yes.

The nurse cleared the path for the two detectives and left the room. The detective behind the other one closed the door behind the nurse. When he turned back around it was as if we had each seen a ghost. At first I didn't know where I had seen him before, but then it came to me. He was that same police officer who had showed up at our apartment in Greenbriar that time I called the police on Reese. He was that same officer who left me with Reese to get beat half to death.

He paused for a moment then he shook off his memory of me. Reese didn't recognize him, but I sure as the hell did.

"Hello, ma'am," the first detective said to Reese. "I'm Detective Somore."

"Nice to meet you, detective," Reese said, standing up from the chair beside my bed and shaking the hand that he had extended to her. "Are you going to find who did this to my daughter?"

"Ma'am, Detective Logan over there and myself are going to do everything possible to find the people who did this to your daughter and her friend."

"Thank you. Thank you so much," Reese said sincerely. Reese moved aside so that the officer could question me.

Detective Somore pulled up the chair that Reese had been sitting in while Detective Logan stood up on the other side of me.

"So, Miss Jones, can you tell us what happened, starting at the beginning?" Somore said.

"Morgan and I went shopping. After shopping we walked to my car. Two men drove up, kidnapped us at knifepoint, and the rest I'm sure you know," I said as if I was reciting the alphabet.

I looked over at Reese. I didn't want to explain everything that had happened in front of her. Detective Logan picked up on that and asked Reese if she minded leaving the room. Reese didn't mind at all. She told me that she would be waiting right outside the door.

Once Reese left the room Somore started up again.

"Did you know these two men prior to the incident? Had you ever seen them before?"

"No and no," I said with an attitude.

Somore looked over at Logan like "Can you believe this little heifer? Here we are trying to help her black ass out and she wants to play hard."

"Did you get their names? Did they call one another by their names, a street name, or anything?"

I shrugged my shoulders. This muthafucker was acting too damn anxious, like they had been waiting up at the hospital for two days, like Reese, waiting for me to come to so that they could drill me. I had never known the cops to show such urgency. Then it dawned on me. It was election year. Perhaps the mayor, governor, and who ever else had been riding their department about the rate of unsolved crimes.

"Look, Miss Jones, we're only here to help," Somore said. "But we need *your* help so that we can make sure that this kind of thing doesn't happen to anyone else. You wouldn't want this to happen to other girls out there would you? We only want to help. So you can tell us everything you and you're friend intended on doing with the men who did this to you. No matter why you went to the woods with them, you didn't deserve this. So tell us everything. We just want to help."

My blood began to boil. This officer was basically trying to say that Morgan and I were hoes trickin' with these dudes.

"Who are you two kidding?" I asked. "I know you're not going to really do anything to help. Cops show up at the scene and take notes because they have to. They don't really want to help you, do they, Detective Logan?" I said in a sarcastic tone.

By now Somore had had just about enough of my mouth. He slammed his notepad shut and stood up.

"How would your friend—Morgan is her name right? How would Morgan feel about you not wanting to cooperate in helping to catch the men who did this?"

"I don't know. Why don't you go ask her?" I said.

The two detectives looked at one another then Somore grabbed a hold of my arm. It hurt like hell, but I didn't flinch.

"How about *you* ask her? Come on, let's go ask Morgan," Somore said angrily.

Logan helped me out of the bed in a more gentle motion. Then the three of us walked out of the room. Reese was still standing outside the door.

"Is everything okay?" she asked with a look of concern.

"Everything is fine, ma'am," Somore responded to her, scooting my body that was struggling to move down the hall. Logan was right behind me trying to assist me by taking my arm, which I jerked away. He didn't want to help me thirteen years ago so fuck him thirteen years later.

Somore led me down one hospital corridor after another. I started getting achy and dizzy, but I was a warrior and I wasn't going to let this pig know that he was getting to me. After an elevator ride and a few twist and turns down more halls, Somore finally led me into a room. The curtain was closed. I stood in the doorway afraid of what I might see behind the curtain. Afraid that I would see just how bad my face looked by looking at Morgan's.

"Go on, Miss Big Shit," Somore said.

"Detective," Logan said, almost questioning his partner's tactics.

Detective Somore ignored him and gave me a little nudge towards Morgan's bed.

I walked over slowly and pulled the curtain back. Morgan was lying there sleeping like an angel. She looked exactly like an angel, a bruised up one anyway. They must have drugged her up pretty good because she was out of it, as stiff as a board. Her face was bruised and she had cuts around her mouth. I could see where her earlobe was ripped from her double pierced earrings being snatched out of her ears.

I swear on everything that I wanted to drop to my knees. But instead I stayed strong.

"Go on and talk to her," Somore insisted. "Tell her how you won't cooperate in finding the creeps who did this to her. Look at her and tell her, Harlem."

Somore was really starting to annoy me with his big mouth.

"I don't want to talk to her right now. Can't you see she's sleeping?" I scolded Somore. "She couldn't even hear me if I tried to talk to her," I said, snapping back at the detective. I just wanted him to shut the fuck up and give me a moment with my friend.

"You damn right she won't hear you," Somore said, walking up on me. "Because she's dead. Look at her, Miss. Jones. She's dead. Morgan is dead."

I refused to allow Somore's words to enter my ears. I looked down at my best friend. She wasn't dead. She couldn't be. She was only sleeping.

"She's dead, Harlem, and you won't help us find her killers," Somore said.

"No," I said in a low tone. "No. No."

I could feel my body begin to quiver.

"Yes, Harlem," Somore said. "She's dead."

"No, she's not," I said, shaking my head. I refused to believe it. "You're just trying to play games with me. She's not dead. Morgan is not dead. God would have ended my life before hers. She's not dead."

"Then I guess you owe the good Lord one," Somore said. "He decided to spare your life instead of hers."

I turned my attention to detective Logan. His eyes were moist. He put his head down and ran his hands down his face as if to wipe away his emotions. What he didn't say confirmed the worst. That Detective Somore wasn't using some evil tactic to get me to talk. Morgan was, in fact, dead.

I turned around and looked at Morgan's cold lifeless body. Rage came over me. I kept seeing those fuckers raping her and hitting her over and over again. My body began to tremble and I had to grit my teeth to keep my wails locked in my throat. I clutched my fist so tight that my nails dug into my flesh. I began breathing so heavily through my nose that I thought I was going to pass out. Detective Logan must have thought the same thing because he immediately ran over to me and caught me right as I began to drop.

"No," I said. "No." Those are the only words that I could manage to say. With my jaws still locked, screams seeped out of my throat.

"Are you willing to help us now?" Somore asked over my screams. "Look at her, Harlem. She was your best friend and look at her now. They sodomized her. Then when they were finished doing that, they used their hand to rape her. They tore her insides out, Harlem. She lost so much blood. So much blood. She struggled to stay alive these past couple of days, but this morning she gave up. Are you going to give up, too, Harlem? You have to help us."

"No!" I continued screaming. "No. Morgan, No! God, I hate you! I hate you, God! I hate you! No!"

Somore walked over and pulled me away from Logan. He made me look at Morgan. He wanted me to lock in my head what those bastards had done so that I would do everything possible to help them bring Tiny and his partner to justice.

Looking at Morgan didn't make me want to cooperate. Looking at her made me angry. I was at a boiling point so I closed my eyes. I closed my eyes and thought about how I wouldn't rest until I saw those two son of a bitches who did this to us dead. Those muthafuckers definitely needed to hear footsteps behind them in the dark. My footsteps.

I didn't even want to go to Morgan's funeral. Nothing had changed over the years. I still didn't want to step foot inside of a church. I was devastated. I couldn't believe this was happening, that I was burying my best friend. I still didn't want to believe that she was dead and I knew that seeing her laying there in that casket would be final confirmation. All hopes would be gone of Morgan calling me up on the phone or ever walking into the store again.

Losing Morgan was incomprehensible. I felt like God would send me an angel every so often and then Indian give. Morgan was more to me than anyone will ever know. How could she die? Why didn't she fight? She never was a fighter. I told her ass she had to learn to fight. Why didn't she learn? I felt so betrayed and once again abandoned.

It took everything in me to get dressed to go to Morgan's funeral. I can't even tell you what clothes I had on because I don't even remember getting dressed. I could have shown up at that funeral butt naked for all I know. The day was just that much of a blur to me and that's how zoned out I was. But I do remember that something drastic occurred at the funeral. It was something that was a true life changing moment for me.

When I walked into the church the first person I saw was Reese. She smiled, but my face was too frozen to return one. Then I saw York and Jazzy. My eyes briefly met with theirs.

I was to be seated on the front pew. Morgan's family considered me family so they had a space for me. They had even offered for me to ride in the limo, but I declined. Limo rides were too much like a celebration to me, like a prom or wedding or some shit. I didn't want to celebrate. I wanted to mourn. I wanted to be sad and angry at the loss of my best friend.

As I was escorted down the aisle, I saw Morgan's casket at the head of the church. I honestly felt as though my legs had given out. Like they had went numb. I felt like I was in a fuckin' Spike Lee Joint, floating down the aisle and shit.

I don't know who the usher was, but he asked me if I wanted to go up and see the body. I couldn't do it. I couldn't stand there over Morgan like that. He sat me down as others proceeded to view the body.

All I kept saying to myself was *this is some sick shit.* How muthafuckas just gon' go stand over her like that? She's dead. Let her rest in peace for Christ sakes. Get the fuck out of her face. I was so angry. When I die, send me straight to the oven. Fuck that!

Folks passed by to pay their respects to the family. Everybody was sorry. Every goddamn body was sorry. But it was me who was really sorry. I was sorry that it wasn't me in that casket instead of

Morgan. I wondered if everybody else in there thought that, too. When they walked by and offered their condolences, I wonder if they were really saying to themselves, "Why couldn't it have been you, Harlem? Why did they take Morgan and not you?" Their guess was as good as mine was. But I could assume that God wanted me to stay here and suffer.

As the funeral service took place, I pretty much stayed zoned out, stone-faced. It was surreal. I still couldn't believe I was at my girl's funeral. And I wanted to cry. I really thought today of all days would be the day that I cried, but I was much too angry to be sad. I was consumed with revenge.

I hadn't paid much attention to the program that was handed to me when I entered the church. I was so distraught that the words danced around the pages. I hadn't even tried to put the words to-gether on the program, that was until I saw what I thought was my name printed in the program. I know my own name when I see it, no matter how blurry or twisted the words appeared.

I took a deep breath and calmed myself down. I rubbed my eyes clear and realized that my name was next to the word of what I thought read eulogy. My heart dropped to my stomach. Once again, the words started dancing around the pages like crazy. They be-came far too scrambled and blurry for me to make out. I wanted to find the person in charge and confirm that that is what the program read. And if it in fact read that, I needed to let them know that it was a misprint. But before I could do anything, I was introduced by the church pastor to read the eulogy.

I just sat there frozen stiff.

"Go on, Harlem," Morgan's mom said, putting her arm around me. "Morgan would want you to."

I couldn't say no after that heap of a guilt trip Morgan's mother had just placed on my shoulders. I walked up to the podium and the pastor handed me the eulogy to read. Sweat was pouring from my forehead. I looked out and saw everyone waiting patiently for me to begin. I didn't know what to do, so I did the only thing that came to me.

"I can't read the eulogy," I said.

"Go on, sistah. You can do it. It's all right," someone shouted out.

"I really can't read it," I said. "You see, I can't read."

The church sighed. Morgan's mother looked up in shock, not to mention Reese.

"You see, when it came to reading, Morgan was my eyes. She's the only person who ever knew about my problem. It's not that I can't *read* read. I mean sometimes I can go just fine for a paragraph or two, but then the words start flipping around 'on the paper. I confided this to Morgan, not because I wanted to, but because she forced me to. It was back when she was selling those magazines. The girl wouldn't take no for an answer."

Some giggled, remembering back to her days as a persistent magazine saleswoman.

"Morgan wouldn't get off of my doorstep until I told her exactly why I didn't want to purchase a magazine from her," I continued. "And when I told her that I didn't read she went on that spiel about my ancestors."

Once again, folks let out a chuckle. It was obvious that they had been forced to purchase a magazine or two from her back in the day.

"She just kept pushing. She knew there was something more to it. Why I confided in her I have no idea. But I did. I told her that I didn't read because I couldn't read. I explained to her how the

letters played tricks on me by changing their directions and flipping on the pages. It was Morgan who told me that I was dyslexic.
And she told me, "If you buy these magazines, I'll do everything I
can to help you read them. And if that doesn't work, I'll read them
to you myself."

I had to pause. I had to fight and choke back tears before I
continued.

"Morgan tried her best to get me to go back to school. She said
since I knew what was wrong with me that I could get special help.
But I had used her so much for a crutch that I didn't see the need
for school anymore. Morgan helped me with my business. I would
have never been able to have a business if it wasn't for her. And now
she's gone."

People started wailing. A couple of folks even had to be carried
out of the church.

I continued. "As I stand here today, unable to read these kind
words about my best friend, I feel like I have failed her." My voice
broke up.

"Oh, no, baby," Morgan's mother cried. "Morgan loved you."

"So I'm going to make this promise to Morgan's spirit in front of
all of you." I paused and gathered myself. "Morgan, I don't know
how long it's going to take, but one day I'm going to be able to read
this eulogy out loud. So if that means I have to go back to school to
learn to do so, then that's exactly what I'm going to do."

Everyone began to clap. Morgan's mother managed to walk up
to me and put her arms around me. She was crying so hard. I put
my arms around her.

"That was brave, Harlem," she said to me. "I know Morgan is
so proud of you."

"Thank you," I replied.

Morgan's mother took the eulogy from my hand with her trembling hand and said, "I know I'm no Morgan. God knows no one could ever replace my daughter, but if she were here, I know this is what she would do. Now let's read this eulogy, Harlem. Together."

I felt like a first grader trying to read big words as Morgan's mother used her finger to go over the eulogy word by word. She was crying and I was stumbling on the word bereavement and others here and there, but no one seemed to mind. After we finished they all clapped as Morgan's mother and I embraced. There are no words for how significant that experience was to the rest of my days on this earth.

I was burying my best friend that day, but at the same time I had to dig up a painful and embarrassing part of myself that I had wanted to stay buried forever.

But I felt like a part of me had been set free, along with Morgan's soul. And even though Morgan's soul was free, I still felt as though it wouldn't be at peace until a certain matter was taken care of. It was a matter that I didn't feel comfortable leaving up to the police to handle. It was a matter that if I myself wasn't careful at handling, just might land me in a plot next to Morgan's.

Trying to recall that address I had seen in the *Essence* magazine while in the back seat of the kidnapper's car was hell. It was hard enough trying to unscramble the words as I saw them on the paper. But I was relentless in remembering until the address popped into my head. 5734 Aqler Peak. That was the address.

I went to the library and asked a librarian to help me locate the area on a city map or something. She directed me to the city atlas. My adrenaline was pumping so fast after remembering the address, that even if I did know how to read up to par, I probably still wouldn't have been able to read an atlas. I knew that every letter on the map was going to be backwards so I told the librarian that I had forgotten my reading glasses and wouldn't be able to see.

The librarian kindly walked me over to the city atlas and performed the search for me.

"There's no such a street name," the librarian said after searching for a few minutes.

"Yes there is," I said with certainty. "There has to be. I saw it."

"Where did you see it?" she asked.

"I don't know. I can't remember," I said, becoming agitated. I buried my fingers into my forehead and massaged my temples with my thumbs. I was tensing up. Maybe if I relaxed the right letters would come to me.

"I'm sorry ma'am, but I just don't see it," the librarian said. "How about we try to do an Internet search on Yahoo!?"

I followed her over to a computer where she sat down and began punching in keys.

"Now what was that address again?" she asked.

"5734 Aqler Peak," I said.

Once again she started punching keys on the keyboard.

"Nope," she said. The only street that is remotely similar is Agler Park."

The librarian moved her head over slightly and pointed to the street name. Those were the letters I had seen. That was it and I knew just where that street was.

"That's it! That's it!" I exclaimed, hugging the librarian. "Thank you so much. Thank you so much." I even kissed her on the cheek. She was in shock at first, but then felt happy for being so much help to a patron.

As I ran out of the library door I ran smack into a gentleman that was entering. I had to take a double take. No it wasn't who I thought it was.

"If it ain't Harlem," DC said in this aggravating tone. A little girl was holding his hand. I imagine it was his daughter.

"DC," I said in a cold tone.

"You go on in, honey," he said to the little girl. "Daddy will be right in."

"Okay, daddy," his little girl said as she went into the library.

"I'm sorry to hear about what happened to you and your girl, Morgan," DC said in a sincere tone. "That shit was foul, even for me. And you know I'm known to be treacherous."

I couldn't believe this fool was standing here bragging about his gansta persona.

"Yeah, well thanks," I said, trying to brush pass him, but he grabbed hold of my hand. I looked down at his hand on my hand as if he was crazy.

"Seriously, I am sorry," he repeated. "I mean, I know I might have maybe done some dumb shit in my time. You know, dumb shit like flattened the tires on a car, make crank phone calls to scare a muthafucka, or even broke up some shit in a bookstore. But no way would I have ever done something as sick and perverted as that. I hope they get the psychos who did this to y'all. I really do."

I was silent. I couldn't move. Everything was spinning. I guess I started sleeping with both eyes closed too soon. DC's snake ass had bitten me. I knew his fuckin' MO. I should have known it was him who fucked up the Suga Shop.

"You take care now, Harlem," DC said as he let go of my hand.

He winked and let go of the door as he went into the library to join his daughter. The door hit me on the shoulder. Words can't explain the rage that came over my body.

I walked to my car and grabbed my gun from out of my glovebox. I cocked it and headed back into the library like a warrior. Folks got the fuck out of my way when they saw me raging through there looking up and down the isles in an attempt to find DC's punk ass.

Just as soon as I spotted him he looked up at me. He smiled, but when he saw what was in my hand his smile quickly faded. Before he could move I let one off right between his muthafuckin' eyes. I hated doing that shit in front of his daughter, but payback is a muthafuck and it can't tell time.

"Excuse me," a woman said as she attempted to enter the library door. I was standing there daydreaming about putting one in DC.

Her words knocked me back into reality. "I'm sorry," I said, moving out of her way so that she could enter the library.

Everything inside of me wanted to act out the vision I had just fantasized about in my head. There's nothing I would have enjoyed more than putting a bullet right between DC's eyes. I wanted so badly to walk to my car and get my piece for real, but fuck it. Him tearing up the store was some bitch ass material shit. Morgan's life had been taken. I had bigger fish to fry than to worry about DC. That one I would have to take Reese's advice on and let God handle.

After leaving the library I went home to begin executing my plan. It was getting late, but I couldn't wait another minute. I had to go case out that house. I just had to. Sooner or later I was going to run up on one of those fuckers and put a bullet through his head.

I put on some black jeans and a black long sleeve ribbed shirt. I put on my black shoe snow boots with the hard rubber bottoms. There wasn't any snow on the ground, but they had good traction just in case I had to chase one of them bastards down.

I stood in the bathroom mirror and parted my hair into six sections straight back. I put them in cornrows and then put on my black Gucci fishing hat. My gear was right for the job. Now all I had to do was get my mind right. I walked over to the mirror that was attached to my dresser. I stood there looking at myself.

"Harlem, is this what you really want to do?" I spoke to the mad woman in the mirror. "Do you really want to take someone else's life?"

After all, what right did I have although I saw it as an eye for an eye? Did I have the right to play judge and jury?

The mad woman in the mirror ran her index finger down the scar on her face that was healing up well, but that was a permanent reminder of the assault.

"Hell, yeah," the mad woman responded. "I have every right to play judge and jury."

I grabbed my keys, hopped into my ride and went searching for my prey.

It took me a minute to find the address numbers but it took me no time at all to find the street. At first, I passed the house right up. Once I realized that I had done so it was too late. I didn't want to back up and bring extra attention to myself. So instead I circled the block and parked a few houses down from the targeted address.

One hour went by and there was no activity. Two hours went by and then two hours turned into four. No one came and no one went. The night was a bust. I gave it another half hour or so and then I dipped.

I felt like a failure driving home. And in addition to that, I worried as to whether the next day I would still have the balls to carry out my plan.

When I pulled up into my driveway there was someone sitting on my porch. Off the bat I realized that it was Reese. She was wearing this cute little white terry cloth hooded jogging suit and her hair was pressed down straight. She really looked good. It seemed as though each time I saw her she was looking better and better. It was kind of like seeing Halle Berry play the crackhead in the movie *Jungle Fever*, then seeing her today on the red carpet.

When Reese saw me pull into the driveway she stood up with excitement. I could tell that she had something that she really wanted to share with me.

I pulled the Mustang into the garage. Reese hurried in behind me.

"Baby girl, I've got great news," she said as I stepped out of the car.

"Let me guess. You saved money with Geico?" I joked with a faint smile, closing the car door behind me.

"No, silly," Reese said. "But I'm glad to see you joking. It's been a while since I've seen you smile. And that's a shame considering you have one of the most beautiful smiles in the world. But anyway looky herre, looky herre."

Reese pulled a piece of paper out of her jacket pocket.

"Tah dah," she said, whipping it out and handing it to me.

I took it from her hand, wondering what it was.

"What is it?" I asked, without even looking at it.

"It's an acceptance letter," she said with excitement. "I got accepted into the community college. Financial aid is going to pay for me to go."

I was honestly thrilled for Reese. It really looked as though she was dedicated to getting herself together. Although I was happy for her, at the same time I couldn't believe that my mother, the crackhead, was going to college and her daughter, a business owner, didn't even have a GED. All the same I was truly proud of Reese.

"I'm happy for you, Reese," I said with a smile.

"Thank you, baby girl," she said, staring down at the paper with a big Kool-Aid smile on her face.

"So where you headed to now?" I asked her.

"Back to the shelter," Reese said. "I caught the bus over here. I just had to share the good news with my baby girl."

I looked at my watch and said, "It's late. You're not going to lose your bed at the shelter are you?"

"Nah," Reese said. "They love me there. I got pull." She winked.

"Well, all right then," I said as I unlocked the side door garage entrance to my house.

"Then I guess I'll talk to you later," Reese said as she turned and headed down the driveway.

"Be careful," I said as I pressed the button to close the garage door. Slowly the door came down and I could see Reese's feet turning left once she got to the sidewalk. I hit the button to open the garage door back up.

"Hey, Reese!" I yelled.

"Yes," she said as if she had been hoping I called out to her.

"Do you wanna come in and celebrate over a drink or something?" I asked.

"It will have to be soda." She smiled. "No alcohol for me."

"How does ginger ale sound?" I asked her.

"Celebrating with you, Harlem," Reese said heartfelt. "A glass of water would be just fine."

I invited Reese into my home. She had never been inside, but she always knew where I lived. A few times I had looked out of my window and had sworn I seen her out there just watching the house.

"I got ginger ale and Cherry Coke," I said to Reese, peeking into the refrigerator.

"Cherry Coke," she said as she looked around my house in awe.

"Harlem, I am so proud of you," she said as tears came to her eyes. "Look at you, girl. This home is lovely. It doesn't even look like the same house as Grandmother Jones's. And it feels like a home too. And I bet the beds are soft."

I knew a hint when it was being thrown at me so I decided to catch it.

"You'll be sure to lose your bed tonight for certain," I said. "Why don't you just spend the night here?"

"Really?" Reese asked in disbelief.

I nodded my head yes.

"I would love to," she said, again her eyes watering.

We both stood in silence until I broke the mode.

"Oh, yeah, let me grab those Cherry Cokes."

"You got any ice cream?" Reese asked. "Praline Pecan. You know that was always our favorite."

Suddenly I thought back to when I was five years old and Reese would take me to Clown Cone ice-cream parlor to get a Praline Pecan cone almost every Saturday. When I opened the freezer and she saw two pints of Borden's Praline Pecan, she smiled. I could tell that she too was having the same exact memory.

I fixed Reese and I each a glass of Cherry Coke and a bowl of ice cream. We then went into the living room where I turned on the television. Of all the damn shows to be on it was *Imitation of Life*. I immediately picked up the remote.

"Don't turn," Reese said. "I've always loved this movie."

I left it on that channel then sat down on the couch next to Reese. We watched the movie in silence for a moment before Reese broke the silence.

"So how are your friends, Jazzy and that other guy?" Reese asked.

I was surprised she even remembered them, let alone Jazzy's name.

"Ahh," I said in an I don't want to talk about it tone.

"That Jazzy sure is a cutie pie, don't you think?" Reese said, waiting on the edge of her seat for me to respond.

"Yeah, he's all right," I said, shrugging my shoulders.

"Do you two see each other?" Reese asked.

"What's with all the questions about Jazzy?" I asked.

"I want to get to know you, Harlem, and the people you know."

"Oh," I said, gearing my attention back to the television, thinking about how many times I would have beat Sarah Jane's ass by now if she was my daughter.

"So is he your boyfriend? Jazzy I mean?"

"No," I said. "I was dating his friend, York. He was the other guy that came to the hospital. Jazzy and I could barely stand to stay in the same room together."

"Oh, good," Reese said. "I mean, I was just wondering."

I suppose Reese was just trying to be motherly and didn't know how to go about it. Watching her trying to converse with me about my love life was kind of funny. By the end of the movie Reese was snorting, snotting, and crying a river. The movie was a bit of a tearjerker, but you know me.

"I don't know about you," I said, yawning and stretching, "but I'm beat."

"So am I," Reese agreed.

"I'll show you up to the guestroom. You can sleep there."

"Where do you sleep?" Reese asked.

"Back there," I said, pointing to my room. "That's my bedroom."

Reese stood silently.

"Is something wrong?" I asked. "Don't tell me you want to sleep in my bed and have me sleep in the guestroom."

"No, it's not that at all," she said.

"Then what is it, Reese?"

She sighed before saying, "I know this might be a crazy request, and you can say no if you want to. But can I tuck you in?"

Reese was right. It was a crazy request. The thought of Reese tucking me in like she did when I was a little girl was . . . Shit, I was at a loss for words.

"Can I?" she asked.

I nodded and her face lit up. How could I tell her no?

"It will be just like it was when you were a little girl," Reese said, rubbing her hands together. "I don't care how big and mean you are now. You'll always be my sweet little girl."

She followed me to my bedroom and before we walked through the door I stopped and said, "But don't think for a minute you are about to dress me in footed polyester pajamas like you did when I was little."

Reese started laughing then hugged me. It was the kind of touch that I had almost forgotten about. I can't explain it, it was just different. My arms raised to hug her back only they just wouldn't wrap around her. Not yet.

After I put on my sleep gear, Reese pulled the covers down for me and allowed me to climb in bed. I felt a little silly.

Once I was in a nice and comfortable position she pulled the covers up to my chin. She kneeled down beside the bed and leaned over to talk to me.

"Harlem, I love you," Reese said, her hand on mine. "I might not wake up in the morning. None of us are promised tomorrow. So I don't want to go one more minute without you not knowing how much I love you."

I didn't know how to reply to her.

"I know you can't say it to me. But I swear to God, I will earn my place back in your life. I'm going to do everything in my power and God's to make sure of that," Reese swore.

I could see the tears forming in her eyes as she continued.

"Pardon my French, baby girl, but I fucked up. I fucked up big time. I'm sorry. I'm so sorry."

Reese began to cry. She cried so hard that the bed shook with her body as she belted out cries.

"I hate how you call me Reese," she said. "It just reminds me that I stopped being Mommy to you a long time ago. I hate looking back, Harlem. I really do. Now, I'm going to keep striving forward no matter what, but it would make my journey a lot easier if I just knew that you had it in your heart to someday forgive me."

I couldn't speak. There were so many mixed emotions going through my head right now. I did want to love Reese, but I was scared. If God knew that I loved her, he might take her away. Those were the kind of games he played with me. Although I wanted to tell Reese verbally that it was possible that someday I could forgive her for everything, I just couldn't get the words out of my mouth. Instead I just placed my hand on top of hers and smiled. She knew exactly what I was trying to say.

Bright and early the next morning I drove Reese back to the shelter. It was Friday, the last day of the work week for some, and she had a couple of jobs she had to look into. After dropping her off I went home and went back to sleep. I must have really needed to catch up on my rest because, other than to get up and go to the bathroom, get something to drink and get my mail, I stayed in bed until about four o'clock in the afternoon.

What got me out of bed was the thought of some unfinished business I had to tend to. All that doubt I had the night before of maybe not having the balls to go back out there and handle mine faded away when I did a repeat of the tasks from the day before. With the same hairstyle and the same attire, I staked out 5734 Agler Park.

My heart was racing ninety miles per hour. It was now going on 6:00 P.M. After about an hour and fifteen minutes of waiting, I saw a figure come out of the house. It was Tiny. When I saw that black son of a bitch my heart filled with lead and it was pushing me to get out of the car and put a bullet right between that fucker's eyes. But my head insisted that I be smart. So I took deep breaths and sat back and watched this snake slither.

As he stepped off the porch and down the walkway, the garage door opened and there sat the red Nissan Altima. I gritted my teeth.

Just the sight at that bloody red car reminded me of the blood Morgan and I had shed at their hands. Just as cool as a breeze, and without a care in the world, Tiny waltzed over to the car and got in. I waited impatient and uneasy. I didn't know how much longer I could sustain myself.

Tiny situated himself inside the car. There was a pink lai hanging on the rear view mirror. It was one of those scented car air freshners. While adjusting the rearview mirror he took the lai down and flung it in the back seat. I guess he didn't want the rest of the world to know that he was driving his woman's car. The pink lai was a dead giveaway that it was a chickmobile.

After a few moments he slowly backed out of the garage. I thought he might have seen me at first because I was so infatuated with the idea of putting one through his head that I forgot to duck down. But he didn't even look my way. I sighed a sigh of relief then I immediately started my car and followed him.

Traffic was light so dodging him was a challenge, but somehow I managed. At one point I ended up being right behind him at a traffic light, but he was too busy bobbing his head to the beat of whatever song he was listening to. I sat there watching him, wondering if it was his favorite song that he was listening to. Did that nigga know that that would be the last time he would ever hear his favorite song? I bet that nigga didn't even know that shit.

We had driven about ten miles, which felt like a hundred, before Tiny pulled up to a mint green, one-floor house. He blew the horn and a few seconds later, standing in the doorway, was the other bird that I was going to kill with my one stone.

The guy who had driven Morgan and me to the wooded area stuck his head out of the door and held up his finger, signaling Tiny to wait a minute. At the sight of that cocky bastard my eyes watered with anger, but I choked that shit up. I had to keep clear vision. I had to handle these muthafuckas proper like.

After a couple of minutes he came out of the house and hopped into the passenger seat. For a moment there I thought about running up on them cats with my Mustang, blocking them in the driveway. But not only did I want to kill them, but I wanted to get away with the shit, too. So once again, my street-smart head overruled my anxious heart.

I laid low and allowed them to cruise off. I could see them giving each other dap before Tiny drove off. Sick ass partners in crime.

I spent the next three hours trailing them. Their first stop was at a carryout, then they stopped at a house that had several cars parked in the driveway and in front of the house. It was safe to assume that there must have been some type of party going on.

While they were inside laughing, drinking, and shooting the breeze, all I could do was sit outside in my car and think about Morgan. Fuck what they did to me. I survived it, but my girl. Fuck them niggas! They had to die. Grimy bastards!

As I waited in my car biting my nails, I noticed that I had had bitten them down to the skin. A couple of them were even bleeding from where I had unknowingly chewed to my flesh.

After hanging out at the party, Tiny and his sidekick decided to leave the party scene with two broads. They were young looking, too. I'd say one was about nineteen and the other was barely legal, if she were at all.

When I saw them come out of the house, my adrenaline pumped. I could hear my fucking heart beating. I swear I though it was going to beat right out of my chest. I sniffed. Death was in the air.

When they came out of the house they walked down the drive-way and stopped to chitchat. My window was down so I leaned my ear out to make out what they were saying.

I heard one of the girls, the oldest looking one, say, "We'll follow y'all."

But Tiny quickly replied by saying, "Why don't my boy ride with you, and your girl can ride with me?"

"I don't know you like that," the youngest girl said, twisting up her mug in a ghetto-like manner. Her girlfriend gave her the evil eye as if to say "bitch you better get your ass in the car with him and quit cock blocking."

The girls would foolishly agree to Tiny's suggested arrangement.

When I saw the women climb into the cars with the two men my heart sank down into my stomach. I don't know if I even thought about the fact that what happened to Morgan and I could very well be about to happen to them. The first thing that came to my mind was "Fuck! Witnesses."

At first I was going to jump out of my car and warn the girls, to tell them to run for their lives. But that would jeopardize my operation. So instead, I remained calm and followed both cars.

We drove for about thirty minutes when they ended up turning off onto a dark wooded road. I didn't make the turn. I was trying to be inconspicuous. I only drove a few feet before U-turning and then heading down the dark wooded road myself.

I could hear this loud ass thumping noise. Oh, shit. It was my heart again. But that voice in my head telling me to turn off my headlights shut out the pestering sound of my heart beating.

I crept slowly down the road. I could see the last car's taillights. I got an eerie feeling in the pit of my belly. My intuition warned me that I had been there before in their company. This is where they had brought Morgan and me. This is where our lives would be changed forever. Now it was time for me to change theirs.

Tiny parked his car and turned off the ignition, leaving the headlights on. The girl following in the car behind him did the same. Tiny walked around and opened the door for his female passenger. The girl following and her male passenger got out of the car. I watched from a distance as the men began to spit game at the young girls.

"Stupid bitches," I mumbled, shaking my head. "They could fuck up everything.

I watched Tiny put his hand on one of the girl's ass. She brushed it off with a silly schoolgirl-like gesture and giggle. I started getting sick. I felt the tart vomit come up from my throat. I didn't need to be hurlin' now. Not in my ride, and I couldn't just open up the door and start puking all over the place. So I did what I had to do. I swallowed the clumpy vomit and kept my hawkeye on the situation at hand.

What looked to be the oldest girl of the two was starting to get a little uncomfortable with the situation. I could tell this by the way that she was starting to fight off the advances in a less playful manner.

"Just spark the fuckin' izm!" she yelled at Tiny. "I thought y'all niggas said y'all had the chronic."

I couldn't believe those weed-head hoes. They fell for the oldest trick in the book. Going off with some dudes, strangers to say the least, for some smoke. These girls had no idea what they were getting caught up in. So before any more time, or lives, were wasted, I made my move.

"Get away from the goddamn cars," I yelled, jumping out of

my car like a damn Charlie's Angel with my gun in hand and running up on them. I nervously fired a shot off so that they knew that I was packing and meant business. It was a loud crack and I almost dropped the muthafucker. But I stayed strong, maintaining a tight grip.

"Reach for the muthafuckin' sky," I yelled. All four put their hands in the air.

"You two, put your face in the dirt," I said, pointing the gun at the two men.

They proceeded to drop without hesitation and without saying a word. After all, what could they say? It's the muthafucka with the gun that is supposed to do all the talking.

"We'll do anything you want," the older girl said, stuttering. "Just don't hurt us."

I froze. All I could hear was Morgan saying those same exact words to the men on this same exact road. My jaw locked and I gripped the gun. It was now as light as a feather.

"It's not you I want," I said to her, calmly, but firm. "As a matter of fact, you and your friend get in your car and get the hell out of here."

The two girls just stood there like I hadn't said a muthafuckin' word. I guess they feared that I might have been bluffin', that if they moved, I was going to shoot them anyway. But nonetheless, their disobedience pissed me off.

"You heard me, hoes. Get the fuck out of here now!" I ordered them. They could tell by the tone of my voice that I wasn't fuckin' around. If I had to, I was willing to take them bitches out too. I was on some ole gansta shit at this point. It was payback at all cost.

The girls slowly began to take a few steps forward. The men

looked up and had these looks on their faces as if they couldn't believe the girls were actually about to bail on them.

"We can't just leave them here," I heard the younger looking girl whisper to the girl who had been driving.

"Feel free to stay and join them then," I said, cocking my gun. I didn't have anything against the girls, but I had to scare them enough to get the fuck off the scene. But I, too, had to make sure they knew that I would only spare their lives once.

"We just met them sorry niggas," the driver said to her friend. "We out."

"Fuck y'all hoes," the cocky one said to the girls.

"You shut the fuck up!" I yelled at him. "Didn't I tell y'all to put y'alls face in the dirt? Say another word and you'll feel this shit, for real."

The girls headed for their car.

"Not so quick," I said to them as they neared me. "Open your purses."

"What?" the younger girl said.

I clinched my lips and gave her a look of death.

Tears fell from her eyes. I wanted to tell her that she would be okay, but I couldn't get soft with them. They'd take that as a sign of weakness and run off and bring the boys in blue into this shit. Fear keeps a muthafucka silent. I had to put the same fear in their hearts that was in mine.

"Bitches, open your fuckin' purses," I reiterated.

The girls nervously opened their purses and held them open as if they were getting ready to get them checked by security at a club entrance.

"Give me your IDs," I said.

"What?" the younger girl said.

"Bitch, who the fuck are you? Lil' Jon?" I screamed at her. "You fuckin' heard me. Don't *what* me. Fuckin' *what* me again and see what happens." By now, I really was starting to get pissed off. They were wasting time.

The girls fumbled through their purses, pulling out wallets, and managed to give me their IDs, neither with a steady hand.

I looked down at their IDs then looked back up at them.

"Look, bitches, y'all don't know who I am, but now I know who you are," I said in the best Clint Eastwood voice I could muster up. "The same way I followed y'all here, someone followed me. When you leave this spot, if you even try to go to the police, you'll be dead before you even make it through the precinct door. Now my partna back there is gonna follow you and keep an eye on you. You know, to make sure y'all get home safe and sound. We don't have no beef with you. Like I said, you don't know who I am. You were never here. This shit never went down." I made sure that the barrel of my gun stared them down as I spoke. I could hear a trickling sound. The oldest girl had pissed on herself. "Do we have an understanding?"

"Yes," they replied with shaky voices in unison.

"Now get the fuck out of here. And remember, not a word. Pow!" I said, motioning as if I would blow their brains out.

The girls damn near fell over one another trying to get out of there. They got in their car and drove off down the road of which they had come, full speed. I felt bad knowing that my words and the barrel of my gun would haunt them for weeks, months, hell, maybe even years to come. But at least they were alive.

Now turning my attention back to the men, who had laid on the ground patiently, waiting for the Grim Reaper to kiss them upon the lips. I looked at them lying there and remembered that it wasn't too long ago that I had been lying there in the mud, that cold, sticky mud that felt like shit. I cringed. I felt disgusted. I could feel them inside of me, fucking me against my will. I could smell them. I needed to vomit again, but I didn't. I had to keep it together. I just had to. I had come too far now.

"Now you two bitches stand the fuck up and put your hands high in the air where I can see them," I ordered them.

The two men did as they were told. I took a couple of steps back away from them just in case they tried some ol' dumb shit like rushing me.

"So we meet again," I said to the men, breathing heavily. I could taste their blood. I could hardly wait to see it ooze. I needed to see it ooze the same way blood oozed from Morgan. The life seeping out of her.

They were standing there confused, and blinded by the headlights of their car.

They didn't even recognize me until I walked closer into the light. The scar on my face reminding them even more of just who the fuck I was. Just then, the one who had driven Morgan and I to that spot grinned at me.

"It's you," he said. "The one with the fly ass mouth. So I see you came back for more. I knew you couldn't keep away from this dick." His sarcasm ate through my bones like acid.

He began laughing a horrible laugh. His laugh to me was like nails down a chalkboard.

"Shut the fuck up!" I screamed. "Shut the fuck up."

"Come on, Roland, man," Tiny nervously said to him. "You heard her. Shut the fuck up, man."

Tiny was smart. He knew that pissing me off wasn't the right thing to do.

"Look, we're sorry," Tiny pleaded. "We're sorry about what we did to you and your friend. But, we'll make it up to y'all. We'll pay you. We'll pay you money for the rest of your life. Please, dear God, don't let her shoot us."

Funny how muthafuckas can go a lifetime without saying two words to God. But it's just like a nigga to call up a muthafucka out of the blue when they need something. Little did he know anyway that he was wasting his breath. God don't listen.

"There's not enough money in the world, you sick bastard," I said, gritting the words between my teeth.

"Hmm. You're uptight, too," Roland said to me, laughing, ignoring his partner's plea. "Looks like Mr. Good Dick is just what you need."

I couldn't believe this cat. I guess he really thought he had nine lives. I couldn't believe that I was standing there with a gun in my hand, and he still wanted to play the role of a cocky son of a bitch.

Roland started to put one hand down and reach for himself, but my instinct fired off a shot before he could. All I could think about was him pulling his dick out to fuck Morgan, to fuck me. I couldn't stand there any longer and take it.

The bullet went right between his legs, grazing his nut sack through the slacks he had on.

"You fucking bitch!" he moaned in pain, hunching over grabbing his wound.

Tiny was now standing there crying, but Roland was trying to be a champ, still talking shit.

"Oh, you fucking bitch!" Roland said in agony. Then he stood up again. "You shot me in my fuckin' nuts! You crazy bitch! I can still take care of you, you little cunt!"

Roland lifted a leg to step towards me and I fired again, wounding him in the right knee. He dropped down to his left knee.

Tiny freaked out and started backing up as if he was going to make a run for it. I looked at him, he looked at me. His eyes pleaded with me. I had to shoot. He was getting ready to run like a deer. I put one in his stomach. He grabbed his stomach as blood seeped through his fingers. He looked up at me then fell to the ground in agony. He lay there moaning. Once again, he called on God.

All of a sudden I felt a hand grab me by my leg and I screamed. Roland had made his way over to me and had my pant leg in a tight grip. I took my loose leg and kicked him dead in his grill. I wish I had worn my boots with the four-inch heels.

"Bitch! Bitch! Bitch!" Roland yelled. "You better believe I'm gonna get your ass now, for sure!"

Spit was flying out of his mouth with every syllable. "Did you hear what I said, bitch?" Roland yelled.

I leaned in closer to him and with a mellow tone I said, "No, muthafucka. I didn't hear what you said because dead men don't talk."

I stood up, cocked the gun and aimed it at his head. He was looking dead at me and I at him. I envisioned him dead in a hospital bed, just like Morgan. I saw him lying in his casket. I could tell by the way that he was looking at me that he saw the end of his life through my eyes as I put a bullet right between his. I looked over at Tiny, who was in misery, moaning and groaning over his wound. I walked over to him. He looked up at me. His eyes made one last plea. I aimed the gun at his head and put him out of his miserable existence as well.

"Oh my, God!" I said, realizing that I had done it. I had killed those bastards. I trembled. I took deep breaths and trembled. For months I had not been able to breathe knowing that they were walking around still breathing. I stood there for a few seconds looking at the sight of those animals, that roadkill.

Donald Goines said you should never die alone. Well, at least those two bastards had each other. I lifted my head up high and I walked away.

As I walked to my car I could breathe again. I could live without fear and know that, yes, I had taken two lives, but I had probably saved many more.

I got in the car and started it up. I looked down at my hands that were gripping the steering wheel and noticed that blood had splattered on them. I looked up to the sky and before driving off I said, "Morgan, now your soul may rest. Justice has been served."

14. Love Don't Live Here

Taking another human being's life didn't feel like how I thought it would. I didn't get a high and I didn't go through that God syndrome. I hurt for the families and friends of those two men who didn't know just how badly they deserved to die. I felt bad that I had taken a life. But I figured that God already had it in for me in this lifetime. I might as well really give Him a reason to shit on me.

I got word from the contractors that the store would be ready in a few more weeks. I should have been excited, but I wasn't. No way was running that store going to be the same without Morgan and I knew I couldn't do it by myself. Some decisions had to me made and had to be made fast. I owned the building my store was in, but I didn't want to keep paying taxes on it if I wasn't going to do shit with it.

While contemplating my next step I signed up and started taking classes at North Adult Education Center to get my GED. It

was tedious, but I had to do it. Pretty soon, running a bookstore
became the last thing on my mind. Maybe it wasn't meant to be,
not right now anyway. Perhaps one day I would run another bookstore, have my chain and all. But not now. I really wanted to focus
on getting my education and learning to read properly. Who knows?
Maybe someday I would even go to college. But first thing was
first. A sistah had to get her reading skills on point. Besides, how
ironic is that, a chick that can't read up to par running a bookstore?

It was a hard decision to come to, but I would decide that giving
up the bookstore was the right thing to do. I had done a great job
with starting up The Suga Shop. I could do it again for certain,
maybe in another city even. Looking at these city walls were
getting tiresome. Picking up and starting over in another city like
New Orleans or something might not be such a bad idea.

I ended up putting my business up for sale, the building, the
business books, the name, etc. . . . I had even posted a sign in the
store window announcing the sale. We actually got an offer in a matter of days. Morgan's mom handled everything for me, the drawing
up of the contracts and whatnot. Some man named Jason Fields was
going to purchase the store for well over what it was worth. Well,
maybe for what it was worth in value, but not in my heart.

The day we scheduled an appointment for me to sign over the
deed relinquishing the store I decided to go back just one last time
to say goodbye. Perhaps it was for some closure as well. Besides, I
hadn't even seen it since the contractors finished working on it. For
all I knew it still looked like shit. But the new owner had an in-
spection done. It must have passed because he was still willing to
buy it so I supposed it looked halfway decent anyway.

The store looked like new again, only it wasn't stocked. There
were tables and chairs, but no merchandise. Never getting around

to doing that was the first sign that I was going to give up the store. I just couldn't bring myself to reopen it, not without Morgan. And it wasn't even that I needed her to read stuff for me. After weeks of excruciating reading classes at North Adult Education Center, that and the sessions with the private tutor I hired who specialized in teaching persons with dyslexia, I finally got my GED.

Being able to tell the instructors that I was dyslexic enabled them to provide me with the proper teaching techniques. That gave me a break and let me work at a pace that was comfortable for me. It was a struggle, but I did it on my own. The day I got my GED I went to pick up Morgan's mom. We drove to Morgan's graveside and it was there where I read the eulogy by myself and without stumbling over a single word.

Morgan's mother couldn't have been more proud of me than if I were her very own daughter. She told me over and over again how proud she knew Morgan was for me. But I knew better. I knew once people passed over onto the other side that they didn't think twice about what was going on on planet Earth. But I still appreciated her saying so.

A tap on the front store door interrupted my thoughts, and on top of that, scared the holy shit out of me.

When I looked up I saw Reese peeking through the front door glass. What was she doing here?

Reese and I had been getting along pretty well. She spent the night with me so often that she might as well have moved in with me. I even gave her a key to my house. Her being there also played a roll in getting my GED. She would help me with my work. She'd stay up all night if she had to, working out every problem until I solved it. If only she could have done that when I needed her to do it most, when I was just a child.

But I have to keep telling myself to live for the present. Often, it was easier said than done, but I was working on it, and Reese was too. She was determined to be the mother that she should have been to me growing up. I had to give her credit for that.

I walked over and unlocked the front door. When I opened it the bell jingled. That was the only original item left in the store that the vandalizers didn't destroy.

"Hey, Reese," I said. "What are you doing here?"

"I saw your car around back," she said, entering the store. "I walked around and peeked in and saw you standing there."

Reese stood there staring at me for a moment, not sure of what her next word should be. I could tell that something was on her mind.

"So what's going on with you?" I asked her.

She got straight to the point. "I need to talk to you about something, Harlem."

Oh, Lord, I thought to myself. *Now what?*

"I have been tearing myself apart debating whether or not I should have this conversation with you," Reese said. "But if I'm going to work on forgiveness from you, then I need forgiveness for everything that has affected your life because of the choices I made. I figure I need to start somewhere."

I closed my eyes and braced myself for the blow.

"It's about your brother, Harlem," Reese said. She paused then walked over and sat down at one of the tables.

I could tell that she didn't know where to begin. She just sat at the table, trying to keep a straight look on her face.

Watching Reese sit at the table reminded me of when I used to sit on the living room floor and play Barbies while she sat at the kitchen table and worked out crossword puzzles. The look on her face would be so intense. There she would sit at the kitchen table in a house gown and slippers. Normally something was in the kitchen boiling or frying for dinner. But for those few minutes she rested, entertaining her mind with a crossword puzzle from the daily newspaper. I saw that same Reese sitting there. I saw the Reese who had loved me and cared for me so much. The Reese who would have died for me. For once, I decided to spare her the drama and pain of rehashing up the past and ease her task.

"It's okay, Reese," I said. "I already know about my brother. I know everything. I've always known how it was really you who let him drown in the tub and not daddy. I overheard you telling Aunt Mary on the day of Daddy's funeral. I'm sure you've probably blamed yourself for daddy's death for years. It probably ate you up inside. And I can't lie. I did get some satisfaction in knowing that you had to bear the weight of that awful burden. There were so many times that I felt you deserved to suffer for what you had done. I saw it as God's way of punishing you for your evil acts."

Reese looked up at me in shock. She couldn't believe that I knew about Ray taking the blame for my baby brother drowning when it was her who let him drown all along and never said a word. There were so many times I could have snitched her out, but I didn't. By her own belief, I let God take care of her. From the looks of things she had paid her debt. I was glad to see Reese cleaning herself up.

"You knew?" Reese asked surprisingly.

I nodded yes.

"I had no idea, Harlem."

"I don't want to talk about it, Reese, not now. I've got too much other stuff on my mind. Let's just move forward. The past has nothing good for either of us."

"I know baby girl, I know," Reese said, standing up and walking over to me. "I do want to move forward with you and I'm glad that that's one thing we've gotten out in the open about your baby brother. That was something I was going to wait and tell you later. I hadn't yet found the courage to talk to you about."

I stood there confused. "What are you trying to say, Reese?" I asked.

"Harlem, that's not what I wanted to talk to you about. I wanted to talk to you about your other brother."

Nothing could have prepared me for what Reese was about to tell me.

"Remember how when you was just a little girl you used to ask me about Grandmother Jones?"

"Yes," I replied.

"You asked why she never came around. Why she didn't like us. I told you how she was, about how she refused to accept Ray's and my marriage and my being pregnant with you. Well, it wasn't because she felt we were too young or anything."

"You told me that Grandmother was heavy into church and that you getting pregnant before you and daddy had even married was an abomination in her eyes. She didn't care about the fact that you two married while you were pregnant. She felt that I was still conceived in sin," I recalled.

"Yes, I know. I know what I told you, Harlem. But now I need to tell you the truth."

Reese walked back over to the table and sat down.

"Your father and I had this big fight right before I got pregnant with you. We split up. Well, while we were apart I got involved with this man. I wouldn't really say involved. It was just one night because when Ray got word that I had been seen out with him, he came running back after me. You know how men are," Reese said, chuckling. "They don't want you until you're gone."

I, on the other hand, didn't find a damn thing funny. I stared at her with a cold look waiting for her to continue.

"Needless to say your father and I got back together. He even proposed to me, but by then I was already into my second trimester. Ray knew that there was a chance that he might not be the father and you know Ray was close to his mother so he confided our situation in your grandmother. Oh, she flipped the script. Came over to our house praying tears with a crucifix around her neck, a Bible in one hand, and a bottle of holy water in the other. She forbade your father to marry me. She vowed that if the child wasn't her blood grandbaby, that she wouldn't have anything to with it, or us. Well, Ray married me anyway and three months later I gave birth to you. Your grandmother wouldn't even spend money on us for a shower gift but paid three hundred dollars for a paternity test to see if you were Ray's baby."

"Well was I?" I asked nervously. "Am I? Was Ray my daddy?"

"Oh, but he was," Reese said, jumping up and walking over to me. "He was the best daddy you could have ever had."

Reese tried to put her hand on my shoulder but I jerked away.

"You know what I mean," I snarled at her. "Was Ray my biological father?"

Reese's eyes filled with tears. She closed her eyes and the tears fell.

"No, baby. No, he wasn't," she sobbed.

"Oh, my God. Oh my God," I said in shock. My hands were trembling. I didn't know what to say, but then it came to me, what I needed to ask Reese.

"Who is my father, Reese?" I asked in a demanding tone. "What's his name?"

"His name is Parker," Reese said, opening her eyes. "But everybody used to call him Peanut."

"Peanut," I repeated trying to recall where I had heard that name before. Once I remembered my eyes bucked and I grabbed my stomach. I ran to the back room to the bathroom. I leaned over the toilet and vomited. I was sick. I couldn't believe it. Reese ran in after me.

"Oh, God, Harlem. Are you okay?" she asked, not knowing what to do for me. "I'm so sorry. I'm so sorry, baby girl. I wanted to say something when I saw his boy at the hospital. I just didn't know where you two stood. I was going to tell you just as soon as you recovered and got out of the hospital. Honestly, I had planned on it because I didn't know what that boy's role in your life was. But when you told me that he was just a friend and that it was his buddy that you had a relationship with, I was relieved. I figured that there was no need in telling you then. It was just going to be another family secret that I carried around with me. But I know for a fact that the truth always comes to light. I figured in this case, though, that it would be better if I was the one who hit the on switch."

Reese's words weren't registering. I didn't want to be hearing what she had to say. What she was telling me was that I had been feeling an attraction to a man that was my very own brother. We shared the same father.

I finally understood why Jazzy and I had this connection. Maybe it wasn't sexual after all, not on his end anyway. It was just me and my sick way of thinking. I insisted on believing that I had to have him and that he was meant to be in my life. Even after my best friend took to him.

This was not happening to me. My life had been one low-budget horror flick and I didn't know how much more of it I could take. I wanted to die. I truly wanted to die.

"Harlem, please talk to me," Reese begged as she stood in the bathroom doorway.

I was still hunched over the toilet throwing up. Just when I thought I would be okay, I would reminisce back to how I fantasized about being with Jazzy sexually. I would throw up again.

I sat over the toilet drained as Reese stood in the doorway watching me, not knowing what to do for me.

"I know it hurts to hear this, baby girl," Reese said. "But like everything else we can get through this. I love you. I just need you to find it in your heart, after all is said and done, to love me too."

I looked up at Reese and took a deep breath. I then took my foot and kicked the door close right in her face.

How could she even ask me to love her when all she kept doing was hurting me? Besides, fuck that. Love don't live here anymore. Not in Harlem's heart. And it never will for as long as I can help it. It never will again!

15. Harlem's Blues

I could see it now. The morning paper would read: Harlem Lee Jones was pronounced dead at the scene. Her heart was beating, but she couldn't breath. When Reese discovered me lying in my bed she softly whispered, almost under her breath, *"Oh, my God. My baby girl is dead."*

It had been the same exact scene as it had been with Morgan and myself the time she found out her father was cheating on her mother.

Reese and I hadn't talked in four days, ever since the day in the bookstore when she told me about my biological father. I needed a few days to cool off, so I hadn't been answering my phone or door. Finally, when she couldn't seem to get in touch with me, I guess she panicked, thinking something was very wrong. The next thing I knew, she was at my bedside.

"Harlem, baby," Reese said as she approached the bed. "I almost called the police."

"Go away," I said to her. "I don't want to talk to you, Reese."

"Baby girl, I know you're mad at me, but—"

I sat up in the bed and cut off her words. "Reese, I don't have the energy to be mad at you anymore," I said.

Reese was stunned to see my face. Tears were flowing down it. She hadn't seen me cry since the day I fell off my bike and scabbed my elbow.

I was just as stunned. I had been crying for four days straight. And in a weird kind of way, it felt good. There were so many times I had wanted to cry and didn't. There were so many times that I had been hurting so bad, physically and mentally, and wanted to cry but didn't. Well, yesterday I cried, and the day before that one too. And tomorrow I was probably going to cry again. I realized that I should have cried a long time ago.

"It's okay, Harlem," Reese said. "I'm here for you."

Something about Reese saying those words ticked me off. They fell off of her tongue like she had been the mother of the year. Who did she think she was thinking that she could just jump back into my life like nothing happened? The same way it was long overdue for me to cry is the same way it was long overdue for me to tell Reese exactly what I thought about her.

"You're here for me, huh?" I said raising up off of the bed. "You're here for me? Well where in the hell were you when I was at home by myself as a child with nothing to eat? Where were you when I had to miss school to stay home and take care of my baby brother? Where were you when I was being thrown into foster homes, trying to keep the foster mother's boyfriend from poppin' my cherry? Where were you when I was fixin' to turn tricks for twenty dollars just so I could get money to eat?"

Reese had a look of horror on her face. She couldn't believe what

I was enlightening her on. I was so angry with her. I was so angry as I continued on.

"Where were you when I was sitting in class humiliated because I couldn't read? Where were you when I was sent to live with Grandmother, a woman I didn't even know? Where were you when I became a young woman? Where were you then, huh? Where the fuck were you, Reese?" I yelled at the top of my lungs as I began to cry harder.

Reese just stood there with her hand over her mouth.

I looked up at Reese. I could see the pain I was feeling on her face. "It hurts!" I screamed as I threw myself on the bed and balled up in a fetal position. "It hurts. Oh, God it hurts. Please, God. No more. No more."

Reese still had her hand over her mouth and tears were falling as she laid witness to my pain, then out of nowhere she got the strength to wipe her own tears and come to me.

"Listen here," she said, grabbing me by my arms, pulling me up in a sitting position on the bed. "I know it hurts. I'm hurting too, baby girl. I'm hurting for the both of us. And it's okay to hurt. And it's okay to cry. And it's okay to be mad at the world. Harlem, it's okay to be mad at me. But you ought to know by now that I ain't going nowhere. For years you been putting me out that store of yours, calling me every name in the book, but I still came back didn't I? I love you, Harlem. I love you. These aren't just words. I do love you. I am your mother. And I'm here for you and I'm going to be here for you. Child, I've stood outside of this house and watched you, even when your grandmother was alive. I'd watch you walk up that porch after school. It broke my heart that I couldn't call out to you. It broke my heart."

Reese began crying hard. The harder she cried the harder I cried. The harder I cried the harder she cried. I just had so much hate and anger in me for so long, that this was the only way I knew to release it. I finally had to just let it go, and once I started, I couldn't stop.

"So you can be mad at me all you want," Reese said. "But it doesn't change the fact that you are my baby and that I love you. It's okay to love somebody, Harlem. It's okay to love me back. I love you."

Reese's words were like medicine to a chronic ailment that I had been trying to shake for years. All I ever wanted was for her to be there for me and be a good mother. That's all I ever wanted. Pride never allowed me to put my guard down long enough to forgive her. Long enough for me to give her a chance. But after all I had been through I felt as though I had nothing left. Not even pride. What did I have to lose now?

Reese held me. She held me tight. As tears continued rolling down my face I found that some were even tears of forgiveness. I was forgiving Reese, Ray, my baby brother, my grandmother, Morgan, York, and even that police officer from when I was a little girl, Detective Logan. I was forgiving everyone who I thought had abandoned me.

As I sat there I thought about the movie, *Imitation of Life,* Reese and I had watched together and I remember when Sara Jane was finally able to tell her mother that she loved her. I didn't want that to be how it would turn out with Reese and I. So I went down way deep in my heart and soul and found the strength I needed to throw my arms around Reese.

"I love you, too," I cried as I squeezed my arms around her. "I love you too, Mommy."

∎ ∎ ∎

About a month after I opened up to Reese and decided to give her a second chance, I decided that I needed a second chance myself. I was definitely going to give Columbus, Ohio, a break. I needed a new scene.

"So where you moving to?" Reese asked as she watched me box up my upstairs office.

"I don't know," I replied. "I was thinking about New Orleans."

"That sounds nice. You got the house sold yet?"

"Nope. But I'm sure that for-sale sign won't be out there for long. I'm selling it well below market value."

"Seems odd, you packing up with nowhere to go and nothing to do with this place."

"I'll manage," I said. "I've always seemed to manage even when I didn't know what my next step was going to be."

"I'm going to miss you, Harlem," Reese came right out and said.

"And I'm going to miss you to, Mom," I said, looking at her in her eyes.

"I feel like I'm losing you again, Harlem," she said as she began to tear up.

"You're not losing me. I just need to make a change. That's all. Who knows? Maybe if things don't work out there, I'll come back here."

Reese didn't seem hopeful of that. She knew that once I blew this joint that I was never coming back. I was trying to feel good about my decision to pick up and move. There was just so much pain for me here in Columbus. I had to get away and venture out elsewhere. I wish she could be happy for me, but I can imagine how she must feel after all these years. She and I finally got back on good terms and were getting close again and now I was heading off. But I couldn't stay. Not even for her.

I took the battery-operated clock off the wall to pack when I noticed the time. It was one thirty P.M. and I had to meet the new owner at the store so that I could give him the keys.

"I have to get out of here," I said to Reese. "I have to meet the new owner at the store in a half hour."

"Oh, okay," Reese said sadly.

"I'll be back, Mom," I smiled at her. She smiled back. "I won't be long and when I get back how about we eat a bowl of Praline Pecan ice cream. And I'll stop at Blockbuster on my way home and rent the movie *Imitation of Life*, how does that sound?"

Reese laughed. "Sounds good," she said.

"All right then. I'll see you in about an hour." I put the clock down in a box then walked pass Reese, who was sitting in my desk chair, and headed out the door. Then something stopped me in my tracks. I turned around and walked back over to Reese and kissed her on the cheek.

"Just in case I get into some crazy car accident or something," I said. "I love you."

I gave her a huge smile then headed out.

When I arrived at the store, the new owner hadn't yet arrived. I entered through the storage room, just like old times, then walked to the front of the store to unlock the front door.

Standing there alone I was able to give the store one last good-bye for real. It was so hard. I kept picturing Morgan and me behind the counter talking and laughing, waiting on customers, guy bashing and just doing the things that best girlfriends do.

I thought about how Reese would walk through that door one day after the next after my shooing her out a thousand times. Such a big part of me was at the store. But now it was time for me to leave it all behind.

I heard the bell over the front door ring so I knew that the new owner had arrived. I turned around to greet him and to my surprise, Jazzy was standing there.

"What are you doing here?" I asked him, in complete shock. I hadn't seen him since Morgan's funeral.

"I'm Jason Fields," he responded. "I'm the new owner. I have a two o'clock appointment with you today."

I didn't know what to say. I was stunned. Not only because Jazzy was Jason Fields, the gentleman who purchased the store from me, but because of his appearance. Instead of the laid back, part casual, part thug look he normally represented, he was in a suit. His high fade was now low and he was workin' this handsome goatee that was very becoming on him.

"You look surprised," he said with a smile, his one dimple showing.

"I guess I am," I replied. "I had no idea that you were the new owner. I thought you said your name was Jay that day you and York first came in the store."

"First off, I didn't say my name was anything. York did all of the talking, remember? But some people do know me as Jay, short for Jason."

"But I specifically remember you saying that your last name was Brown the first night we all went out," I said, confused. "That's what you told the host at the restaurant."

"No, the host asked the name of the party and I replied Brown,"

Jazzy corrected me. "I do business under The Brown Corp. I made our reservations under the name Brown."

"Well Morgan and I just assumed—" I paused. "I just assumed all kinds of names for you then, huh?"

"Hell, I got all kinds of names out there in the street." Jazzy closed his eyes and nodded his head to correct himself. "Had all kinds of names. Now I'm just Jason Fields, bookstore owner."

"Does that mean you're no longer Jazzy, car wash owner?"

"Yeah, well. I decided to get out of the car wash business," he said with a wink.

A slight smile crept across my face. I guess Morgan was right. People do change.

"After all," Jazzy continued, "the book business was pretty good to you. I figured, why wouldn't it be good to me, too?"

"What made you decide all of this?" I asked. "I mean, the car wash business wasn't necessarily mean to you."

"Lots of reasons I suppose," he said. "For one, my pops died a few weeks ago."

"Peanut," I said, trying to restrain my feeling of anxiety.

"Yeah, Peanut," Jazzy said, looking down at the ground.

"I'm sorry to hear that," I said. "I don't know how close you were with him, but I'm sure either way it goes it's a great loss."

"Yeah. Even though he wasn't my father by blood, he was the only man I had ever known as a father. He treated me and my mom good, damn good," Jazzy said with a smile of remembrance.

"So Peanut wasn't your biological father?" I asked. I needed him to repeat it. I had to make sure that I was hearing what I was hearing.

"No, but nobody really knew that. He couldn't have treated me any better, though, than if I had been his biological son. See, he met my moms when I was only a month old and he played the role of daddy right off the bat. He taught me everything I knew about the game. He even taught me how to get out. Unfortunately for him, he didn't follow his own advice and get out soon enough. He was shot by his best friend over money. It was over some small paper at that."

I was sadder for Jazzy losing the man that raised him as his son than I was about the fact that I had lost a father whom I had never even gotten to meet. My never knowing this Peanut didn't allow me to feel extra sad about his death. But I did have some sadness in my heart. I think I was more concerned with finding out that Jazzy wasn't my brother after all.

"I'm really sorry, Jazzy," I said in the most sincere voice I could manage. Inside I wanted to scream with excitement that he wasn't my brother. All those feelings of guilt and shame I tortured myself with for being attracted to a man who could have been my brother was no more. I could breathe again on that aspect.

"Thank you," Jazzy said, looking around at what was about to become all his.

"I guess I better give you what you came here for," I said, walking slowly towards Jazzy.

"What's that?" he asked.

"These," I said, dangling two sets of keys in his face. "Here's two sets. The silver key if for the front door and the gold key is for the back door."

I handed the keys to Jazzy and he just stared at them.

"Thank you," he said.

"You seem hesitant," I said.

"It's not that. It's just that I don't know who I'm going to get to be a partner and help me out in running this store. I know you and

Morgan did the damn thang," Jazzy's eyes got sad thinking about Morgan.

"What about York?" I asked.

"Didn't you hear? He got ten to twenty-five years in the federal pen," Jazzy said as if I should have known what the word was on the street. "That fool changed lanes without using his turn signal and got pulled over by the police. He was on his way to make a drop off for me so he was holdin'."

"Word?" I asked. "I take it the drop off wasn't a bag of pine tree car air freshners."

"Nah," Jazzy said. "And you know the cops tried to get him to talk, to rat out everybody else in the game, but he kept quiet. I got him a good lawyer and he's appealing the sentence, so hopefully he shouldn't have to serve his full time. I'm going to take care of him no doubt, make sure his books are tight and shit while he does his bid. That's the second reason why I'm getting out of the car wash business. Niggas get pulled out in threes, like three strikes. But a brotha like me gon' take my balls and walk."

"I see," I said, putting my head down. "That's really fucked up about York. I'm sure you'll find somebody else to help you out, though."

"Perhaps," he said. "Do you have anybody in mind? It would definitely have to be someone who knows a little somethin' somethin' about running a book/music/coffee shop?"

This was another one of those moments. It was a time when opportunity knocked and you either let him keep knocking before his knuckles got sore and he stopped, or you answered the goddamn door.

Well, I wanted to answer the goddamn door, but before doing so, there was something else that I wanted to do even more.

I walked over to Jazzy, nose to nose, and kissed him softly. I leaned back to get his reaction. He was just standing there. I kissed him again, and again until he finally kissed me back.

The two of us stood in the middle of the store like long lost lovers kissing one another passionately. I couldn't pull myself away from his deep kisses, then finally I did have to pull myself away and come up for air.

He stood there, lips shiny from my lip gloss.

"I was wondering how long it would take you to do that," Jazzy said with a wink.

I smiled. I knew he knew all along. I knew he knew.

"So you need a partner to help you run the store, huh?" I asked him.

"Yep," he said. "Are you positive you don't have anyone in mind?"

I paused. I twisted my lips and put my index finger on my chin as though I was trying my best to think of someone. Then finally I said, "Come to think of it, I just might have the perfect person in mind."

"Oh yeah?" Jazzy smiled.

"Yeah," I said. "But the thing is, this person is going to insist that you are only allowed to have *one* partner."

"Only one partner, huh?" Jazzy said, licking his lips.

"Yes," I replied. "Me."

I took back one set of the store keys from Jazzy's hand and kissed him again.

Epilogue

Dear Reader:

Once Jazzy and I reopened the store, business was better than ever. We added three computers to the scenario and we charged for their use, kind of like how Kinko's does. We even added a small copy machine where we charge ten cents per copy.

Our music selection, which before had consisted of mostly hip-hop, now had a mixture of old school music such as Billie Holiday, Al Green, Otis Redding, Marvin Gaye, and B.B. King.

The store became more of a social spot than just a regular bookstore. We hold open mic contests and give away prizes.

Our bookstore is the go-to bookstore in Columbus, Ohio. Jazzy even negotiated contracts with major publishing houses guaranteeing that when their authors toured in the city, that our bookstore was their designated stop. We got those publishing houses on lock.

With so many additional services to the store, it became overwhelming to handle sometimes, but I've never been happier running the store. It's more than I could have ever dreamed up alone.

Starting over wasn't as hard as I thought it would be, especially now that I could read and understand more of what was coming across the table. Morgan was right. Having an education really makes a difference in how far one can go in life. With that being said, I decided that college was to be my next step and I didn't waste anytime in making it a reality.

Not only did I get accepted into Columbus State Community College, but Reese graduated from it. And little did I know, but Jazzy already had a college degree in art and design. His favorite pastime is drawing. We even sell some of his original prints in the store now. People come in and ask for his work by name.

With Reese graduating with an Associates degree in Business Management, I'm proud to say that she is the official store manager. Thanks to having her around, I get days off now. At first Jazzy and I alternated working in the store with Reese. Then we started letting her open and close by herself. Never once did inventory or the drawer and bank deposits come up short. As a matter of fact, Reese treats the store as if it were her very own. Granted, Jazzy has her hooked up on a nice little salary so her interest in the store is genuine. I told Jazzy that I thought her salary might be a little too excessive, but he said it would keep her honest.

She spends most of her money furnishing her new apartment. Anything she has left she saves. She won't even splurge on eating out or anything. She says why spend on something she wants to do today, when there's something she needs to do tomorrow. She reminds me of Grandmother sometimes. Just as long as she's not spending it on drugs and alcohol, more power to her.

Reese even had the idea of putting in a jukebox on the latte side of the shop. She also came up with a way to set up the store so that it allowed us to add two more table and chair sets. And get this, it was her idea for us to start selling deli sandwiches along with the latte. We're like a one-stop book and music shop.

Oh yeah, and it's not The Suga Shop anymore. Jazzy, since he is the official owner, changed the name. It's now called Harlem's Blues.

I would have never dreamed that my life would have fallen into place such as it did. I can honestly say that I feel as though I'm reborn. Starting over with Reese was the best thing that ever could have happened to me at that point in my life.

Reese constantly reminds me that she can't make up for the past, but that she can take advantage of the present. She says that she didn't teach me to read when I was little, but now that I am a grown woman, she can teach me to be a loving and compassionate person, as well as a forgiving person. Not to toot my own horn, but toottoot. I think she's done a great job so far. She started by getting me to step foot back into a church building again. Reese said that until we do three things, tell God that we are sorry and asked for forgiveness, thank God, and love everybody, we would be blocking blessings. I've apologized for taking those two men's lives. It was bad enough playing judge and jury. It was dead wrong playing the executioner. I believe God has forgiven me. But I don't know. Maybe someday I'll have to account for it. I thank God every day for my blessings. As far as that last one, loving everybody, I'm still working on it. I'm trying to accept that it's okay to love a person, but not love the things they do.

Sometimes Reese and I have even been able to talk Jazzy into joining us. That girl, Zondra, from the club and the car wash, saw us up in church together one Sunday and couldn't wait to write

York and tell him about it. So Jazzy had to pay York a visit just to holler at him about the situation man to man.

At first York wasn't cool with Jazzy and my being together but he got over it. He didn't have a choice. He told me that he didn't have any hard feelings against me. He just wanted me to always remember that no matter what man I was seeing, that Harlem knew York first.

Jazzy and York were still good friends so it made our relationship easier getting York's blessing. Jazzy and I made sure we kept his books tight and that we both would go visit him so that he knew that he was being thought about on the outside.

Sometimes Jazzy and I would go visit him together, and sometimes I would go alone. One time I went and he was telling me about this guy in the cell next to him who thought that he was big shit until one day he got broke down in the showers by three men who literally ripped him a new asshole. I felt bad for the guy until I found out that it was DC.

I still keep in touch with Morgan's parents, who didn't end up getting a divorce, but went to counseling and mended their relationship. Morgan's death ended up bringing them closer together. It's sad that it took the loss of their daughter to make them see how much they really loved and needed one another. It's sad but true.

I'm always sure to visit Morgan's grave frequently. And I always take a book with me and read to her. Just last month, while at her grave, I finished reading *Yesterday I Cried* by Iylana Vanzant. I wished I had had the privilege of reading that book years ago. To make up for it though, I read that book every chance I get. It helps me to heal some wounds that I have yet to stitch up.

But life is good. It's strange sometimes, but good. I know I could have never predicted years ago that things would have ended up the way they have. Even now, I'm still clueless as to what the next day holds. But at least now I know what I'll be doing for the next sixty-one years of my life. I'll be living, and I thank God for carrying me through every trial and tribulation that has molded me to be able to live. That has molded me to survive.

All along God had a plan for me. Even when I doubted him and cursed him, even when I lost faith in his greatness, he didn't lose faith in me. He didn't abandon me like I had felt so many others had, like I had felt that he had done too often. But he hadn't abandoned me. He was carrying me through life so that I did not create my own plan to live by, but so that I could live by his plan and his plan alone. And you know what's so great? That if God had a plan for me, his problem and sometimes disobedient child, then he has a plan for all of his children. Imagine the plan he has for you.

One Love

Ya Girl, Harlem